THE LAST ANGEL

–

RICHARD VALANGA

For my father Charles and my mother Elizabeth…xx

Book cover design for The Last Angel
And book cover art 'When Angels Cry'
by Richard Valanga

Books by Richard Valanga

Complex Heaven
Complex Hell
Complex Shadows
Blind Vision
The Sunderland Vampire
The Wrong Reality
Colosseum
The Last Angel

"Richard Valanga writes about the Afterlife like nobody
else today, he's the 21st-century Dante of the North."
– Tony Barrell, The Sunday Times.

"The author's talent for writing engaging tales of the
paranormal is second to none."

"The author Richard Valanga writes like a poet and has
a brilliant and impressive imagination to match."

ABOUT THE AUTHOR

Richard Valanga lives in the North East of England.
His previous life in the world of work included
Advertising Creative Director and Teacher of Art.
All of his time is now devoted to writing…
"Painting with words is just as cool as painting with paint."

For a long time I had an idea for story called The Last Church, over time it faded then disappeared to the back of my mind while other stories took priority. It was only after I had finished The Last Angel that I realised that the story had originated in my idea for The Last Church which just goes to show that the engines of your subconscious mind can work in mysterious ways.

Now it is time to start work on The Next Reality which is a cross-over sequel to my alternate reality novel, The Wrong Reality and my murder mystery with a paranormal twist, Colosseum… stay tuned booklovers, the story must go on.

Richard Valanga
28th November 2020.

"We are all in the gutter,
but some of us are looking at the stars."

- Oscar Wilde

THE MAN
WHO FELL TO THE MOON

STEPPING STONES

Neil Armstrong, Buzz Aldrin, Yuri Gagarin…
Famous faces from the history of space travel appeared on the large silver Skyroom screen, changing each second as the digital clock ticked down.
5 4 3 2 1…

"I would like to declare the Stepping Stone Moonbase fully functional, operational and officially open for business and the adventure will not end here, the quest to reach the stars has only just begun."

A loud raucous cheer swirled enthusiastically around the large circular room combined with the encouraging popping fizz of multiple Champagne bottles. Most of the moon-base personnel were in the Skyroom but a few staff still remained at essential workstations, the last thing Major Tom Savage wanted was some sort of unexpected glitch due to sloppy neglect to spoil the celebratory proceedings. The music of David Bowie's Space Oddity began to fill the Skyroom, this song was a personal favourite of Major Tom's for obvious reasons and instantly brought a wide smile to his affable face.

Doctor Susan Eden sipped her refreshing bubbly drink and stared out towards the heavens she was now part of. Part of planet Earth was visible on the horizon; a giant blue ball that sat in the black sky as a reassuring reminder that home was not that far away.

The Stepping Stones Moonbase was situated in the Sea of Tranquillity, which was a fitting tribute to the first moon landing. The moon-base was destined to develop and grow rapidly as the initial purpose of the base was to construct a gateway to the stars. Phase one had been completed, the next phase was the construction of a vast orbital space docking station.

Susan Eden looked to the serene vision of the Earth and tried to forget. The cruel death of her husband-to-be had propelled her into the Stepping Stones project; it was a real way of detaching herself from a world that had begun to crush her with memories.

"Beautiful isn't it?" said Major Tom Savage who was now standing beside the doctor.

"Do you mean the Earth or the moon-base Tom?"

"Mother Earth of course, the moon-base looks cool but it cannot compete with nature."

The Skyroom was situated at the top of the biggest dome and vast panoramic windows encircled the entire the room giving a three hundred and sixty degree view of the moon from the base. The Skyroom was the nerve centre of the moon-base; all the other domes sprang out from it like tentacles on an octopus's legs. From above, the moon-base was a beautiful sight, almost like a silver flower in bloom. It was some thought that the moon-base was man's first colony on another world, a world that still had many secrets to reveal.

"Nature will always top man-made Tom, even the great artists cannot compete with it."

"You said it Doc, whoever is painting the canvas of the universe, he sure is doing a fine job" replied the Major and this comment made them both laugh.

"Vincent Van God maybe?" said the doctor and this made them laugh even more.

"I thought Vincent was God, I mean look at Starry Night" suggested Savage.

"Yes I do think…"

Then the doctor paused, she seemed puzzled, disorientated all of a sudden.

"Are you alright Susan?" asked a perplexed Savage.

"Did you see that?"

"What?"

"That movement in the distance."

"Where?"

Savage was scouring his viewpoint but could see nothing unusual

"Straight ahead, beside the first drift to the left."

"I was still looking at the sky and thinking about Van Gogh's painting. What did you see?"

"A… shadow… moving" said Eden and voice trembled slightly.

"Moon shadows Doc, tricks of the light, triggered also by movements inside the base."

"I'm aware of that Tom but this is different, it was not a shadow… it was more solid."

"What did it look like?" asked Savage and now his curiosity was aroused.

"A… man" was the doctor's blunt reply.

"Was he suited, there should be nobody working outside now?"

"No, he was…"

Both went quiet, as quiet as the moon itself then Savage asked "Was it Vincent Van Gogh?"

This broke the ice and the Major and the doctor began to laugh at the absurd thought of Vincent Van Gogh moon-walking.

"If only" said the doctor, "hey, how strong is this Champagne anyway?" and again they both laughed, relieving a moment of real tension.

"Okay Doc, I need to circulate, let me know if you see Salvador Dali or Picasso out there will you?" said Major Tom and then he left the doctor to join the rest of his colleagues.

The Major had lifted the doctor's spirits as she had been getting a little too maudlin staring at the home world…

But what had she saw?

She had seen a man… but that was absurd, there was no man in the moon.

That night though, the man in the moon appeared to her in her dreams.

2

Susan Eden's sleep was restless. This was not unusual as periodically her fiancé Samuel Hayden would often visit her in her dreams. This night was different though, this night it was not him.

A shadow was moving in the distance; that is all it was, a shadow. Everything was moon grey, even the sky, even the Earth. The shadow was pure black and it was moving towards the doctor… not walking, but drifting, hovering… and the shape was that of a man…

"No… no" Susan Eden moaned, "It can't be?"

Why she said this she did not know; it was only until the man was standing directly over her did she realise…

It was Samuel Hayden.

Or something that looked like him.

The doctor sat up suddenly, her breaths short and stuttering, her heart racing, her naked body covered in sweat. It was as if there was no oxygen on the moon at that moment, as if her bedroom had become devoid of gravity.

The doctor's room was spacious as befitting her status, a quarter of a standard dome. She had a separate bathroom and she went for a much needed glass of water. The water cooled and calmed her as she returned to her sleeping area to gaze at the soothing lunar landscape that was visible through her porthole. There was no need to dress; there was no bustling world outside to be embarrassed by.

"Another Sam dream" she muttered to herself, "You even followed me here…"

And tears filled her eyes that blurred the moon sky; black became grey, much like her dream. Doctor Eden sobbed heavily like she always did after dreaming of her lost love.

Eden checked the time, she had woken early, there was still another four hours until the start of her shift even though she knew that her working hours were completely flexible, one of the perks of this moon job she always thought and again the real reason why she was there resurfaced in her mind. There was still work to be done though, medical files to be updated and checked on a routine basis. There had been no serious medical crisis as of yet and she thanked her lucky stars for that. It was not just a question of being there to regularly monitor staff health though, Susan Eden was also an accomplished surgeon but since the death of Samuel Hayden, it was an area she had tried to avoid, she hoped that this skill was never to be needed on the moon but she knew what they were doing there was extremely hazardous at times and maybe it was only a question of time.

The porthole became a giant looking glass the more she stared through it, a magnifying glass that illuminated a scene that never seemed to change. *That is the wonder of the moon though* she thought, the stillness, as if time did not exist there, as if eternity itself was waiting for something to happen. Well it was about to now, the moon had indeed become a stepping stone and that stillness was about to be broken by the impending construction of the space station.

Eden sipped at her water and as she was about to leave the hypnotic view from her porthole, she thought she saw a slight movement in the distance...

A shadow, like she had seen in the Skyroom.

Like her dream.

"Your dream" she said, "It's just the remnants of your dream."

Then the shadow moved again, away from the side of the small crater.

It moved closer.

It was not a shadow anymore, it was a man!

Eden dropped her glass; it fell to the floor as if in slow motion and what remained of the water splashed on Eden's rigid feet.

She had frozen.

Her mouth tried to move but she could not speak.

The figure moved closer, slowly; then it stopped. The man was clearly visible to Eden. He was completely naked, a man with wavy jet black hair that touched his wide shoulders, a man that looked exactly like Samuel Hayden.

Eden fainted and fell to her nearby bed. Only moments later her eyes opened, "A dream, it must have been a dream." Eden stood up, instinctively robed herself then went back to the window. He was still there. She began to shake...

Was she having some sort of psychotic episode finally, had it cruelly waited for the moment when she was close to closure?

Why did this being look so much like Samuel?

Why did it just stand there as if taunting her?

How was it possible, there was no spacesuit?

Why was it there?

Eden needed answers and fast, she needed help... her trembling fingers activated the videocom; she had to speak to Major Tom.

"Uh... hello... doctor? Boy, you're an early riser. What's the problem, has Vincent Van Gogh woken you?"

Eden stuttered her reply, "Not... Van Gogh... check your base monitor Tom, check my dome; tell me what you see."

There was a moment's silence; then the face of Major returned to the screen, it appeared white and totally flabbergasted...

"Who the... what the Hell is that?"

"You tell me, I thought that maybe I was imagining it."

"No I can see it too... though I just don't believe it. Join me in the Skyroom as soon as you can, I'll assemble my team."

3

Doctor Eden raced through the moon base 'Labyrinth' as it was affectionately known by the Stepping Stones personnel, her heart pounding louder with each step and she arrived at the Skyroom like an athlete who had just ran a thousand metres. The Major and his select team were already there, deep in heated conversation as they looked down to the lone figure, who was now standing at the main entrance to the base.

The Major turned to Eden, his face was solemn but he managed a smile...

"You were right Doc, it's not Van Gogh."

The crew members nearest to them were puzzled by this remark but it brought a smile to the doctor's face.

"Not even Picasso, I was thinking Dali though because this is all way too surreal."

"I know what you mean" replied the Major and his smile faded.

"Any clue as to who or what this man is?" asked the doctor, she thought it best not to mention the resemblance to her dead partner.

Major Savage simply shook his head, "I simply have no idea; it is not possible and yet there he is."

Jon Dawkins, the Major's second in command had to intervene, "It has to be an alien."

"My guess is robot or advanced hologram" said one of the scientists present.

"Have you made any preliminary sensory readings?" Doctor Eden asked the scientist.

"We have tried…"

"And?"

"And what we have is nothing; we need to get him to the isolation lab."

"Are you out of your mind? You cannot let that 'thing' inside the base, there is no way of knowing what its intentions are, what it could do… if it can exist in a God forsaken environment like this naked, then think what it could be capable of."

"You're right Jon, we need to try and communicate with it first out there, I will suit up but I will need another" said the Major.

"I will go with you" said Eden.

"No Doc, it is too dangerous, Jon is right, we have no idea what this thing is."

"Blast it with a laser cannon" shouted a big muscular black man with short spiky hair that was standing behind them.

"And that is your advice for a possible first encounter Ray?" asked the doctor who had turned to face him.

Major Tom wanted to laugh but the seriousness of the situation prevented him.

"That would only happen as a last option Ray and you being head of security should know that. No, we have to meet this… alien."

"You believe it is first contact then?" said Eden.

"What else can it be, there is no other explanation. You suit up too Ray, I will go and notify Earth Command first, provide them with what we have which is not much at the moment then I will join you."

"Not me too? I was the first to see him; he was standing looking at my bedroom…"

"Yeah, a pervy fucking alien who gets his kicks hanging round moon bases fully naked, hoping for a bit of 'first contact,' have you noticed how well- endowed it is?" interrupted Raymond Gunn with a wide ironic grin and this comment made some of the team laugh.

"Do you have to swear all the time Gunn? This is not the Nostromo" was the doctor's quick retort and she had noticed how large the stranger's penis was but she was not giving Gunn the satisfaction of replying to such a comment.

"Sorry Doc, if we do get it to the isolation lab, your assistance there will be obviously needed at some point. I am going to request all staff to remain calm and alert, duties to be carried out as normal. Right Ray, let's go and meet our unexpected guest."

4

Major Savage and Security Officer Gunn stood at the moon-base doorway, Gunn held a spare helmet for communication with the entity as they had decided to call it. Savage was silent and still, gathering his thoughts, still trying to get to grips with what was happenng.

"Are you alright sir... we need to do this now."

"I know that you are impatient Ray, it is in your nature but this... what we are about to do is... monumental in the history of mankind. Whatever that entity is, it has to have an alien origin; this is first contact."

"All those movies sir... they were fucking right then?"

"It looks that way Ray, I thought that the moon-base was mankind's greatest moment, I think we're about to shatter that."

"Let's hope it does not shatter us."

"Let's go then, whatever happens Ray, keep a cool head, remember what we agreed."

"I hope it does not come to that."

"Me too."

Major Savage pressed OPEN and they stepped out once again onto the lunar surface.

The entity did not move; it was now only a few yards away from them. Savage and Gunn advanced slowly until they were face to face with their mysterious naked visitor with the black hair. Major Savage was taken aback by the beauty of the entity. Savage had not noticed it from the Skyroom or on the monitors but the skin of the entity was simply amazing, it gleamed and sparkled like it was polished diamond... and the entity's eyes were pure white with a violet blue that shone brighter than any star that Savage remembered. The look of this entity was mesmerising but Savage knew all too well that looks could be deceiving. The entity held its right hand up with the fingers all open, this somehow reminded him of Spock from Star Trek but he thought it best, considering what was happening, to not mention this.

Savage turned to look up at the Skyroom, his adrenalin was pumping like it never had before, there had been moments in the construction of the moon-base that had set his heart racing but this surpassed those moments a thousand fold. In his mind he had rehearsed what he was going to say but his thoughts were now muddled by the enormity of the moment, the memory gone, he held up his right hand to mirror that of the entity...

"I... I am Major Thomas Savage, the man in charge of the Stepping Stone Moonbase... your presence here is... unexpected."

Before he could say anymore the entity shook his head, its lips began to move but the Major could not hear him."

"The helmet Ray; put the helmet on his head."

Savage pointed to their helmets then pointed to the spare helmet then to the entity's head. The entity seemed to understand and smiled. Its smile was warm and reassuring and this helped ease Savages' nervous state of mind slightly.

"I think he understands Ray, go ahead."

Gunn lifted the helmet above the entity's still head. Gunn noted that the entity was taller than him and his lean muscular frame suggested that he might be stronger too. Gunn lowered the helmet and Savage spoke, repeating his original words but again the entity shook its head... then it spoke...

"Jhar nar dir ston diar Lunar."

"Damn Ray, he does not understand and his speech is alien to me."

"Where's a Star Trek Universal Translator when you need one goddamn it?" said Gunn trying to lift the tense mood.

The entity looked thoughtful for a moment then it reached down to the lunar surface and drew a crude graphic in the soil.

"What the Hell is that?" said Gunn then the entity stood up and smiled.

"A... head and... fingers? It... wants to touch our heads, I think."

"No way sir, no way is that thing touching me" and the memory of what Gunn had said to the doctor returned to him.

"Of course not Ray but maybe it is their way of greeting."

"You can greet him sir."

"Yes I will" and the Major held out his hand...

"Apologies, I should have done this first."

The entity looked slightly puzzled by this but eventually touched the outstretched hand, it did not shake it but it was gentle as it caressed the Major's fingers

"Still think that it could be a threat Ray?"

"My impression at the moment is that it would not harm a mouse, but..."

"Good, I think we need to get it to the isolation lab then, work on communication."

"I did not finish sir; I was going to remind you of the Trojan horse."

"I appreciate your honesty Ray but I have made my decision."

The entity smiled as if it knew what the two Earthmen had just said.

Major Savage pointed to the three of them and then to the door to the base. The entity nodded and Savage smiled. Savage held his arm up to the Skyroom, a pre-arranged signal for his team to meet them at the isolation lab.

The men and the entity entered the moon-base.

Inside the airlock there were two doors, one of which led directly to the isolation lab. The Major opened the door to the left of them for the entity and waved his hand to point him in the direction of the lab. Without hesitation the naked entity walked on, he had removed his space helmet.

"Right Ray, let's see what the lab reveals about our guest."

"You're not seriously going to let it touch your face are you sir?"

"It shook hands with me; the least I can do is return the favour."

Gunn shook his head.

"But only after it has been checked out and I have clearance to do so."

In the isolation lab, Doctor Eden and two scientists were waiting for the entity. They were dressed in contamination suits as a standard precaution and they had prepared a Stepping Stone uniform for the entity as its nudity would be a constant embarrassing factor.

When the entity entered the lab, it placed the space helmet on the first table it saw. Then it looked at the three nervous Earthlings that were standing waiting for it, looking at it in disbelief. When the entity saw Doctor Eden it smiled which caused the doctor to blush instantly. Eden was not embarrassed by the entity's nakedness; she was embarrassed by the fact that the entity had obviously recognised her from her bedroom window. Eden's heart raced even faster now that she was close to the entity, the resemblance to Samuel Hayden was remarkable... and the entity's skin and eyes, *it's like this being is some kind of a god* she thought.

But there was important work to be done and after the scientists had managed to persuade the entity put the uniform on, they set to it.

Savage, Gunn and a few select members of the Stepping Stone crew watched through the protective screen. An hour later, one of the scientists left the lab to speak to Major Savage.

"And what do you conclude Neil?"

"The physical frame and internal organs suggest that it is human apart from the glowing skin and those remarkable eyes. The problem is Tom, that nothing shows up on our equipment; no readings, no DNA, no cells in the blood... it is... as if it were dead in some ways."

"Dead? You mean we have some sort of ghost on our hands, c'mon Neil you can do better than that surely."

"Not a ghost Tom, it is solid, it is definitely there..."

"Is there anything to suggest that we could be contaminated by it?"

"No nothing, there is no strange radiation of any kind, not even a particle of moon dust, my guess is that sparkling skin protects it. I would say that if offers us no danger in that respect."

"Good, we need to communicate with it somehow. I am going to join you in the lab, without a suit."

"It's your neck Tom and your decision but I will bet my reputation that you will be quite safe."

"That's good enough for me Neil."

Major Savage entered the lab without a protective suit and the entity looked pleased to see him, it held out its hand as Savage had done and Savage took it, then with its other hand it touched the side of Savage's head… everybody gasped and it was as if time suddenly stood still…

Savage murmured as if in a sudden momentary trance and the team became worried, Gunn began to put a protective suit on…

"Stop it Neil, it is doing something to the Major" Gunn cried out.

But incredibly Major Savage then held a hand up as if to say no, his eyes looked different, they looked violet and seemed to sparkle like the entity's skin.

The entity released its hand from the Major's head.

"I have learnt your language, it is not one I am familiar with" said the entity and everybody was struck dumb except the Major.

"It is called English."

"English? I shall remember that."

"And you, who are you?" asked Savage, still reeling slightly from the entity's touch.

"I am… Mastema."

6

"Where are you from Mastema, do you have a second name, a surname perhaps… and how can you survive the moon environment without a space suit?"

Savage's mind was racing fast, it was as if a multitude of questions were trying to come out of his mouth as one

"Mastema the Fallen might be appropriate… I can see you have many questions and there is much I can tell you but also much I want to ask of you… but this is quite some audience, maybe we can go somewhere more discreet?"

"Of course… of course" said the Major and it felt as if he was fumbling his words, "We have a primary meeting room we can go to."

"Good, we shall go there then" said Mastema as he turned to Doctor Eden, "and maybe the female could join us?"

"She is called Susan Eden; she is the moon-base doctor."

"I assume you mean a physician, I had guessed. Good, you will probably need a physician Thomas Savage after what I will reveal to you."

Everyone went silent; they knew that this was probably the most important moment in the history of mankind. What was the entity now known as Mastema the Fallen about to reveal?

In the meeting room they sat at a round table that displayed a map of the moon on it with Eden and Savage sitting together and facing Mastema. The primary meeting room was secure and private but Savage did want the conversation recorded. Mastema did not seem to know what 'recorded' actually meant explaining that he only searched the Major's mind briefly concerning language, after Savage had explained, Mastema agreed.

"You have progressed beyond all imagination and I have watched in amazement as you constructed your lunar dwelling here."

"Why did you not contact us earlier?" asked the Major.

"Quite simple really, I did not want to disturb you. Your dwelling now seems complete so I thought that the time was right."

"Are you alone Mastema or are there others like you?" intervened Doctor Eden.

"You ask questions from the heart Susan Eden, I like that. Yes, I am quite alone, I have been for eons."

Eden looked to Savage and both were quite stunned by this statement.

"Eons?" stuttered Savage.

"I feel as old as time itself dear Thomas, but maybe it is because I have been so alone for so long" Mastema replied and his remarkable eyes seemed to glaze over, they even seemed moon grey and angry for a short moment. Doctor Eden knew that this meeting might be too much for her and Savage but she continued, "So you... you are saying that you are immortal?"

"Oh I was once mortal, just like both of you."

"You died then?" asked Eden anxiously knowing how ridiculous she sounded.

"I was taken after death, hand picked, I suppose, I had a life but I was needed to serve a higher purpose."

"Who...what?"

"Aenor."

"What is Aenor?" asked Savage.

"Aenor is the God of Everything" replied Mastema then he smiled, "Maybe you have another name for Him?"

"Another name would be... Yahweh" added Savage who was now trying to comprehend what Mastema was saying.

"Yahweh... is God!" exclaimed Eden, her voice gasping like a dying fish.

"Yes, He is" was Mastema's simple reply, "And I loved Him completely for years... until I could take the pain and suffering no more."

"Pain?" asked Savage who was still reeling from this revelation.

"The pain and suffering of mankind."

Eden stood up and paced nervously around the meeting room…

"My God… Yahweh cast you out of Heaven!"

"Yes, He grew tired of my constant arguing and requests to end human plight… and the day my son died I confronted Him."

"You… you are…"

"I am one of the Fallen."

"The Fallen Angel!"

Savage moved back in his chair away from Mastema and Mastema seemed concerned by this.

"You're saying… that you are the fucking Devil!?"

Eden knew that Savage did not usually swear but on this occasion she had to forgive him.

"Devil… of what Devil do you speak?" asked Mastema.

"You do not know do you?" said Eden, "The mythology of the Devil is unknown to you or are you simply toying with us?"

"There were many devils and demons in my world, of course, as I have told you, I was banished here, not the world known to you as Earth, I would have to delve deeper into Major Savage's memories to find the specific Devil you speak of."

"My God… my God" Eden repeated in an almost hysterical state, "How can any of this be true?"

"I am here dear Doctor Eden, am I not?"

Eden tried to calm down as did Savage, they felt sure that this fallen angel was no Devil but there was a still a nagging doubt and as Eden became sympathetic to what Mastema had said, she was also aware that Mastema's resemblance to her dead fiancé might have had something to do with that.

"How… have you kept sane Mastema… even an obviously strong being such as you would go mad stranded on this forsaken place for so long?" asked Eden and she knew that the doctor inside of her had asked the question.

"My dwelling, I have carved it out with my bare hands, it kept me busy… I always believed that I would not be alone forever, I had to think that and now you are here."

"Your dwelling… could we see it; go there?" asked Savage with renewed excitement. Savage now felt like an explorer whose discovery was about to change the world.

"Of course, we could go there now if you want?"

"No not now, we need to rest, I am guessing that you do not?"

"Oh sometimes Thomas, I like to think, to reflect, to imagine and… to remember" and his last words he said with some sadness.

"We are not so different then" said Eden who felt she was looking at her dead lover.

"No, you remind me of what I was" replied Mastema and Eden blushed again because his deep violet eyes had seemed to enter her very being.

"Tomorrow then, we will go to your dwelling" said Savage, "after our batteries have been recharged, I assume you understand how your presence here has tested us?"

"Of course… and will it be just the three of us again?" asked Mastema.

"I will need my security officer I think, it's a matter of protocol" replied Savage.

"So be it" proclaimed Mastema and his disarming smile lit up the meeting room.

"How far away is your dwelling?" asked Savage still curious as to how it was never revealed by any sensors.

"Not far, if we ride in one of your strange chariots."

Savage laughed, "Moon buggies, you mean" and then he had to ask Mastema, "How did we not pick up your dwelling on our sensors?"

"Maybe you were simply just not looking for it?" replied Mastema, "but it is well hidden in the depths of the caverns."

"In the lava tunnels?"

"If that is what you call them, I call it my palace not that I was a king but I came to think of Lunar as my kingdom."

As Savage and Eden prepared to leave the meeting room, Mastema managed to brush his hand against the skin of Eden's hand. Eden was not aware of this.

8

Back in her dome, Eden could not rest, her adrenalin levels were sky high but she knew that she had to try and get some sort of sleep before what was probably going to be the greatest day of her life. *An angel's abode* she thought to herself, *how can this be?* The Stepping Stone project had indeed become a stepping stone, a gigantic one. What would this mean to humanity? Surely it would mean that God, Yahweh or Aenor as Mastema had mentioned did indeed exist, that maybe life after death was true. What would be the impact of all this when it became known on Earth?

Eden poured herself a large brandy in one of those big wide glasses that were used on special occasions, she did not believe in sedatives as such even though she would prescribe them to patients when needed and just after she had taken a much needed drink, Savage came on the videocom…

"Hi Susan, I was just wondering how you are? I have just finished briefing those that need to know about tomorrow."

"Tomorrow? You know where we are going Tom, the home of an angel!"

"I… it's just mind-blowing, I'm struggling a bit with all this I guess."

"Do you need anything? I am having a large brandy but if you need me to prescribe something for you I will understand, no-one will need to know."

"No… I'm fine, a brandy sounds like a good idea, bring something with you tomorrow though just in case" and Savage managed a smile. "What do you make of him Susan?"

"I… feel that there is a great sadness about him, a deep loneliness within him."

"Yes, and when he suggested that he was the fallen angel; that just freaked me out!"

"We have to ignore what we may have imagined before… think Tom, if what he is saying is true then he knows God, he has spoken to God; he bloody well knows what Heaven is like!"

Eden drank some more of her brandy.

"If what he is saying is true remember."

"But how would he know about our belief in God?" surmised Eden.

"I… don't know, my mind is mixed up, paranoia I guess… I was thinking alien technology, maybe he is a product of that somehow?"

"Your imagination is running away with you Tom but that is understandable given the circumstances. I can only suggest that we take this one step at a time."

"Of course, you're right Doc; I will see you tomorrow… not too early though, try and get some sleep."

"I'll try, this brandy should help."

***

The brandy did help and eventually the mind of Eden switched off and drifted uncomfortably towards sleep.

Strange images assailed her thoughts as she slept – men with wings, clouds, colourful rainbow gardens; a light so bright it burnt her eyes… and from that light came the naked form of a man…

His skin sparkling in the surrounding light.

A man that came closer to her and whispered her name…

"Susan my love, I have missed you" and Eden turned in her sleep, aroused by the figure's presence.

It was Mastema, Samuel, the same…

And they joined her on her bed and caressed her slowly.

The doctor moaned…

As Samuel kissed her mouth and Mastema kissed her breasts.

"My love, my love" Susan Eden repeated.

"We are here" they said in unison as they both entered her and again she cried out in ecstasy.

The three moved as one and it was as if they had joined with eternity, like the night would never end, in love forever…

Together.

And when the doctor reached her climax, it was as if she had joined the heavens, as if she had become a star that would never stop burning.

The universe had opened up for her and she lay exhausted between the two men she knew as Mastema and Samuel.

And she slept.

Soundly.

And when Susan Eden opened her eyes the next morning, she felt calm and not afraid. She was excited by what the lunar day held in store for her.

And her dream was nothing but a warm memory.

9

It was midmorning moon time when they left in the moon vehicle. The vehicle was executive class, totally self-contained and driven by Security Officer Gunn.

Gunn was one of the few who had seen the recording of the meeting. He had not spoken much about it to the Major and remained sceptical and wary of the entity known as Mastema.

***

Mastema guided Gunn to the entrance to his dwelling and he had been proven correct in his estimation that it was not far using the 'Chariot' as the Major now called the vehicle.

Eden, Savage and Gunn suited up and stepped out into the quiet of the moonscape with a still clothed Mastema who also had a helmet for communication.

There was an opening ahead of them in the side of a tall rocky structure. To all purposes it was an opening to a cave, to Mastema it was something else completely.

"The doorway to my palace my new friends, please enter with me, you will need the shining light from your helmets."

Savage looked at Eden and knew that she was trembling.

Mastema and the Stepping Stone crew members entered the cavern. It was totally dark and it was immediately obvious that Mastema's eyes were accustomed to this. Gunn was prepared for this though and carried a powerful lantern that illuminated the wall completely.

They were indeed inside a lava tunnel that displayed a series of words and phases in an unknown language carved along it. Shortly they came upon wide steps leading downward that looked they had been smoothed out, *by hand* thought Savage as he remembered what Mastema had said. The steps led down to an enormous wide open space that was obviously Mastema's palace.

Eden and Savage gasped in amazement. The cavern was circular and the walls were covered in a glorious multitude of carved relief images, the majority of which were below head height but some figures did soar above them which made Savage wonder just how that was achieved – various men, women, places, gardens, meetings, a variety of scenes in one continuous circular movement of activity, all leading to a large stone seat in front of a wide round moonstone table... and behind that seat was the large carved face of a woman... a face that held a chilling, vague resemblance to the face of Doctor Eden.

Savage turned at Eden, his eyes wide with wonder.

"Is that you?"

"Of... course not, how could that be? Coincidence that's all, please do not dwell on this Tom."

"Of course not doctor, I'm sorry."

"How the Hell has he done this?" asked Gunn.

"By hand, with crude tools carved from the rock" interrupted Mastema.

"It's... incredible, a marvellous work of art" said Savage in utter appreciation of what Mastema had accomplished.

"Thank you Thomas, your words please me greatly."

Eden took pictures and Mastema did not object, she knew that he probably did not understand what a camera was.

Eden, Savage and Gunn studied the walls for some time and eventually Eden had to ask who the woman behind his seat was.

"My wife, before I was taken, her name is Meliah... I loved her greatly and still do" and for the first time the doctor noticed tears in Mastema's eyes, they seemed pure violet and for some reason this did not surprise her. She laid a hand on Mastema's shoulder in an attempt to lessen his sudden grief.

"Thank you Susan for your kindness, but it was such a long time ago, maybe she has forgotten me?"

"I think not Mastema."

"I hope not too."

As they stood in silence looking at Mastema's large sculptural portrait of Meliah, a sudden thought hit Eden, "And Yahweh, what of Him, is He depicted here Mastema?"

Eden suddenly felt an ice cold feeling in her suit, was she about to see the face of God!

Mastema's demeanour changed suddenly, he appeared irritated, angry... "No, Aenor is not depicted here. Why should I glorify somebody who cast me out because I defied His cruel intentions?"

Eden knew that this conversation could well escalate in a negative manner and would she be capable of comprehending what Mastema would say? She thought it best to leave such a discussion for a later date and a more appropriate place so Eden did not press Mastema further on this subject but she did ask him about the two narrow entrances each side of Meliah's large face, "More rooms?" asked Eden.

"Private chambers Susan, I would be grateful if you did not go in there."

"Private chambers? do you have possessions there, clothes even?"

Mastema laughed "Clothes? My clothes come to me if I think about them and I now understand your embarrassment at the sight of my naked body... you have no need for clothing when you are alone, I do apologise."

Eden was embarrassed again, "Of course we will respect your privacy" she eventually managed to say.

Suddenly Gunn intervened, "We have to head back to the Chariot sir, to renew our oxygen packs."

"Thanks Ray but I think we need to get back to the base now... do you want to come with us Mastema?"

"Of course Thomas, my palace seems even more lonely and desolate now that I have met you. My ambition is to return to Earth."

Savage was speechless as was Eden and Gunn, "I... I will see what I can arrange for you. There will be formalities; I have not fully informed headquarters yet but I think that we are now ready... and boy will this report be interesting" said Savage smiling.

"That has to be the understatement of all time sir" added Gunn.

"Your new world will be interested in me then Thomas?"

"Just a little bit I think" replied Savage with humour, "but I think secrecy will be paramount."

Mastema seemed excited by Savages' words but Eden was apprehensive, she knew that Mastema's fate could be far from what he imagined.

"Okay Ray, fire up the Chariot."

It was three weeks before it was agreed that Mastema could set foot on the Earth. During that time he was subject to more routine testing, scientific, medical and psychological and in that time he grew to both like and know more about Eden.

On the eve of Mastema's historical return to the land of his birth, Eden had to ask him about Meliah, about how she looked so much like herself.

"You are aware of my resemblance to Meliah?" she asked of Mastema.

"I am Susan."

"Are you aware of your resemblance to a man named Samuel Hayden?"

"I am Susan" was his same reply.

This declaration stunned her...

"How... how do you know this?" Eden demanded... then his hand gently grazing her hand surfaced in her memory, "I... see now, have you been visiting me during my sleep every night?"

Eden's question was blunt but without malice. Mastema simply smiled and in that moment she felt a great love for him.

"I must go now; a great adventure awaits me, one that I have dreamt about for an eternity."

Mastema lent forward and kissed the doctor, it was the first time he had done such a thing.

Suddenly Samuel Hayden appeared in her mind, he seemed alive, he seemed happy and all her grieving seemed to leave her at once.

"I love you Mastema."

"I love you too Susan."

Then Mastema left to prepare for his great journey home.

***

As Eden watched the shuttle leave from the Skyroom, she felt the sharp pang of an acute depression descend upon her but knew that she would see Mastema again as she had decided to resign from the Stepping Stone Project.

Three weeks later, Doctor Susan Eden became aware that she was pregnant.

WHERE ANGELS FELL

MASTEMA

The man with the old style horn-rimmed glasses sat staring pensively on the black leather chair that should have been much more comfortable. His neatly ironed white shirt was showing large patches of sweat under his armpits and as he loosened his thin black tie that had suddenly decided to strangle him seemingly, he swiped through the notes on the large tablet in front of him.

The man was nervous, he moved the small silver standing microphone closer to him and then shuffled uncomfortably as he thought about what he was about to say.

Opposite the sweating man sat the being known as Mastema, who was calm and composed and did not show the demeanour of someone who was now effectively being held as a prisoner.

It had been seven days since Mastema had arrived on Earth and he had no idea where he was as the authorities that were taking care of him, had not told him. Mastema knew that he was in a large protective complex and that his spacious living quarters were hidden deep underground.

Mastema had used his time wisely and been quick to learn how to use the contraption known as a computer which had been given to him for information; this knowledge he had gained from the mind of Major Savage but he had no idea though that the activity on his computer was being monitored.

Mastema had requested that Major Savage and Security Officer Gunn accompany him to Earth but Savage had not been able to leave the moon base until a replacement for his post had been arranged.

As soon as Mastema had arrived on Earth, Mastema had been subjected to physical examination and once again the results were unbelievable and astounding for all concerned, just as they had been on the moon. The scientists at the security establishment were totally baffled by the entity known as Mastema, they had no idea what he was... their conclusion was that he was of alien origin.

Now it was time for verbal examination, the only thing they required of Mastema was that he wore the protective gloves they provided; they were well aware and wary of his telepathic capabilities as advised by Major Savage.

"Please let me introduce myself" said the nervous man sitting opposite Mastema, "My name is Doctor Corrigan, I have been asked to speak to you on behalf of the American government. These interviews are meant to be advantageous for all concerned."

Mastema said nothing but simply continued to smile.

"I hope you find our talks very beneficial" added the

Mastema pulled softly at the gloves on his hand, "Indeed Doctor Corrigan, I am sure that I will... and I am intrigued by what more you want to know of me as I confided much to Major Savage.

Corrigan straightened in his chair, pushed his glasses towards his eyes and thought awhile before replying... "You are a great mystery to us Mastema..." then Corrigan hesitated... "Is Mastema your only name?"

"Me-han, I was known as Mastema Me-han."

Corrigan looked surprised by this reply.

"Your creators gave you two names then?" said Corrigan and his face looked solemn and confused. Mastema was puzzled by Corrigan's words and was quick to reply, "My creators? There is only one creator, you should know that."

Corrigan consulted the notes on his tablet again... "I think that depends on what you believe, don't you think?"

"I know it to be true."

"That God created this world and all on it?"

"I am not saying that."

"What are you saying then?"

"One day you will understand."

"I want understand now."

"You sound impatient Doctor Corrigan, I am not sure that you are ready for such information."

"Me?"

"The mortal race... some maybe... we shall see."

"The mortal race? So you acknowledge that you are not mortal, not of this world?"

"I was once, an eternity ago, but you are aware of this are you not from my discussions with Major Savage."

"Yes we have a complete record of that... but surely you are aware of what you are saying?"

"Of course."

"And you understand how difficult it is for us to believe such a thing?"

"No, because I speak the truth, how else would you explain my presence on the celestial place you call the moon?"

"You do not call it so?"

"No, I call it Lunar."

Doctor Corrigan became extremely nervous, as if he could not believe the conversation that he was having...

"Our conclusion is… that you are of extraterrestrial origin… that this is our first contact so to speak… our problem is… your motive, why you are here?"

Mastema's face was blank as he considered what Corrigan was saying, "I am here because you brought me here" was his straightforward reply.

Once again Doctor Corrigan shifted uncomfortably in his chair because he was about to ask another serious question, "What world are you from?"

"Your world."

"I still think that you are playing games with us."

"Why would I do that?"

"We could make you talk, we have ways of doing that" said Corrigan and now the tone of his voice was threatening.

"You could try… I might even let you… but you would not prevail."

Mastema's eyes suddenly seemed to change; as if they had suddenly become sparkling violet diamonds, he had noticed a movement in the interview room undetected by Corrigan. A faint shadow was moving slowly behind Corrigan, almost hovering over him. Mastema focussed his eyes more acutely.

"I notice that your eyes have changed" said Corrigan and he was worried, turning to the wide window behind him…

"Your eyes…"

Suddenly the furtive shadow encircled Corrigan then disappeared slowly as it entered the doctor's body. Mastema was intrigued as Corrigan's face slowly changed before him, his features contorted and blurred as if other faces were vying for control.

WHO ARE YOU?

"Who are you?"

YOU SAW ME?

"Yes"

WHAT IS YOU NAME?

"I am Mastema of Lolar."

I HAVE NOT SEEN YOUR KIND FOR SOME TIME

"My kind?"

YOU ARE ANGELIC ARE YOU NOT?

"Yes."

WHAT IS YOUR PURPOSE?

"What is your purpose and you have not told me your name?"

I AM NAMELESS

and the face of Corrigan began to change rapidly, woman man boy girl repeated…

AND I EXIST BECAUSE MORTALS EXIST

"You have no purpose then?"

I AM THE ANSWER
WHAT FEEBLE MORTALS CRAVE
I AM THEIR DARKEST DESIRES
THOSE THAT CHOOSE MY PATH LIVE IN

"You are Death then?"

NO

"You are Evil."

There was no answer and suddenly Corrigan's face stopped changing…

"…your eyes are sparkling like tiny bright diamonds!"

Doctor Corrigan's mind had returned but he seemed confused as if he did not know what had just happened; only one second of his time had passed. Mastema's eyes no longer sparkled.

"Are they?"

"No, not now… but in my notes it says that your skin was like diamond… but not now?"

"No, it has adapted again to the atmosphere of this world, much more favourable than that of Lunar don't you think doctor?"

Corrigan did not answer; it was as if he could not suddenly.

"Sorry" he stuttered, "I… think I need to end this interview now."

Mastema smiled, "You do not seem well Doctor Corrigan?"

"I'm… I'm fine, we will continue later."

Corrigan switched his tablet off and as he stood up he visibly swayed to one side, his glasses crashing to the floor. The door to the interview room opened immediately and a man came inside to help the doctor. Mastema knew that it was a reaction to his body being possessed by the entity called Nameless. After Corrigan was helped out, two hefty armed security guards escorted Mastema back to his living quarters.

As soon as he was back in his quarters, Mastema became reflective of his situation. There was no doubt now that he was being held as a prisoner by the people known as Americans but he was appreciative that his place of confinement was luxurious and comfortable compared to his rocky abode on the moon. There was a study room complete with a range of books covering various topics; all in the language that he now knew was English. The bathroom was lavish with a low level walk in bath that was almost like a small pool and reminiscent of his bathing area when he was mortal.

The bedroom was spacious with a king-size bed and there was a small kitchen area that was fully stocked even though food was delivered regularly. Mastema did not need to eat but he did, it was he considered a novelty and after an eternity of exile in a desolate barren place, it was something he enjoyed immensely. Mastema was particularly fond of red and white wine and was surprised that he actually felt slightly intoxicated when he drank them but this was something he knew he was activating himself. What Mastema really liked about his accommodation though was the large metal fireplace in the main room, he knew that the flames were not real, that somehow they were being simulated and that no heat emanated from them but fire was something that he had sorely missed during his exile. Watching the flames made him think better as it had always done when he was alive.

Mastema sat in the large comfortable brown leather chair next to the fireplace and stared into the flickering flames... what his accommodation lacked was a window, a view of the outside world. Mastema wondered about this new world and how vastly different it would be to the one he remembered, of course he had seen pictures and moving pictures on the marvellous thing known as the internet but they were no substitute for experiencing the real thing.

Mastema decided that he would wait for the arrival of Major Savage before making any further decision about his time with the Americans but he did know that he would not be staying in his confinement, no matter how luxurious it was, Doctor Corrigan's attitude had more or less confirmed that.

Mastema then thought about the entity that had called itself Nameless, he searched his memory of his angelic time on Earth but there was no recall of meeting such a being. Of course he knew that pure living evil existed, it was part of his argument with Aenor but he had never met it, never communicated with it, his work as an angel of Aenor had been to care for vulnerable people in their time of dying, to guide them through the portals to the place that was known to them as Enolan and Heaven. However, he did know that other angelic had experienced servants of Nameless, in the portals and on Earth and the souls of angels and mortals had perished in such meetings... Mastema began to think of the time before the argument, of the time when he was mortal... and warm tears filled his eyes.

Mastema could not remember the last time he had cried, he had cried constantly when his son had died but there had been many times since then, too many times which resulted in the 'argument.' Since then though he thought that his well had run dry, that he was hardened and unmoved by such thoughts, his banishment to the moon had done that to him, stripped him of all emotion. Was that part of Aenor's plan for him then, when emotion is gone, there is no feeling, no breeding ground for argument?

Being back on Earth amongst the mortals had revived his spirit, revived his soul and he knew that he had made the right choice in revealing himself to them – it was a message to Aenor, that he still existed, that he had survived his banishment. If Aenor was love then let Him show it.

Mastema wiped his tears; he knew that he was being monitored constantly, but he was not concerned by this, *"Let the mortals think what they may!"*

Mastema was surprised to suddenly feel that he craved a drink, *a white wine maybe, something that might help soothe my troubled mind* he thought, he went to the kitchen and poured himself a large glass of wine, he knew that he could drink the entire bottle in one go and a whole lot more but he decided that would not be wise. Mastema returned to his comfortable chair and gazed into the caring flames once more.

The beautiful face of his wife appeared, long dead but he knew that her soul was safe in Enolan, at least he hoped so, his argument with Aenor had happened before her death so he had not been the one who had guided her there. She might not have needed help though, through the portals or the Blue Veins as they were known to the Angelic. The majority of mortals did not need such help, only the troubled and confused were the concern of the Angelic and this was why the number of the Angelic was vast. This had been another prickly thorn in Mastema's side, why so many Angelic were needed... but Mastema was not ready to fully remember again, at least not yet, the 'argument' would only sadden, anger and frustrate him, he had to remain focussed on his main object, to return to Enolan!

To see his wife and son again...

The flames of the steel fire blurred as once again his eyes filled with sudden tears.

Another face appeared in the dancing flames, not his wife but similar.

Susan Eden.

Mastema had been truly astounded by the fact that she looked so much like his wife but he had tried not to show it... and why did he look so similar to the man that Eden had loved? Some cosmic coincidence, some strange twist of fate or was there a reason for it? Mastema knew that he was over-thinking things – he drank more wine but still the face of Eden stared back at him.

Mastema had not been able to control of himself, an eternity alone had compelled him to go to Susan Eden... he had not been making love to her though, he had been making love to his late wife... and now he loved both of them. Would he see Eden again? Mastema sincerely hoped so, to explain everything to her as he wanted to do with Major Savage.

Mastema became tired, not physically but mentally, or maybe it was the soothing wine, he went to his king-size bed and rested, he hoped for the feeling of light sleep, he was capable of catatonic sleep, sleeping for years at a time; this was how he had survived his banishment. Here on

Earth though there would be no need for such extremity, for some reason he felt that if he did go catatonic then that would be fatal. Mastema closed his eyes and his mind began to wander...

And he began to dream.

Of the first time that he had flown through the endless sky.

His wings of light shining brightly behind him.

He had never known freedom like it.

Across the never-ending fields of Enolan he flew, up amongst the new stars and beyond, the entire cosmos surrounded and protected him as he flew like a new fledgling...

For he had to master this new ability.

He would need perfection of flight for the Portals.

EDEN

Immediately after the departure of Mastema to Earth, Doctor Eden video messaged her resignation to Moonbase Headquarters, a decision not taken lightly but one she felt compelled to do.

On the eve of Eden's return to Earth three weeks later, the cold realisation of what had happened to her became apparent, she had been experiencing regular acute morning sickness which eventually forced her to conduct a self pregnancy test which incredibly proved positive.

How is this possible?

The erotic dreams of Mastema and her beloved Samuel were just dreams surely?

The test results did not lie though and this hit the doctor like a sledge hammer to her belly.

"My God... my God" she kept exclaiming to herself, "I am carrying the child of an angel!"

This was the only explanation, there simply was no other.

Eden's hand shook as she poured herself a large glass of wine; she then went to the window of her room and stared out blankly at the still lunar landscape.

He walked out from there, from the grey darkness, lit by the lights of the moon-base and the blue of the Earth... naked... a being who claimed to be the Fallen Angel, the angel cast out of Heaven by God!

Eden trembled violently at this thought, it was too much for any single mortal to truly comprehend; she then began to shake uncontrollably as this thought finally gripped her like a suffocating metal vice. Slowly warm tears filled her eyes that blurred her vision of the moon, not because she thought that she was losing her sanity but because of the all-consuming love she felt for Mastema.

But what if he was not an 'angel' What if he was an alien or some sort of highly advanced android, an other worldly avatar that was being controlled from beyond the stars or somewhere closer? This was a sinister thought and Eden felt that she was on the verge of a panic attack, she had to talk to someone and the only one she could trust was Tom Savage, she went to her video com.

"Hi Tom... I..."

"Hey Sue, are you alright, you look..."

"I'm... not, Tom... I..."

"Stay there, I'll be right over."

In the living quarter's area, Savage's room was not far from the doctors and after entering her room he went immediately to Eden and noticed that she was trembling; "Okay Doc, what's up?"

They both took a seat beside the window and Savage poured himself a drink. Eden looked out to the stillness and so wished that she could see the stars but only one or two were faintly visible, like tiny dying lights in the distance, she knew that the rest of the stars had been swallowed up by the light of the sun reflecting from the Earth.

Eden took a big gulp from her glass of wine then refreshed her glass, she had calmed down somewhat since the arrival of Savage, her shaking hand had greatly subsided... "I'm pregnant Tom" she blurted out and the Major nearly fell off his chair.

"Who... how?" he replied and he began to mentally try and picture which member of the crew it was and none came to mind, if the doctor had been involved in a relationship then she had managed to keep it well under wraps. Savage could not believe her answer when Eden finally summoned up the courage to reply...

"Mastema."

The Major gulped down hard, the result of not believing his ears.

"I thought I was dreaming" Eden continued, "he came to me during the night... he looked so much like my beloved Samuel."

"Are you sure Susan?"

"Of course, there was nobody else"

"But how?"

"How? Was his room locked?"

"It would have been" replied Savage then he became thoughtful... "But he could have accessed the unlocking code from my mind... damn!"

"Do not blame yourself Tom, it is what it is."

"You seem suddenly at ease with your situation?"

"I think I am now... I was worried; worried about who and also what Mastema was... but there was something about him. I know that this will sound unbelievable, but I actually believe him."

"What, that he was cast out of Heaven and banished here to the moon?"

"Yes… and you Tom, what do you believe?"

"I'm afraid I cannot accept that, my scientific brain just won't allow me to, he has to be of alien origin."

"But you saw his carvings?"

"Savage became thoughtful, "Mastema is now the greatest enigma mankind has ever known, the world and the universe as we know it, is now changed forever."

"Nobody will know though, we have all signed the secrecy document, taken an oath."

"Of course and we will be watched. Mastema will be taken to the highest security unit."

"Then what?"

"Mastema has asked for me to be his confidante, both me and Gunn but I am not convinced that I will be given access to him, at least not immediately, to be honest, I cannot ever see them releasing Mastema."

"That sounds so cruel, so he is now effectively a prisoner?"

"You know how they work Sue but I will try my best to see that he is treated fairly, it all depends on what this will lead to… if he has a purpose or not?"

"But he has been stranded on the moon for centuries."

"So he says" said Savage and he sounded frustrated, "This is a mystery that only Mastema himself can answer… maybe I can help, maybe he will truly confide in me?"

"And what if he is not happy being a prisoner? If he is the father of my child then surely he will have rights?"

"But he is not human."

"But maybe he was once, what if I decide to talk, to tell the world about him?"

Savage immediately looked concerned, "They will not let you, and let's be honest, who is going to believe you, that an alien or even an angel maybe, is the father of your child! You will end up in the funny papers, a joke, and an embarrassment to your profession and family."

Eden looked sad, she knew that Savage was right, she would be a laughing stock, they would probably think that she'd had some sort of mental breakdown or even that she was suffering from some sort of moon fever, "I'm sorry Tom, and of course you are right."

"We will just have to take this one day at a time Sue, and I understand why you have resigned your post now."

"Well I made that decision weeks ago when Mastema was taken to Earth."

"It was not your pregnancy then?"

"No, I have just found out today."

"Of course... so what are your plans now Sue?"

"Just to go back home, to England, and do what you suggested; take it one day at a time."

The Major smiled, he knew that it was all that both of them could really do.

MASTEMA

It was a few days later when Doctor Corrigan returned. Mastema noticed a distinct change in Corrigan, his nervous demeanour had gone, this time he seemed more assertive, more focussed, his facial features even looked different but behind his glasses his eyes were bloodshot and sickly looking.

They were in the same interview room, facing each other and this time Corrigan was smiling, Mastema could not remember Corrigan smiling the last time they had met and it was not a nice smile, it was a cruel smile.

"It has now been some time since our last meeting Mastema, I hope that you have used this time wisely and have reconsidered."

"Reconsidered what?"

Again Corrigan smiled, "Your situation basically, you are obviously withholding information from us, information we need."

"I thought that I had made everything clear to Major Savage when we spoke on the moon-base?"

"We have read the report but unfortunately we think that it is a fabrication, a lie."

"That is your prerogative doctor but it does not change the reality."

Corrigan began to laugh in a slightly maniacal way, "That you are in fact some sort of an angel, do you really expect us to believe that?"

"It does not really matter to me what you believe doctor" was Mastema's stern reply. Corrigan then became thoughtful, stood up from his chair and paced around the floor.

"Think about what you are implying; that you have spoken with God, seen Heaven... and now you want to make yourself known to mankind, and what would be the consequences be if what you say is true, surely global chaos would ensue?"

"Not chaos, peace and love I would imagine, from what I have seen so far, I think it is time for mankind to believe again."

Again Corrigan began to laugh as he sat back down, "So you see yourself as the new Messiah?"

"No, I see myself as simply Mastema, someone who has returned home."

"You lie Mastema; you are not and never have been of this world, where are you from and what is your purpose?"

Corrigan's face became cruel and angry; his red eyes began to burn as if the fires of Hell had just consumed him.

"I do not like your tone of voice doctor, this time I am declaring the interview over."

Then the room darkened and Mastema smiled, he knew what was happening again.

Corrigan's face began to change but not as fast as the last time it had happened. The face of a woman with dark skin looked at Mastema...

YOU ARE NOT WELCOME HERE ANGELIC

THE TIME OF YOUR KIND IN THIS REALM

IS NO MORE!

Mastema slowly took off his gloves and reached across the table and touched Corrigan's hand.

IF YOU TRYING TO REACH MY SOUL

THEN YOU WASTE YOUR TIME

"Your soul is not my concern Nameless, information is."

Mastema withdrew his hand, he did not like the feeling of touching pure evil but it was not Nameless he sought, it was the mind of Doctor Corrigan.

"Why have you come back to converse with me Nameless?"

TO WARN YOU

TO TELL YOU THAT YOU WASTE YOUR TIME

"How is my time wasted here?"

YOUR WONDERFUL AENOR HAS ABANDONED THIS WORLD

THE GATES OF YOUR ENOLAN ARE CLOSED

"You are the father of lies I think Nameless, the Aenor that I knew would never abandon his flock!"

Mastema was now looking at the manic face of an aged man, spittle dribbled down his chin and dark sunken rings encircled his eyes, this face was displaying a sickly smile...

HOW LONG IS IT SINCE YOU WALKED THIS EARTH?

THERE ARE NO MORE ANGELIC

THEY ARE LOST IN THE PORTALS THAT I CONTROL NOW

"I do not believe it!"

The entity known as Nameless began to laugh and it echoed around the interview room making the walls shake with its unearthly vibration. The face of Nameless then changed to that of a young boy and the laughter began to fade as did the haunting face of the young boy...

SEE FOR YOURSELF THEN ANGELIC

THIS WORLD IS MINE

Suddenly the face of Doctor Corrigan reappeared, "I am waiting for your response Mastema."

"Then you will wait forever doctor and forever is a very long time."

An eerie silence filled the room then Corrigan stood up with his computer tablet in his hand.

"This is disappointing Mastema and I have so many more questions for you, the two long scars on you back for example. I am afraid we will move to Level Two now."

Mastema said nothing, just stared intently at the doctor as he left the room with a sinister smile on his face.

Mastema's two security guards walked him back to his living quarters. Mastema had no idea what Corrigan had meant by Level Two but he guessed that it was unpleasant by the way Corrigan had informed him.

CORRIGAN

Corrigan woke up sweating, he felt feverish and weak and his head was pounding like it was about to burst, he ran quickly to the bathroom where he was violently sick. This nightly occurrence had started since his first meeting with Mastema, he did not mind the sickness so much though, it was the voices in his head that worried him... mumbling incoherent voices, in changing languages that he did not understand. Some of the voices did break through in English though, fragmented words...

Kill

Destroy the Angelic

Do it

His kind is no more

Corrigan had begun to hate Mastema, the sight of his gleaming, shining skin repulsed him, his overbearing confidence that seemed to state that he was superior in some way irritated him. Corrigan was glad that they were now moving to Level Two...

Humiliate

Torture

Destroy

Corrigan looked in the bathroom mirror and saw a myriad of faces looking back at him, scowling at him with deathly glares and open mouths that moved unnaturally as they said...

Do it

Do it

"Yes, I will... we will" Corrigan answered and he smiled to himself, content in the knowledge that the angel known as Mastema was soon about to suffer.

It was a Saturday morning; Mastema was feeling slightly apprehensive for some reason, he had a strong feeling that something was about to happen... and sure enough it did. In the main room of his living quarters, a portion of the wall slid silently open, it was a hidden door to a secret adjacent room. The two large guards that were assigned to Mastema entered. Mastema saw them from the kitchen and went to them.

"Ah, hidden entrances, I suspected so, I guess that you want me to come with you?"

The two surly men in uniform nodded together in unison. Mastema knew their type, soldiers who only responded to orders; he had saved so many after fatality on the battlefield.

"Then lead on my good men" added Mastema.

"This way" one of the men said and Mastema followed them through the doorway.

In the next room, Mastema was quite impressed by what he saw; he was inside a room as big as his entire quarters, a room that was full of all types of different electronic equipment, wall to wall computers with men sitting operating every one of them, who all turned on their seats to see the strange entity that they had secretly observed.

In the centre of the room was something that oddly seemed out of place to Mastema, it looked like a vertical standing single bed or board and what was ominous about it was the thick leather arm and feet straps. The board looked like it would adjust to become horizontal. Suddenly, the two security guards grabbed Mastema's arms and Mastema did not resist.

Another hidden door on the wall opposite Mastema opened and three men in smart green military jackets walked into the room, Mastema knew immediately that these three were the men in charge by the array of small coloured bands on their chests. The room that they had emerged from was obviously a briefing room and Mastema knew that this was what Corrigan had meant by Level Two.

The man in the middle of the three military leaders spoke first.

"Entity known as Mastema, I'm afraid that you have been less than cooperative with Doctor Corrigan so unfortunately we will have to move to Level Two. I think that this will result in the correct information which is what we need as I am sure you will understand."

"You have not introduced yourself" said Mastema with some disdain, "And I do understand but this is all unnecessary as Major Savage is witness to who I am."

"My apologies Mastema, I am General Stobbs, supreme commander of the American forces... and you are an enigma that needs to be resolved."

The general's eyes seemed to burn bright when he said this, then he nodded to the guards that were still holding Mastema. The two men took him to the standing restraint board in the middle of the room, opened up his shirt and rolled up the sleeves then strapped him to the board. Mastema did not resist, he was surrounded by mortals who were all staring at him in silence, it was as if they were waiting for someone… and then he entered from the briefing room. It was Corrigan in a white medical jacket and Mastema noticed immediately that his appearance had somewhat deteriorated. Corrigan looked unkempt, his face was pale and his eyes looked bloated and dark behind his glasses, even his walk was different, his posture and gait was uneven. When Corrigan spoke, his voice was deeper and his words slurred, "This is better Mastema, I now have you exactly where I want you, and I have the authority to do what I want."

"Do what you will doctor" was Mastema's calm reply.

"Oh we will Mastema, and we will enjoy it."

Suddenly the standing board began to tilt until Mastema was lying flat in front of the doctor. A big steel attaché case was handed to Corrigan which he promptly opened, producing a large syringe containing a dark green liquid.

"This will sedate you somewhat Mastema, I have increased the dosage to match your unusual constitution, soon you will tell us what we need to know."

Mastema looked coldly at the doctor; there was no smile, just a look of defiance with a hint of pity.

Corrigan grabbed Mastema's arm and prepared to insert the sharp needle of the syringe into it, there was a wide grin on his face which dropped dramatically when he saw Mastema's skin change.

It began to sparkle like tiny diamonds, reflecting the blue light from the surrounding computer screens… then the skin hardened and crystallised until it looked totally transparent. Mastema no longer breathed or moved… he had turned to pure diamond.

"What the fuck?" exclaimed Corrigan viciously, "Fucking angelic, you only delay the inevitable!" he shouted and stabbed the syringe onto Mastema's arm but it only broke into pieces. Corrigan became even angrier, so much so that he began to shake and he began to swear repeatedly, the sound of his voice changing with every word.

"What is it Corrigan?" shouted General Stobbs, "What has happened?"

"He… he has gone into some sort of protective catatonic state General."

"His skin is like glass, like diamond!"

"Diamond can be cut General, laser beams…"

"And what will we learn then?"

"Bring me the right equipment and I will cut into his heart!"

General Stobbs turned to the other Generals, who both shook their heads, "No, we will wait, wait for Savage, he might just be the key to unlock this."

Corrigan growled and scowled in disgust as he walked away and out of the room.

"Fucking angelic, fucking angelic" he repeated as he reluctantly left the body of Mastema behind him.

"That's one fucking disappointed doctor" said one of the Generals.

"The guys fucked up, did you see the state of him?" said the other General.

"Fuck him" said General Stobbs, "Corrigan has outlived his usefulness for now; as soon as Savage arrives on Earth I want him here!"

Stobbs stared at the unmoving ice-like body of Mastema; he could not believe what he had just witnessed.

SAVAGE

After speaking with Doctor Eden, Major Savage went to Ray Gunn's room where he was preparing for the return journey to Earth. Savage explained to Gunn what had happened concerning Doctor Eden and Gunn's response was, "I knew there was something shady about Mastema, loving the alien springs to mind."

"Susan thought that she was dreaming."

"Under some manipulative spell more like."

"Possibly... I want you to access the monitors to Mastema's quarters Ray, see what we can find out."

Gunn clicked on his computer and found the relevant monitor file and skipped through the recorded footage.

"Look Ray! Slow it down..."

The door to Mastema's room opened but nobody came out, then the door closed.

"What the Hell?" exclaimed Gunn but Savage was thoughtful.

"He can make himself invisible, maybe some sort of cloaking device?"

"We need to log this Tom" was Gunn's immediate response.

"Yes... no, wait; there is no proof, just a door opening and shutting, malfunctioning maybe?"

"What? C'mon Tom..."

"I just think that we need to keep this to ourselves for now."

"Why?"

"I don't know, a gut feeling I guess."

"Okay, you're the boss" replied Gunn reluctantly but he would honour his Major's request.

"C'mon Ray, we need to get ready for the shuttle home now" said Savage but before he left; Gunn had had a question for him, "So what do you think Mastema is then Tom, you've never really said?"

"He has to be an alien Ray, I can see no other alternative, maybe he crash-landed here years ago?"

"And those cave carvings of his?"

"Memories of his own world maybe?"

"I still wonder how he did it" said Gunn thoughtfully.

"Remember, there was a room that he did not want us to enter, he could have the relevant tools there, or maybe it leads to the remains of his ship, he would have supplies there."

"We should order another survey of his dwelling then?"

"Officially we're finished here for now Ray, our replacements might have that in mind, right now I'm more interested in what makes Mastema tick, what's on his mind and where he is from."

"What do you think they will do with him then?"

"I don't really know, informal interrogation initially, he has shown no sign of aggressiveness. I think they will be worried about him contacting his home world somehow although how he would do that I have no idea even access to a computer would not achieve that."

"I hope you are right about that, remember ET managed to phone home" replied Gunn and this caused Savage to laugh out loud then he became serious again.

"What is really worrying me though Ray, is that they will not release him."

**

The flight home on the Stepping Stone Shuttle was rather muted. Eden, Savage and Gunn were all preoccupied about what lay ahead, not just for themselves but for the future of mankind. Whatever or whoever Mastema was, they all knew that their world was never going to be the same again.

As planned, Eden went straight home to England after landing and Savage and Gunn were whisked immediately away to the Area 51 Complex which was not far from Savage's hometown of Las Vegas.

It was a sleek black government helicopter that took Savage and Gunn to the secret destination. Savage looked at the speeding desert below and wondered about Mastema, *how had the security forces treated him? Would he be the same?* One thing was for certain now though and that was he was soon to find out.

Soon after arriving at the Complex, Savage and Gunn were led through the briefing room to the room were Mastema was incarcerated. What greeted their eyes saddened them; the lonely figure of Mastema lying strapped to the restraining bed was not what they were expecting. As they neared the seemingly lifeless body, Savage gasped as he saw the hard diamond-like skin of Mastema.

"My God, what have you done to him?"

"Nothing" said General Stobbs, who was now standing behind Savage and Gunn, "His skin changed... then he died."

"Died, are you sure General?"

"C'mon Major, what do you think, just look at his skin, we have not been able to penetrate it with anything, not been able to do any sort of autopsy."

"Have you not thought that this might be some sort of alternate state, to protect him, I assume that you moved to Level Two?"

"We had no alternative Major, he was not cooperating and we needed to know exactly what he was and where he was from, I am sure that you understand this."

Savage looked at Gunn and grimaced, "You assumed that he was a threat then General?" asked Savage.

"He was withholding information; his story about being an 'angel' was just not viable, I am sure you agree?"

Savage reluctantly had to nod his head, of course Mastema was not an angel, he was of alien origin but that still did not make him automatically a threat... then Savage noticed the odd looking Corrigan, grinning on the other side of the bed. Corrigan had been waiting patiently for Savage's arrival; he was convinced that existence of Mastema had not ended, why he was so sure of this he did not know.

Savage reached out and touched the arm of Mastema as if he was touching a comrade that had just died...

Suddenly to the astonishment of Savage, Mastema's shining eyes opened and looked directly at him, "Ah Tom, it is good to see you my friend. I have been waiting for you."

Everyone in the room gasped in surprise, except for Corrigan who continued to smile, his instincts had proven to be right. Guards quickly surrounded the bed brandishing deadly weapons, all of which were pointed at Mastema. Mastema leaned up from the bed and the restraints broke as if they were made of paper, he then stepped from the bed and glanced around the now hostile room, "Am I a prisoner now Tom?" he asked Savage who looked to the General before replying, "I'm afraid so Mastema, I was hoping that they would not go to Level Two."

"I know someone who did" replied Mastema and he turned to look at Corrigan who was still grinning like a mad Cheshire cat.

"Do not try anything Mastema, you are surrounded and this complex is secure" exclaimed the General with all the authority he could muster.

"Seems to me after investigating the history of this new world that humanity is never secure" retorted Mastema.

"So you and your kind are a threat then?" asked the General. Mastema only smiled like a father would to his child who did not understand, "I can see that it is worthless talking with you and your kind General, it is time to take my leave of you" said Mastema and suddenly he was no longer there.

"What the?" exclaimed General Stobbs and everyone in the room looked astounded...

Except for Savage and Gunn, who just smiled secretly at each other.

The personnel in the room were immediately restless, waiting for the General's immediate orders.

"He's... gone!" said the puzzled General, still looking around the room.

"Teleportation?" said the still smiling Gunn, "Y'know, beam me up Scotty."

The General ignored Gunn's flippant comment then he shouted to the guards, "Search the complex, shut it down, nobody farts or leaves without my permission!"

Savage turned to the General looking concerned, "General, I really need to get home, I have been away some time and I have video conferences to prepare, whatever has happened to Mastema, wherever he has gone, I think that I am of no use to you at this moment."

The General looked around, men were scurrying away, the surveillance team returned to their computers and then he looked at Corrigan who was standing glaring intently at Major Savage.

"Of course Tom I understand, follow me" said a flustered General who now had an excuse to the leave the room.

They went into the briefing room where Savage and Gunn's kit bags were, only the General, Savage and Gunn were present.

"There will be a car waiting for you at the main gate" Stobbs said then he paused for a moment before continuing, "Where is he Tom, what happened in there?"

"I really don't know sir" answered Savage but he was being less than truthful.

"Self destruct?" suggested Gunn, "Or maybe he was teleported out of there?"

"Self destruct? But there is nothing there, no remains... and teleportation, why did he not do that before?" replied the General scratching his head.

"Maybe... he's returned to wherever he came from?" said Savage rather wistfully, "There's a lot we do not know about Mastema."

"We don't know doodley shit, it seems" growled the General then he looked Savage straight in the eye, "You mentioned video conferences?"

"My final report and conclusions sir that will obviously include today's events."

"Well I will look forward to that, it seems we had a genie on our hands, someone who can disappear like smoke."

"I think we had him trapped in a bottle General and I think he did not like it, maybe we should have been more patient?"

General Stobbs did not like Savage's comment and almost growled as he lit his shaking cigar, "I will keep you informed of any further developments."

"I will appreciate that sir" said Savage and both he and Gunn saluted before they left the briefing room.

***

At the main gate a black sporty BMW with darkened windows was waiting for them. A soldier stepped out of the car and opened the rear doors for them.

"Thank you private but I will be driving, there is no need for your service tonight" said Savage to the young man.

"But sir, my orders are…"

"Your orders have changed private, do not worry about the car, I will see that it is returned."

The private saluted then reluctantly marched away. Savage and Gunn put their kit in the boot then Savage looked up to the clear night sky and the moon, "Look at that Ray, not so long ago we were up there, looking out to the stars and where our future lay."

"And now?"

"And now we are back to where we started and maybe this is where our future lies?"

Gunn looked slightly puzzled by what Savage was saying.

"C'mon Ray, let's get moving, I think that genie may have a few more magical surprises for us yet."

Savage started the car and after going through security they headed towards Las Vegas and Savage's home.

It was about an hours drive to the outskirts of Las Vegas and Savages home, a house that he had inherited from his parents who had retired to the Californian coast. Gunn noticed that Savage seemed to be constantly checking the car mirror, "What's up Tom, do you think that someone is following us?"

"No… I… I was just thinking…"

"About your final report, is it true what you told the General?"

"Oh yes, they need my final conclusion Ray as to what I think Mastema is…"

"And what is that Tom?" came a soft voice from the back seat.

Gunn turned in surprise but Savage just smiled as he looked at Mastema in the car mirror. Mastema was no longer hardened diamond; his skin was as Savage remembered from the moon-base.

"Well it looks like the genie found a new bottle" exclaimed Gunn and they all laughed at this.

"This bottle is a smooth ride" noted Mastema.

"Courtesy of the army" replied Gunn, "nothing but the best for VIP's like us."

"I find it hard to imagine horseless carriages, but I think I could get used to it" said Mastema and he smiled as he looked out of the window to the swiftly passing darkness of the roadside.

"It seems you have the power of invisibility Mastema?" asked Savage casually as if it was something he asked of people everyday.

"A necessary function for the work we did here on Earth."

"Oh boy, would Stan Lee have loved this" joked Gunn, "So how do you do it?"

Mastema thought awhile before replying to Gunn's question, "I just think it, I seem to remember an angelic telling me that it was something to do with the re-born reflective quality of our skin."

"A reflection of light?" interrupted Savage.

"Yes, I imagine so but I am no scientist" answered Mastema.

"And the diamond-like skin?" asked Savage who now realised that he was interviewing Mastema.

"We have the ability to adapt to the harshest of environments, how do you think I survived on Lunar?"

"They thought that you were dead" said Gunn, referring to Mastema's diamond state at the Complex.

"I decided to go catatonic when that horrible Doctor Corrigan decided that he wanted to stick sharp needles into me" replied Mastema and Gunn had to smile.

"You can do that?" asked Savage who was now beginning to get really intrigued by this new information, *Surely Mastema was of alien origin* he thought, only an advanced civilisation could accomplish such things

"Oh yes, we can sleep for hundreds of years and indeed I did so for hundreds of years on Lunar, if I had not I would have surely have gone insane."

There was a slight moment's silence before Savage asked, "So you were aware of our first moon landings?"

"No, I am afraid I was not, I missed that epic moment, I was sleeping. I would have probably introduced myself to your first astronauts had I been aware of them… what made me awake from my heavy slumber was the activity surrounding the building of your moon-base."

"What, we woke you up?" Gunn asked and the question did sound kind of silly.

"Yes, in a way, I was probably due to awake anyway but I... sensed the movement, in the stars so to speak... before you go to sleep you can set a time to wake up, like one of your modern alarm clocks... but your mind and body can sense things too, a kind of survival instinct."

"Well, I am glad you were not grouchy when you woke up, that diamond skin of yours could have done us some damage" joked Gunn and they all laughed again.

"Oh no, I am not a monster" said Mastema.

"But you are an alien?" Savage had to say almost as if he were trying to catch Mastema off guard.

"I see that you still do not believe me Tom, but maybe we will have time now for me to tell you everything in a more relaxed setting. Where are we heading to Tom?"

"My home Mastema which is near a city called Las Vegas, not far to go now."

"Las Vegas is a nice name, and you Raymond, where are you heading to this night?"

"I'm from Las Vegas too, the other side of the tracks to Tom though" replied Gunn and Savage laughed again.

"Good, perhaps when we get there I can tell you my story; I have been waiting so long to do this."

"Well I was going to go straight home but that can wait" said Gunn, "If that's okay with you Tom?"

"Sure, you can crash at my place as long as you want, there's plenty of room, plenty to drink but we might have to order pizza though?"

Mastema stared out of the car window, up to the clear bright moon, he felt strange because it was as if he was looking to his home. Mastema knew that time had done this to him, if you stay in a place long enough then it becomes your home. Then the surrounding stars seemed to suddenly shine brighter, dazzling and glittering in the night sky, almost dancing before his eyes as the car moved through them. Seeing stars on the moon was rare and Mastema revelled in this sight, he wanted desperately to soar through them but he knew that might never happen again. Suddenly the car stopped and Major Savage interrupted Mastema's daydreaming.

"We're here, Savage Ranch at last."

All was dark and quiet; Mastema adjusted his eyesight to view the large house and surrounding land.

"All this land is yours Tom?" asked Mastema.

"My family home, my parents left it to me when they retired to White Palms."

"It is a farm then?"

"Not anymore, I just don't have the time with my job, maybe one day. There are wild horses though."

Mastema looked wistful and sad standing before the house and Savage and Gunn noticed this...

"I had a farm with horses... in Hibrasil."

HIBRASIL

1

Once inside the farmhouse they walked down a wide hallway to the main room which had a spacious modern feel to it which was almost at odds to the outer façade of the house.

Savage turned a few side lamps on and then was about to close the vertical blinds of the rooms main windows when Mastema pleaded, "Please leave them open Tom, the stars comfort me, I have not seen them sparkle in abundance like this for quite some time."

Savage then turned to Gunn who had to say, "Y'know they're not going to like this Tom, we should have taken Mastema straight back to them?"

"Back to what, more attempts at torture?" growled Savage as he thought about what they wanted to do to Mastema.

"Hey, I'm totally with you on this buddy, but you're harbouring an escaped prisoner now."

"A prisoner without rights" replied Savage sharply and he knew that he was echoing Doctor Eden's words.

"I can't send Mastema back to them, could you?"

"No like I said, I agree with you, but we have to be careful from mow on… closing those blinds could be a wise thing to do."

"Nobody's out there, they won't be looking here already surely?" Savage said but he did not realise that they had been followed.

"Of course not, but better safe than sorry I guess."

Savage reluctantly closed the blinds, "I'm sorry Mastema."

"I understand Tom, and if you feel I am a danger and a burden to you then I will leave now."

"No… no, you can stay, where would you go anyway?"

Mastema realised that Savage was right, where would he go?

"Ray is right Mastema, we have to be very careful from now on. Look, we all need to unwind a bit, to say that it has been a long day is an understatement, I'll get us some drinks."

Mastema and Gunn sat on separate low leather chairs that had steel arm rests. Black and grey was the theme of the room and Mastema noted, "Tom has, how would you say it, style?"

"Oh yeah, and he's bloody tidy, it's a little different to my modest flat" replied Gunn and Mastema thought that he was fooling with him.

"You are both military men, I know that you are trained to keep things orderly."

"Sure, but that is work buddy, when I am at home I like to kick my boots off, relax a little."

Mastema seemed to drift away, Gunn's words had made him think about his home again and Gunn sensed this. At this point Savage returned with the drinks and put them on the coffee table next to them.

"Cool beers and bourbon if you want it, I also have pizzas in the freezer so we will not starve" joked Savage.

Savage poured out the beer for Mastema, Gunn and himself then reclined back onto the elongated leather sofa opposite them.

All the tension of the last few weeks seemed to visibly evaporate from Savage immediately as he supped his beer; it was obvious that he was home, away from the pressure of running a moon-base, away from the pressure of worrying about the entity known as Mastema who was now sitting right in front of him. What Savage had witnessed since the arrival of this man on the moon was unbelievable but Savage was a practical man who knew that having Mastema in his house could be a way of finding out what he truly was and this was the excuse he had formulated should it somehow become known to the military authorities. Savage began to relax again at this thought but his curiosity was growing with every sip of his beer.

"You said that you wanted to tell us your story Mastema?"

"Yes I do," replied Mastema slowly, "But it can wait, the both of you must be exhausted."

"We are" interrupted Gunn, "but sleep can wait, what do you say Tom?"

"Of course, tell us what you want Mastema, it seems I have been waiting forever for this now."

Mastema shuffled in his chair, "Alright then, but it is a story that will take me to the depths of personal despair, it is a story that you will find unbelievable and one that will astound you."

Savage poured out more beer and Mastema began.

2

"I was born on a large island know as Hibrasil, the year was about 2,000BC if my calculations are correct. Hibrasil was situated in what you now call the Atlantic Ocean and it was west of the country of Nealan, what you now call Ireland, but Hibrasil was slightly smaller and circular in shape."

Savage and Gunn were impressed; it was obvious he had done his research during his confinement in the Complex.

"I have heard about this magical island" said Savage, "about how it disappeared thousands of years ago."

"I know that it is no longer there and that it is now considered to be a mythical island that only appears every seven years. I find that hard to believe but maybe one day I will try and prove that theory is true. Whatever happened to my beloved Hibrasil, whatever catastrophe occurred, it has not taken my memories away and that is all that matters.

As a young boy, life was idyllic and relatively safe except for the constant threat of the vicious and demonic Vaagen but I will speak more of them later. Hibrasil was a highly developed civilisation for it's time, the main city was called Hibar and was situated more or less in the centre of the island and from there it was encircled by many villages, some of which were situated on the coast. Each village had a speciality, for example, mining, ship-making, construction, steel, glass, clothing and household goods and every village was prosperous. In-between the villages were military bases and camps, a tight network for defence of the whole island.

The village that I lived in was called Lolar and my father Miro Me-han was the village Protector, the man who enforced the law of Hibrasil. Our village was situated on the west coast and it was one of the coastal fishing and farming communities. My father owned a small vegetable farm which was also full of horses and a variety of other animals. I can see him now; out in the fields during the day, then at night he would change into his Protector attire complete with broadsword, axe and knife. This is what impressed me the most when I was young, seeing my father dressed as a warrior.

Before he inherited the family farm, my father had been a warrior in the Hibrasil security guard. When my grandparents retired to their cosy home overlooking the sea, my father married and moved into the main farmhouse. My grandparents were still daily visitors though as their house was only a stones throw away, my grandfather would often joke that he was just checking that my father was looking after the farm properly. But my father knew that not only was working the farm important but being able to defend it was important too, so from an early age I was instructed in the art of self defence and battle, hand-to-hand combat without weapons, then combat skills using sword axe knife archery and horse riding ability. By the age of ten cycles I was a skilled young warrior, fully capable of defending myself and it was at this age that my father took me to Hibar for the Hi-Council of Blood to acknowledge my Coming of Age as a warrior.

3

The Coming of Age ceremony was a daunting prospect for me but my father prepared me well for it. My father explained that it was no long a drawn out affair, that it was a swift but painful necessity for anyone born to be a warrior... the hand of Aenor would be imprinted onto my chest, close to the heart by red hot metal and not by small needle like most people would do.

"This scar will be the sign that you are a true warrior" he said to me and he showed me his scar on his chest. I touched the scar gently, felt the hardened skin and this made me more determined to go through with the ceremony. Of course my mother did not want such a thing for me, her sign of Aenor had been applied by needle, she thought that the hot metal branding was barbaric and unnecessary but my father disagreed intensely; "It will prove that he is a warrior trained, something nobody can ever take from him. Mastema will fight two others, no weapons just hand-to-hand and the victor will be branded first, there is no shame in losing, that fact that you have fought will be evidence enough for Aenor."

"Exactly what I mean, 'branded' like cattle" exclaimed my mother.

Father just laughed at this statement, "So if we had no warriors, who do you think would protect you from the Vaagen?"

"Do you not think that I can fight?" retorted my mother immediately.

"Oh you can fight all right" laughed my father, "maybe you should come with us and be branded with Mastema?"

"Maybe I will, I have not visited Hibar for sometime. I do need some new clothes; see what the new fashion is, but nobody is coming near me with a hot iron!"

My father roared with laughter and eventually my mother and I had to join with him... but I was still scared.

"Good" my father eventually declared, "we will take the cart then, Mastema can ride his horse there like a true Lolar warrior."

HIBAR

It was the Season of Hetta, which was our summer. The weather would be hot and dry for months; perfect for the long ride to Hibar which father said would take about a week.

I was to ride my favourite horse that I called Thundar, his coat was a deep reddish brown but his frontal hair and mane displayed streaks of jagged white which always reminded me of bolts of lightning. The horses of Hibrasil were magnificent creatures, standing taller than the average man in height. Their appearance was that of a hybrid, half horse, half bison but there was no horns and their strength was unsurpassed by any other creature known to me

The night before we were to depart I was restless, a young boy who was on the verge of losing his youth. I felt a great sadness; did this mean no more toys, no more playing games? I did not know but what I did know was that I was soon to have a place of worth in the community and that made me smile as I looked out to Lunar above who seemed to be smiling back at me. Little did I know that one day I would call this moon my home, how could one even imagine such a thing?

Lunar comforted me and calmed my nervous excitement and soon I drifted off to a deep sleep beneath his caring eyes.

I was a man.

Fighting the Vaagen, who had deathly white faces...

With black zig zag VVV patterns

The Vaagen were nomadic cannibals...

Their ships were crude but sturdy

With the skulls of those eaten along the sides

The sails were made from human flesh...

And they sailed through our nightmares constantly.

Thankfully there had not been any sighting of them for some time...

But my father knew that their threat had not gone away.

I awoke from my dream as soon as it was light entered my room...

"It is time for you to become a man Mastema"

I heard the dawn whisper to me.

5

Everything was packed and ready, mother and father had obviously been busy the night before preparing for the journey. All we had to do was wash and eat breakfast then it would be time to go.

What father had flippantly called a 'cart' was a large wooden caravan full of supplies for the week long journey with room to spare for the three of us to sleep in. Two of the strongest horses were chosen to pull it.

My grandparents came to look after the farm while we were gone and father had instructed his Second to protect the village. My grandmother kissed and hugged me tight before we left, tears falling from her eyes because she knew what was in store for me.

"Be brave little Mastema, be brave."

"I am no longer little greatmama" I declared.

"No of course not, young man" she replied and little did I know that these would be the last words she would say to me.

***

All the villages of Hibrasil had straight roads leading to Hibar in the centre of the island. Father said that it would take seven to days to get to Hibar and at the halfway point we would stay in the village of Midlen which was a mining community, "Comfortable beds for the night at the village tavern will do us good" he said and this brought a broad smile to his face.

I had been camping before with my father but this journey seemed more exciting, more of an adventure at the end of which I was to be the hero.

The journey was slow and relaxing, there was no need to exert the horses so we kept at a leisurely pace. As darkness approached our fourth night on the Hibar road, we reached the village of Midlen. My father had stayed at the tavern he had chosen before and as soon as we had checked out our rooms, we went to the bar area for food and refreshments.

The people of Midlen were hard working people who liked to relax after work so the tavern was boisterous and full. The barman and owner of the tavern remembered my father and was pleased to hear why we were going to Hibar. The barman found us a quiet corner table and brought us a variety of large bowls containing hot beef in gravy, potatoes and vegetables: he also brought wine for my mother and a large jug of black Necal beer for my father. I was given cold milk and I must have scowled at this.

"Just a few more cycles son" said my father who had noticed my discerning face, "Then you can enjoy a Necal or two with me."

Mother smiled, "Fifteen cycles to be exact and not a day before mind!" she added and my father laughed.

After we had finished our meals I noticed that my father had been quiet for some time, as if his mind was somewhere else. I saw him look to the bar where a group of large rowdy men were drinking. The largest seemed to be looking over at us and I knew that my father was aware of this.

"Farmers, all they do is pull up potatoes all day, what do they know of real work?" I heard one of the men say.

"Quiet" said the barman, "Miro is a Protector; they are going to Hibar for the Coming of Age ceremony for his son, after that the boy will be acknowledged as a true warrior."

"What, that scrawny runt? I have seen bigger rats down the mines" said the largest man. After hearing this remark my father stood up. My father was as you see me now, tall, muscular with dark shoulder length hair, he had left his axe and sword in the room but I noticed that he still had his knife in his belt. My father took the knife and placed on the table in front of me.

"Miro no, they are not worth it, ignore them," my mother pleaded.

"I cannot Marta, you now that, he has insulted my family."

I stood up to walk with my father but my mother held me tight, she was clearly worried and I had not seen her so frightened, I could feel her trembling as she held me.

My father walked toward the group of men and the large one moved to the front of them.

"Well Protector, who is going to protect you then?" slurred the man who seemed to be a giant, he had thick hairy arms full of scars and abrasions and his clothes seemed dirty and unkempt. His bald head seemed as big as Lunar and his teeth looked broken and sharp when he smiled.

"I protect myself and my family, that is my main concern and I did not like your comments. I can see that you may have had too much Necal so if you apologise then we can forget all this."

The tavern went deathly silent for what seemed like an eternity then the large man clumsily lunged toward my father.

With his right boot my father kicked the aggressive man hard between his legs...

The man groaned out loud in pain and as his head lowered, my father then hit him below the chin with his hands that were clenched together. The large man dropped to the wooden floor like a huge sack of potatoes.

I broke free from my mother, grabbed my father's knife and ran to the man on the floor then held the sharp blade tight to his throat. When the man opened his eyes and looked down at the knife that was pressing against him he was clearly scared.

"Not bad for farmers eh?" remarked my father grinning, he then grabbed my shoulder, "Take my knife back to your mother Mastema, we do not need it... do we?" he asked the man.

"No" was the man's sullen reply then he began to smile as my father held out a hand to help him up from the floor. The man then put his arm around my father's shoulder and roared, "Necal and wine for the Protector, drinks for everyone!" and the whole bar cheered.

"You have still not apologised to my 'runt'" my father said rather sarcastically.

"That is no runt, that boy is a true warrior!" the man replied and again everyone cheered.

I had never felt so proud before or scared but deep inside me I knew that I would have cut that man's throat.

***

The next morning, we left the village later than we had anticipated, my father complained of food poisoning but my mother knew that it was due to the amount of Necal that he had consumed.

The further we travelled inland the hotter it became and on the seventh day, the mountain range surrounding Hibar came into view.

"Magnificent" remarked my father, "The Hand of Aenor, the mountains of our gods and Aenor lives on the highest." From my temple teachings I knew that this mountain was Mount Aenor, Aenor was our supreme God, the other four were the goddesses of our cycle seasons – Swetta was the Goddesss of Spring, Hetta was the Goddess of Summer, Arma was the Goddess of autumn and Anga was the Goddess of Winter, all were Goddesses except for Aenor. Our village temple was always decorated according to each season.

Of course later I would come to realise that the four goddesses did not exist and that the seasons were purely forces of nature… and it took me a long time to acknowledge Aenor as Yahweh the one God but to this day I still refer to him as Aenor.

Hibar was situated in a deep green valley in the middle of the Hand of God Mountains and two rivers either side of the towering city provided its water supply.

As we descended towards Hibar, the sun was setting and I marvelled at the magical beauty of our capital in the distance. The city was huge and vast in length with tall circular domed buildings that had multiple coloured glass windows. The city actually seemed to sparkle with colour and we were now so near that I could see the colour of the city reflecting in the water of the river, making the river seem like a living moving rainbow on the land. I was spellbound by the beauty of it all but my mother and father had seen the spectacle before.

"Wonderful isn't it?" said my mother.

"Always" replied my father and we crossed the wide stone bridge over the River Brasil and then entered the metropolis.

The city was not as busy as I had expected but it was sundown and most people had returned to their homes for the day, most of which now lived outside of the city in it's surrounding suburbs, the city had increasingly just become a place for work my father informed me.

The roads of Hibar were wide and I marvelled again at the amount of coloured glass that seemed to surround us, shop windows, temples, buildings of great importance. Soon we were at a wide circular white building that had steep steps leading to it.

"There it is Mastema, The Temple of Blood, tomorrow you will fulfil your destiny there."

A shiver coursed through me as I sat on my horse Thundar, the night air was warm but my sweat was cold.

It was not far to the tavern where we were to stay, walking distance to the Temple of Blood, a good choice by my father as the horses were to be fully rested before our return journey.

The tavern was known as The Higate and was not really a tavern as such, more like one of your modern sophisticated hotels. It was painted a vivid green and had wide oblong shaded windows set within its curved walls. When we entered The Higate my mother was almost speechless as she looked at the silver and gold décor, "My Aenor, can we afford such a place Miro?"

"Do not worry Marta, this is funded by the Council of Blood, all our expenses are paid for so make the most of it."

And so we did, we relaxed in a communal pool followed by a deep cleaning steam bath. Then when we were ready, we ordered the most luxurious of filling suppers and just before we retired for the night my father raised his glass of expensive Slaar, "This night belongs to Mastema, the last of his childhood, for tomorrow he becomes a true warrior!"

I had been allowed one glass of Slaar and I sipped the golden nectar with pride, the following day at noon was the initiation ceremony, tomorrow was to be the biggest day of my life thus far.

***

It felt strange sleeping in a bed again and it did take me some time to fall asleep because of the mixture of excitement and fear that was flowing through my veins, but when I awoke I looked at the morning light glittering in my room and I felt truly honoured to be alive. These were the right thoughts I reminded myself, these were the thoughts of a warrior.

***

Father was not present at breakfast and I asked mother where he was.

"He has gone to buy you new clothes, a new tunic and leather belt, new tight fitting boots and a ceremonial gown for the occasion."

This pleased me greatly and I looked forward to his return as I ate the hearty hot meal that had been cooked for me, the last meal of my childhood.

When father returned, he came with gifts of all sorts, my attire as my mother had mentioned but also bottles of perfume, scarves and linens and dresses and amazing sparkling jewellery, all for my mother who once again was speechless. There was also something else in a long wooden box but father did not open it.

"That can wait" he simply said, "Now we have to prepare, it is only a short walk to the Temple of Blood and we must leave now."

***

Inside the temple I was relieved to see that there no crowds, only the immediate family of those that were to be initiated.

In keeping with the rest of Hibar, the temple was magnificent, gold and silver adorned the walls and the light from the coloured glass windows was kaleidoscopic as it cut through the great marble columns that stretched up to the high domed ceiling.

As we neared the front of the temple the columns were replaced by giant marble statues of the four goddesses, two either side of us. And when we reached the altar wall we were greeted by the giant face of Aenor which was also carved in marble. The space in front of the altar was circular and marked as such.

"That is where you will fight" my father said bluntly and as soon as he said this a priest in a shining silver gown entered from the right of where we were standing and in his hand was a gleaming golden broadsword.

When the circular area was fully surrounded by those that were to be initiated the priest lifted the sword and turned towards the face of Aenor which seemed to take up the whole wall.

"Hear me great Aenor, this is The Sword of Blood, the sword that protects Hibrasil, Your sword as You handed it down to us. Today we have those who wish to become true warriors, those who wish to serve You and Hibrasil, to protect our glory forever."

The priest then turned and shouted out three names, one of which was mine.

"This is it" said my father and I detected an urgency to his voice as he removed my new ceremonial gown, "Remember all that I taught you, stay on your feet, use your speed to avoid their fists, do not get held by one of them, the other one will use that to his advantage. Go son, fight for your right to be a warrior."

I stepped cautiously into the circular space and weighed up my opponents. Obviously they were of a similar age and all from different villages. One of them was about the same height and build to me but the other one was much bigger and rotund, this one reminded me of the fearsome miner from the Midlen tavern and my anxiety increased but I did remember how my father had beaten that giant. I also remembered that my father had said that there was no shame in losing the fight as long as I competed and showed bravery… still, I was nervous and anxious to proceed.

The three of us began to walk the perimeter of the circular fighting space, we were obviously waiting for the first one to make their move then a man from the observing crowd shouted "Now!" and the boy of my height suddenly sprang at me. With a swift movement to my left I avoided him and then I turned and grabbed him around the neck. Out of the corner of my eye I saw the large fat boy rushing up behind me so I turned just as he was about to swing his large fist… his lethal knuckles hit the boy I was holding full force and he dropped to the floor unconscious. The large boy had been surprised by my speed and I quickly lunged toward him stepping over the body of the other boy and as I did I kicked him hard with my sturdy new boots between the legs, just as my father had done to the Midlen giant and as the boys head lowered, I hit him below the chin with such force that he reeled backwards and fell to the floor next to the other boy. Neither of them stirred… I stood in disbelief and gazed at the marble eyes of Aenor that seemed to be smiling in approval. All was silent as if waiting for the two fallen boys to stand up and when they did they were still groggy, dizzy on their feet from the swift fight.

"We have a winner!" declared the priest and he raised his sword, "Let the branding begin."

Everyone cheered and I noticed my father smiling, he seemed so proud, but my mother was crying for what was about to happen to me next.

The two other boys were now standing behind me. Two masked men entered from the sides of the altar and held my outstretched arms. Without warning a man dressed similar to the priest entered brandishing a scolding red hot iron and without hesitation pressed it hard against my chest…

"Rejoice young man, you are now a true warrior this day!" I think I heard the priest say as I fought to keep conscious. The heat and pain was intense, so intense that the great marble temple became dark red and the last thing I saw was the face of my father who was looking at me with loving eyes, then my mother whose face was full of tears.

***

When I woke up in the Higate room I noticed that my chest was bandaged and not so painful, later my father would tell me that a special healing balm had been applied.

"Well well, sleepy head has decided to wake up."

I had been asleep all afternoon, it was evening now and the lights of the city were beginning to glow.

"I have slept this long?"

On the bottom of my bed was the mysterious long wooden box that my father had not opened.

"It is yours Mastema, open it."

I reached for the box and inside was the most wonderful of swords; it had a gleaming silver blade with a golden handle that glistened in the sunlight. The sword seemed heavy to me but I was weak from my ordeal.

My mother kissed me gently on the forehead and said, "Rest little Mastema, this has been an ordeal for you and it has eventually taken its toll but tomorrow we will return home."

"So soon?" my father had to ask, "There are more great sights to see here!"

Mother scowled at him, "And the farm will run itself?"

"But my father is there."

"He is too old now, you know that and greatmama has been very ill lately... she told me not to tell you, at least not until after the ceremony."

Father suddenly looked worried in a way I had not seen before.

"Mastema needs to be home too" mother continued, "so that he can recover properly. Mastema will ride with me in the cart, you will ride Thundar" she declared with that authority that only mother's have, "We will visit Hibar again another day, then we will see all the sights."

"Yes... we will" my father said hesitantly and there was no argument from him as he was now very concerned about greatmama.

6

It was late at night when we finally arrived home, a large thunderstorm was raging out at sea and I think my father took this as some foreboding omen.

When we entered our farmhouse we were greeted by a physician whose face was grey and serious.

"Welcome home Miro" he said to my father, "But I am afraid that it is not a happy welcome."

Father rushed through to the spare bedroom where he found my grandfather seated beside the bed holding greatmama's hand, he turned to face his son.

"She is leaving us Miro" he stuttered and his tears marked the side of his face.

We stood at the entrance to the room and I wanted to go to the bed and hold her.

"No" said the physician, "She is too weak, her time is approaching quick."

Father ignored the physician and went and held greatmama's other hand. My mother and I remained with the physician.

Suddenly a great light filled the room but it seemed that nobody else seemed to notice it, "What is that" I asked mother.

"What is what?" she replied and her voice was just a whisper.

"What is that bright light beside greatmama's bed.

"Just the lamp burning Mastema, why do you ask?"

The light was too bright though and within this light I saw something move.

"You… have come for me" greatmama whispered, "I am ready."

Father looked at my grandfather and shook his head; they thought that greatmama was hallucinating.

Beside the bed I saw the shape of a man emerge, the light was emanating from his back like the ripples in a pool… he turned to look at me, and he seemed surprised that I could see him… after a moment he smiled at me and it was as if all the sadness and worries in the world seemed to evaporate from me.

"Who is that man?" I asked mother quietly.

"Ssh Mastema, you are worrying me" mother replied.

"But…"

In the light I saw greatmama arise and stand beside the shining man, her body was still lying on the bed though and that confused me. Both the shining man and greatmama looked at me and both were smiling… she blew me a kiss with her hand and suddenly the bright light in the room faded… and all I could hear was the sound of my family sobbing. I began to cry too but strangely I felt no sadness, I felt that she was now with Aenor in Enolan.

***

The Great Departing ceremony for greatmama was two days later and her body was buried in the garden of her home which overlooked the sea. Afterwards I asked mother again about the shining man but she said that it was just my imagination, probably heightened by the medicine I had been given by the Council of Blood.

At the end of the next cycle my grandfather died but I was not there to witness it. They said that he had died of a broken heart. I had told my grandfather about what I had seen the night greatmama had died and he hugged me greatly.

"You have been chosen Mastema, you have been chosen to be One of the Shining" he said with gusto and he was shaking when he said it.

"What does that mean?" I enquired of him. There were drawings and paintings of the Light People in the village temple but my grandfather and me knew of nobody that had actually seen one of them. I guess I just thought that these drawing were the creative imaginings of various artists.

"All in good time dear Mastema, live your life first; live it to the full. Protect your parents, protect the family you will have… and then one day you will work for Aenor in his Kingdom of Light!"

That day came sooner than I thought it would.

THE VAAGEN

I was about to become fifteen cycles old which would allow me to drink Necal with my father, little did he know that I had been secretly drinking Necal for some time with my young friends; teenagers will be teenagers whatever the cycle it is.

On the eve of my fifteenth cycle my father invited me to the Great Hall to celebrate. Mother stayed at home as she wanted to prepare for the next day's celebrations.

I was much taller and much more muscular. I was not quite as tall as my father yet but I was close. I knew that I was attracting the girls of the village and my father was aware of this. As we stood at the bar with a large jug of Necal between us he asked me, "So who have you got your eye on Mastema?"

"What?"

"You know what I mean, which maiden?"

I think my face reddened as I turned to look around the hall. In the corner I saw a friend from my schooling days who was sitting with her parents. She was called Meliah who was looking at me with red cheeks too.

"Ah Meliah," my father said, "The most beautiful young girl in the village, you have chosen wisely."

"Stop it father, you are embarrassing me" I declared but he was right, I had loved Meliah from an early age and I had always thought that she had felt the same about me.

"She will be at the celebration tomorrow; maybe we can announce your engagement?"

"Father, I am only fifteen cycles."

"And I was only fifteen when I asked for your mother's hand."

"Those were different times father."

"Love is the same no matter what the time. Let's drink to it then, you are a true warrior and tomorrow you will become a man, I am so proud of you."

We did drink, possibly a little too much. It was late when we left the Great Hall and on the way home father decided to walk along the beach, I knew that he wanted to pass on his wisdom to me.

It was the season of Hetta again and the night was still and warm, Lunar lighted up the many fishing boats as we walked past them.

"One day you will be Protector of this village son, like me, and one day your son too hopefully."

Father was being nostalgic and as we walked his words soothed the effects of the Necal.

When we came to the large stone steps that led up to our house, for some reason father suddenly became cautious and after a few steps he stopped, he did not turn but said to me quietly, "Look at those marks in the sand there to the left of me Mastema."

I looked behind him and down and noticed the wide drag marks.

"Turtles?" was my first thought but the marks were too deep and wide in the sand.

"No, I think it is the small boat of a…" he exclaimed loudly and as he reached for his broadsword, the sharp metal point of a three pronged grapple hook cut into his throat.

"Vaagen!" I shouted and immediately became dizzy and confused, the effects of too much Necal.

Father was pulled from the steps down onto the beach and I watched in horror as a large axe pierced his chest and heart… I think he died instantly

In shock and grief I sprang from the steps and unsheathed my ceremonial sword, the sword my father had given me on becoming a true warrior, in the back of my mind I knew that it was time to prove myself even if I was drunk.

I could only see three Vaagen and the sight of them chilled my very bones… white skull faces with black zigzag patterns, standing over my dead father, grinning like the spectre of death itself. I noticed that one of them seemed to be about my age because of his slight build of body and his face was painted blood red not white. This one seemed to be in charge of the other two and he ordered them to attack me.

The first one came at me with a small wide knife, what I think you would call a machete these days… my vision was blurry, double vision even and the Vaagen appeared to be moving in short stages but I sliced that Vaagen's hand off in one go. My blade then turned upwards in the air and cut through his throat like a hot knife through butter, his head dropped grotesquely to the side but did not leave his body as he fell to the bloody sand below him.

The other Vaagen was now more cautious. I wiped the sweat from my eyes and saw that 'Redface' was now beginning to back away towards the sea slowly but I was not concerned about him for the moment.

Redface, it was a name and face I would never forget.

My anger grew and this time I was the one who lunged at the remaining Vaagen but he avoided the thrust of my deadly blade… suddenly he had his hand at my throat and his crude spiked hammer was ready to crush my skull…

A vision of my father in the Midlen tavern appeared in my mind.

Then the large fat boy from the Temple of Aenor.

Instinct and memory told me what to do.

I kicked the Vaagen hard between the legs and he faltered in pain, his gruesome mouth open wide in shock.

This gave me time to send the blade of my sword across his eyes and the bloody remains splattered on my face.

The Vaagen began to turn screaming wildly.

I thrust my sword through his back and through his heart and he fell to the sand and as I pulled my sword from him I looked to the sea and saw that Redface was swimming in the distance… I ran into the sea and shouted as loud as I could, "Come back Redface, come back, I will have my revenge!" tears were dripping from my eyes and my voice was cracked and broken.

I waded into the sea, deeper and deeper after Redface… then I sensed a shimmering light behind me that made me stop and turn. To my amazement, my father was standing with a shining glowing man… he held his hand up and I could see tears on his face but he was smiling, a sad smile but a smile that said he was safe, then he turned to walk into the swirling light with the shining man and the light faded swiftly behind them.

I stood crying… my father was gone… and Redface was gone, drowned I hoped but I knew that there was probably another boat waiting for him in the distant darkness.

I walked out of the water to my father's dead body, the bloody grappling hook had contorted his face but I knew that he was now in another place and I clung onto this thought as best I could.

I was weak and in shock, I made it up the stone steps to the door of our farmhouse then I collapsed…

The world was spinning in my head.

And the eyes of Redface were the last thing I saw.

THE SHINING MAN

Those were dark days after my father's death; I do not think that my mother ever recovered from the shock of it. I joined the Hibrasil Water Guard, the equivalent of your navy, as I thought it could be a way of achieving some sort of revenge. Special ships were commissioned to seek out Vaagen ships and on several occasions we were successful. I satisfied a deep blood lust within me but I never came across Redface again, the real reason I had joined the Water Guard.

After serving five cycles I decided to leave the Guard and return home because news of my mother's deteriorating health had reached me, unfortunately I was too late when I eventually reached our farmhouse.

At this time I was comforted by my friend Meliah and this affection blossomed into the true love that had always been there. Meliah had never married and confessed that she had been waiting for my return although she never expected it to be in such sad circumstances. Within the cycle we were married.

Meliah's beauty was exceptional, golden blonde curly hair shimmered around her face like a summer's breeze and her blue eyes were like deep pools of water that reflected the beauty of her inner soul.

Shortly after my marriage to Meliah, the village voted for me to be the new Protector as my father's Second had reached the age of retirement. I was now walking in my father's footsteps and that filled me with so much pride because I knew that it was always what he wanted for me. I hoped that my father was looking down from Enolan upon me and every time I held the golden handle of my Coming of Age sword, a sword that had now killed so many Vaagen, I felt blessed that he had been my father.

So my days now were more or less as they had been before, working the farm but now I had to protect the village also. There were no more sightings of the Vaagen and their threat once more faded from my mind, out of sight, out of mind is the saying... but this did not apply to Redface, his dark red eyes and mouth always lurked somewhere in the shadows of my memory.

***

The following cycle I was given the most heart-warming news, Meliah was with child. I suddenly felt like a different man, I worked our fields with more vigour, I patrolled the streets of Lolar with a more sprightly gait, in some ways I was like a young boy who was about to be given the greatest gift of all.

As the day of birth approached I became more and more anxious, I visited the Great Hall more and drank more Necal to appease my nervous state. It was on one such night after my nightly patrol that I decided to finish the evening in the Great Hall before returning home.

I was drinking with my old friends from my schooling days, the night was warm and still and only an occasional breeze could be heard. The Necal was cool and soothed my worries about the imminent child birth.

"Not long now Mastema?" said Denim, my very best friend.

"A week or two, maybe three says the physician" I replied smiling.

"But they have been known to be wrong on many occasions" laughed Denim who was trying to agitate me on purpose for fun.

"I know that you are just trying to worry me Den but we are well prepared, all of the young one's clothes are ready, his room and bed is waiting for him."

"His?"

I laughed, "Or hers?"

"What about they?"

"Now you do have me worried" I answered and we laughed heartily and finished our beer.

"More Necal!" I demanded slapping my hand hard on the bar-top and as soon as I said this, the large wooden doors to the hall burst open and a frantic man rushed in.

"Vaagen... Vaagen" he shouted, "Attacking our homes!"

"Grab your swords, defend your homes!" I shouted and the adrenalin immediately surged through my body like lightning, the word Vaagen was a word I hated and despised, a word that triggered instant anger in my blood... and all I could think was *Revenge!!*

When entering the hall, all swords had to be suspended between nails on the wall next to the entrance. There was a mad rush as worried frantic men ran to get their swords.

"Go the hill Den, light the beacon, we will need the Shore Guard this night" I shouted at Denim.

I left the hall with great speed; I had only one thing on my mind now besides revenge and that was to get home to Meliah as fast as I could.

It was a fifteen minute walk or maybe a ten minute run to the farmhouse, I saw Vaagen moving around houses to the right of me, vicious fighting had already broke out. I saw the vile flesh coloured sails of their boats on the beach to the left of me and this made me run faster. I must have made it home in about five minutes...

A dead Vaagen was lying at the door to the farmhouse with my dog Solo at his throat, Solo was dead too, blood seeping from his back.

Then I saw his killers.

Three of them on the beach.

They were dragging Meliah who was trapped in a thick rope net, she was clawing and fighting the best she could and she saw me she cried out, "Mastema, save me, cut me loose!"

I ran down the stone steps, sword and axe in hand, the Vaagen had spears this time and the first one threw his spear at me but I easily side-stepped it. I threw my axe and it instantly split his head in half. The Vaagen to the right of me came at me but I parried his spear aside then slashed his throat open with my sword and blood gushed from it like a grotesque red fountain.

The third Vaagen was more nervous; he did not know whether to keep hold of his spear or throw it. I quickly pulled my axe from the dead Vaagen's head and sent it spinning once more through the air. All my years of combat training and my experience of fighting for the Water Guard were being rewarded as my flying axe hit my target hard in his chest, he fell stunned to the sand and lay dying in the thick pool of his own blood.

I went straight to Meliah and began to cut at the restraining net with my knife but in her eye I saw stark terror reflected.

I suddenly remembered the night my father died...

Redface emerging from the shadows behind him...

I stood up and the spear pieced my back before I could turn.

The bloody blade had torn mercilessly through my chest.

I staggered on my feet and turned slowly...

It was Redface!

Grinning like he had the night he had killed my father.

I will have my revenge I thought as Redface walked slowly and ominously toward me, he thought that I was finished, another meal to add to his gruesome stomach.

But I still had enough strength, enough to throw the knife I still held. The blade hit Redface in the chest, deep into his godless dark heart, and his blood spurted from his body as if it was surprised. I think I smiled because Redface was not grinning anymore... he slumped to the sand then fell face forward. There seemed to be a darkness around him but maybe it was just my fading eyesight. Redface did not move again.

I slumped to my knees, numb but aware of my final revenge has been achieved. I heard Meliah screaming, shouting my name as she tore herself free from the terrible net.

And the last thing I saw was Denim, running down the steps to the blood stained beach. I tried to say, "Did you light the beacon?" but no words came... only a misty darkness.

Then a shimmering brightness; like the light that had circled greatmama on her deathbed.

"Do not be afraid" said a man who shone like he was light itself. His face was that of my father but it was not his voice.

"No... no, I must protect Meliah... our baby, the village."

"You are not able to do that now" the shining man said, "But the Vaagen will not endure, the men of your village will see to that."

I felt frightened, not for myself but for Meliah, I also felt confused, the spear in my chest was no longer there.

Then I felt angry.

"I must go back, I have to!"

"You cannot dear Mastema, this is your time."

"No, no, no" I repeated but the shining man simply smiled.

My anger increased and I wanted to strike out at the shining man...

But I could not, the face of my father calmed me, soothed me, "Come" said the shining man, "Your father waits for you."

"But my wife Meliah?"

"She will join you one day but come now, you need to be calm, and you need to rest."

We turned to walk up the small steps but they were not the steps to my farmhouse.

SAVAGE FARM

1

Daylight had begun to seep through the blinds but Tom Savage did not open them. Like his security officer Ray Gunn, he was sitting in silence, stunned by Mastema's story.

Mastema looked at both of them and he knew that they were in need of sleep now.

"Do you have a warm drink Tom?" he asked.

"Sure... sure, I'll get us some coffee."

While Savage was making the coffee, Mastema noticed that Gunn was unusually silent, "You have nothing to say Ray?"

"I... erm, I don't know what to say which is unusual for me" and he was genuinely struggling to respond to Mastema's story.

Savage brought the hot drinks and Mastema asked of him, "So what do you think Tom?"

Savage supped at his coffee, "I'm thinking what happened next, to your wife Meliah, your friend Denim, what happened to you?"

"I think maybe I will leave that for now, it has been a long night... what happens next you will find hard to believe as did I at the time."

Savage and Gunn acknowledged Mastema's advice and decided to get a few hours sleep. Mastema closed his eyes but did not sleep, he thought again about his life in Hibrasil and his wife Meliah and what was to come and again tears fell from his eyes, the tears of an angel that sparkled in the sunlight like silver rain.

2

It was midday when Savage awoke; as soon as he entered the main room he opened the window blinds slightly. Mastema was still sitting in the same chair, quietly reading a book he had found on Savage's bookshelf,

"The Wrong Reality... it's a book I bought a few years ago, by some English guy if I remember rightly."

"I find his alternate reality quite intriguing... a godless society would be interesting would it not?" said Mastema thoughtfully.

"I'm beginning to think that is what has happened to me; that I have been sent to another reality by that Blue Ripple" mused Savage.

"Why do you say that Tom?"

"The fact that you are here, and now I want to know what happened to your family, what happened next?"

"All in good time Tom, I think you need time to readjust to civilian life first."

"I think you're right, I've just been on the phone to my superiors."

"And?" asked Mastema and at that moment Gunn entered the room looking slightly overhung.

"Too much beer Ray?" laughed Savage.

"Just tired, moonlagged I think" Gunn muttered.

"Well I have some important news for you; we've been given indefinite leave."

"What, why?"

"To prepare for the possibility of a series of top secret seminars worldwide, England, Germany, Europe, maybe even Russia and China."

"They know about Mastema?"

"I'm not sure, the feeling is that they might, spies and all that, they might have picked up Mastema on their satellites, I think that there is a good chance of that... so basically they want us to prepare for possible meetings, of course they might want all of this to blow over like some UFO conspiracy theory, I personally think that this would be their preference should it ever become public."

"But we have submitted our reports; they have video evidence, why do we have to be there?"

"I know that Ray but they think that these governments might want first hand accounts."

"When?"

"Weeks, months, who knows? We just have to check in Facetime regularly."

"Sounds like an extended holiday with full pay to me... great! Did they say anything about the disappearance of Mastema?"

"Just that they are stumped, they sound confused but is something they still have to deal with, they know Mastema exists and they still need to know the whats and the whys. This break is just what we need... and it buys time for Mastema too."

"I hope I have not been too much trouble for you Tom?" asked a regretful sounding Mastema.

"No you have not Mastema, I think we have just been given some breathing space, time maybe to work out where we go from here" said Tom but what he meant was that he had been given time to figure out what and who Mastema really was.

"Okay you guys, I gotta run, a few little ladies will be anxious to know that I am back on home soil" said Gunn and he winked at Savage.

"I'll walk you to the car Ray; I've been told we can use that BMW for now."

"Cool, its top range, my lady friends will dig that."

Before Gunn drove off, Savage had to ask him, "So what do you think about Mastema's story Ray?"

Gunn thought awhile before replying, "I dunno Tom, it was very vivid, I was realy back there with him in Hibrasil."

"You know the connection between ancient alien astronauts and Hibrasil?"

"Yeah, I know those myths, so what are you saying?"

"I dunno, I still think that all those memories could have been implanted in him... or that they are the memories of an android that was stationed there."

"So that is what you still believe?"

"Yeah, I think I do, I think Mastema is some form of an advanced immortal android."

"It makes sense Tom and as long as he is no threat to us and humanity then I am cool with that. Okay, keep me in the loop especially when he decides to tell you the next part of his story."

"Will do" said Savage and then Gunn roared away at top speed, smoke and dirt forming a plume around Savage, "And watch what you doing with that damned car!"

***

Back in the farmhouse, Mastema was no longer reading The Wrong Reality.

"So you still do not believe that I was once human, that in fact I am human, you think that I am some other worldly humanoid robot?"

"You heard all that, how?"

"We can heighten our senses... I did not mean to spy on you but I simply could not resist."

Savage became embarrassed.

"I... just don't know what to think really, like Ray said, your story was so vivid, I felt for you and what your family endured at the hands of the Vaagen... but... but Hibrasil just does not exist, if only there was evidence."

"That is something I intend to try and find out Tom, find out what happened to Hibrasil."

"How will you do that?"

"There should be a way, maybe you can help me?"

Savage felt adrenalin surge through him, was he now about to find out what happened to a lost mythical civilisation?

"Look, before you go all Indiana Jones on me, there are things I have to sort out, food supplies, clothes for you, basics y'know, we can go to the mall now and sort all that out... oh, and we will need to disguise you, sunglasses and a hat should do it."

"Will this suffice Tom?" said Mastema and when Savage turned he was looking at the face of his brother.

Savage staggered backwards in surprise, "How the fuck did you do that?" he stammered.

"Your memories Tom, from when we touched. Remember when I said that the Shining Man had the face of my father when I died... he had touched me, accessed my mind, he knew that it would help calm me, it was an essential gift for the work we did, it helped ease the confusion of the scared and vulnerable. I think I was chosen because I could see the Light People."

"You had the gift, the shining?"

"The what?"

"Y'know, psychic like the Stephen King novel."

"I still do not understand; who is this King you speak of and where is his kingdom?"

"Access my memories and you will understand. Okay 'brother' we'll go to the mall now."

"And then we can look for those that will know."

"Now you've lost me Mastema?"

"I need to find my own kind."

EDEN

Doctor Susan Eden was exhausted when she entered her house in County Durham in the north east of England; it had been well over a year since she had been there.

After unpacking her travel bags, she collapsed onto her bed and went to sleep immediately. It was a deep sleep that took her back to the moon and the being known as Mastema...

Why did she love him?

She had only known him for a few weeks.

Was it because he looked so similar to her late partner Samuel Hayden? Both men moved through her dream as one...

Samuel, Mastema, Samuel, Mastema.

"Sam" she cried out but there was no sound.

Then Mastema was above her, a sparkling, crackling light behind him.

Thrusting gently in and out of her wanting body, whispering to her in a language she did not understand and as his angelic seed filled her he called out "Meliah!"

At this point Eden's eyes opened, sweat was pouring from every pore of her skin which prompted her to go straight to the bathroom and shower. Eden then returned to her bed and when the sun broke through the blinds of her bedroom she sat up, hands caressing her worried forehead.

Eden had not given her future much thought, her only priority was the baby she was carrying and she knew that she would have to see a doctor for a scan as soon as she could. First things first though, she had to phone her mother, she felt that she was the only person she could confide in.

Eden ordered a home delivery of food and essentials from the local supermarket and while she waited she phoned her mother.

"Hi mum, I'm back."

"My baby made it back from the moon safely, I'm so proud of you."

"You might not be soon."

"What do you mean?"

"Oh nothing mum... how are you? It seems like an age since I last saw you."

"Over a year, those video Facetimes are just not the same are they?"

"I know, look, I've ordered some stuff and your favourite scones so you are welcome anytime."

"Great, I will pop round this afternoon; I'll be dropping some flowers on your father's grave first on the way."

"I need... to visit there."

"Now you just get yourself sorted first, get some of that moon dust out of your system."

"I don't know if that can ever happen now?"

Eden's mother was puzzled by her daughter's reply, "Whatever do you mean Susan?"

"I'll explain when you get here."

"Exciting news?"

"Well yes and no, I'll see you later."

What will mother think Eden thought as she put the phone down, *does she believe in angels? Does she believe in aliens?* Once again, Eden's mind began to swirl with uncomfortable thoughts...

Images from that Alien movie franchise.

The alien bursting from her stomach…

Nightmares invading day space.

"Damn it" Eden called out to the empty kitchen, "Focus girl, you're home now, there are no moon aliens here."

Eden waited for the home delivery and prepared for the arrival of her mother.

***

The start of May had been glorious, temperatures were hitting seventeen and eighteen degrees and a clear bright sky languished over the Durham countryside. Eden looked out to her spacious back garden and was pleased that she had arranged for a retired trusty gardener to keep it all in order. The garden was secluded by a large surrounding fence with tall bushes and small trees, the main flowers in her garden were a variety of roses that had not quite blossomed yet.

Eden opened the wide umbrella under a garden table and waited for her mother… she was obviously pensive and was desperate for a gin and tonic but only poured herself a tonic.

At about three o'clock, the kitchen door opened and Eden's mother stepped into the garden.

"I let myself in love; I thought you might be back here enjoying the sunshine."

"Something I have missed for a long time mum" replied Eden and she stood up and kissed her mother on the cheek, "Tea, or gin mother... I think you might need a gin, a large one."

Eden's mother's smile dropped slightly and she immediately became thoughtful as Eden went inside the kitchen.

Eden's mother was as beautiful as her daughter, golden curly locks of hair and a full body shape enhanced her looks, she could have been mistaken for Eden's older sister.

When Eden returned with the drinks tray and poured her mother's gin but not one for herself her mother had to comment, "Okay Susan, what's wrong? It's not just about leaving the space program is it?"

"What do you mean?"

"Come on, I've known you since you were a little girl, I know something is on your mind, that something is worrying you."

Eden was silent but there was no point in delaying the inevitable... "I'm pregnant mum" she blurted out.

Eden's mother placed her drink slowly on the garden table, it was as if she had suddenly been frozen in time... then she picked her glass up and took a large gulp.

"You're what! But how... who?"

Eden's mother did not know whether to smile or frown or cry. "Someone from the moon-base? So that's why you resigned?"

"Yes... and sort of no."

"Sort of no, what does that mean?"

Eden refilled her mother's glass with gin then straightened herself in her chair, "You need to listen carefully to what I am going to tell you mum, and you have to promise not to tell anybody else."

***

After Eden had told her mother everything, her mother sat stunned in silence as if trying to look beyond Eden's garden; she poured herself more gin into her glass.

"I think I am going to get quite drunk at this rate... so what you are telling me that you made love to an ancient angel who just might be some sort of an alien and that you are now bearing his or it's child!"

"Angel or alien, they don't know, they have him in a security complex in the states right now."

Eden's mother stood up twirled round, "Have you seen a doctor Susan?"

"No, not yet, I'll be going for a scan as soon as I can."

"No, I mean a doctor who you can talk to."

Eden was stunned, "You... don't believe me?"

"I don't know what to believe darling, how can I believe that?"

"It's true mum, I'll get Tom Savage to verify it for you if you want."

Eden's mother sat down at the garden table again.

"Not until I've had more gin."

***

The next day, Eden attended a scan appointment, Eden had private medical care and she knew her doctor well, he was a man she could trust implicitly. Lying on the bed, the doctor gently ran the scan monitor over Eden's stomach and looked to the large screen to the left of her.

"I'm afraid there is nothing there Susan" he said in a rather formal way.

"What do you mean, how can that be?"

"Look."

Eden turned to look at the screen that was devoid of any form of developing embryo.

"But the pregnancy test, it was positive, both times?"

"The tests are positive Susan" said the doctor taking off his glasses, "but what we have here is a 'phantom' pregnancy I think."

"What?"

"It is not that uncommon, there can be no other explanation, your body thinks it is pregnant, wants to be pregnant even but it is not."

Eden was speechless but not entirely convinced by what the doctor was saying although deep down she knew that he had to be right.

Eden left the hospital in Washington and drove home to Durham and drank a large gin. *Was she or wasn't she, am I or am I not?* She knew that only time would tell now.

CORRIGAN

Unknown to Savage and Gunn, Doctor Corrigan had followed them in the dark of the night to Savage's farm on the outskirts of Las Vegas. Corrigan parked his car beneath the cover of a large oak tree near the bottom of Savage Farm drive. He looked into the car mirror and his eyes began to change...

"What am I to do?" he asked.

WAIT WATCH SEE

SEE IF THE ANGELIC ARE HERE

A voice hissed back at him.

Corrigan had not seen anybody get out of the car that he had followed; the road to the farmhouse was too long, the night too dark.

"I did not see the angelic... the house is too far away."

WAIT AND WATCH

WAIT AND WATCH

Corrigan became confused; he suddenly became worried that he was talking to himself... *I should see a doctor* he thought, *I should go home now, get help...*

NOT YET

YOU SHALL BE MY EYES

OUR EYES

Yes... not now.

Corrigan looked into the mirror and his own eyes stared back at him, tired eyes, black eyes, eyes that needed sleep.

AENOR

1

Savage decided to take his classic Chevy pickup truck, the truck that his family had owned for years, purely because he had missed driving it.

"Okay then, priority is some clothes for you Mastema, that base wear they gave you at the Complex looks a bit drab and suspicious. I will order home delivery of fresh food supplies when we get back, we cannot live off frozen pizza forever."

Mastema smiled, he really liked Savage, he reminded him of his good friend Denim from all those years ago. Mastema opened the truck window to the right of him, stretched his arm out and opened his hand wide to feel the passing air.

"The wind, the air, the sunlight, I have missed them so much."

"It must have seemed like a prison sentence to you, and your clothes, what happened to them, did they just deteriorate?"

"Oh no, the clothes of the angelic are as durable as we are but when I was burned by the light of Aenor, my clothes were incinerated, part of my humiliation I suppose but my remaining light can replicate any attire I desire."

"Wait a minute; you said that you were burned?"

"I will tell you later Tom but not now, I want to enjoy this moment and I look forward to seeing your home village."

"Well it is a bit more than a village I think Mastema. The mall is not far and after I will drive you around Vegas so that you can see the sights."

"And how far is this Vegas from here?"

"About eight miles or so."

Soon they had parked in the mall car park and as they walked toward the clothes shops Savage remarked, "Y'know, I am not going to get used to looking at the face of my brother Mastema?"

"It is not a good disguise?"

"No, it's perfect; it's just that I used to argue a lot with my brother."

Mastema smiled, "Ah, family squabbles, I remember that."

"You could put it like that, used to end up in fist fights more often than not but we still loved each other."

"I understand; he is a warrior like you then?"

"I wouldn't exactly call myself a warrior, I became head of the moon-base because of my expertise in Lunar studies which has nothing to do with combat although I have completed all the necessary basics in hand-to-hand stuff, I think I can handle myself. But my brother, he works in the movie industry, some sort of art director."

"The moving pictures with actors? I am quite fascinated by them, something I would like to watch and study more."

"Good decision pal; they are a nice way to unwind."

In the clothes department of a large retail store, Mastema chose a variety of faded blue jeans, bright coloured shirts with intricate patterns and plain light blue t-shirts. Mastema then chose black leather biker boots because they reminded him of what he had worn in Lolar and when he saw a thin black leather jacket he just had to have it, "I have missed the comfort of leather for so long, it is fine to take all of these clothes Tom? I cannot repay you at the moment."

"No worries man, you can repay me after you have published your memoirs" said Savage humorously then he had to add, "But the leather jacket, is it not too hot for you?"

"It is a light jacket, not as thick as the other ones and my body temperature adjusts to whatever I want remember."

"Of course, and now you blend in perfectly, a Vegas biker, maybe I should get you a hog?"

"A hog"

"A motorbike, I'm sure you would like riding one."

"Ah yes, I think I would" replied Mastema then as they made their way to the check out. Savage noticed a dark blue baseball cap which had the words I AIN'T NO ANGEL embellished across it in silver. Savage grabbed the hat and placed it on Mastema's head...

"Perfect!"

Mastema smiled, he recognised the irony of it, "Maybe never again" he said with a hint of sadness.

Walking from the mall, Mastema observed all the passers-by, "People... the throng of life, the cycle of life, it endures" and he turned to look up to the sun with his new seventies retro sunglasses and said, "Sol will always bless us, until his time runs out, until the flames of his burning fires finally die out."

**

After dropping the shopping bags into the back of the truck, Savage decided that they would drive around the city. Savage looked at Mastema in his new attire, the fallen angel on the run that now looked like a seasoned biker and that hat just made him smile.

"Okay then Brando, let's see the sights."

As they drove through the city streets, Mastema marvelled at the beauty and size of everything – the shops, the hotels, the casinos, and the intriguing advertising signage.

"Sometimes I think it is just one giant casino" said Savage, I guess it was built on gambling but there is more to Vegas than just money."

"I can see that Tom, you and your generosity are testament to that."

Savage felt slightly embarrassed by these words but he was just doing what his instinct had told him to do which was the right thing in his eyes.

Soon they had drifted into downtown Vegas and the bright lights and busy streets faded, small bars and fast food establishments became more prevalent.

"I thought I'd give you the full tour Mastema, not everything is rich and rosy here."

"I see" said Mastema, "Hibar and Lolar had their rough edges too you know."

Then as they slowly passed a side street to the right of them, Mastema seemed to become instantly alert.

"Stop... stop the carriage Tom please!"

Savage stopped the truck immediately and turned to Mastema.

"What's up" said Savage and he noticed unbelievably that Mastema seemed to be shaking.

"Those men in that side street we have just passed... I sensed something."

"Just some guys, did look like a bit of a squabble though, probably drugs."

"One of them could... I might be wrong?"

"Wrong about what?"

"My kind Tom... angelic."

"Savage stared deep into Mastema's shaded eyes, "Are you sure, I mean... in a back alley?"

"I am not sure but..."

"Okay bud, we'll check it out, wish Gunn was here though."

Savage and Mastema walked cautiously back to the side street that they had just passed, the alley was shaded from the sun but they could clearly see that three men were hassling a man who was sitting on the step to a back entrance to a bar.

One of the men who was thin and weedy looking began to kick the man on the step who was wearing a torn and dirty looking overcoat. The man had long silver white hair but he did not look old.

"Fucking hobo, you dare to come into our bar and beg for a drink, get the fuck outta here you fucking damned leech!"

The other two men who were much larger and big bellied began to kick at the man who seemed confused and drunk.

"I think he has had enough, don't you?" said Mastema and Savage noted that his usual gentle tone had changed; his voice seemed deeper and full of authority.

The three grizzly looking men turned to face Savage and Mastema.

"And who the fuck are you, his guardian angels?"

"You could say that" said Mastema and this made Savage smile.

"Yeah, so what are you going to do about it Brando?"

Mastema turned to Savage and remarked, "Why is everyone calling me Brando?" and Savage had to laugh.

"It must be the biker look and my brother's oiled back hair" answered Savage but Mastema was none the wiser.

The thin man produced a thick chain from his hooded jacket and proceeded to wrap it around his knuckles, the two fat men produced knives.

Savage stepped forward.

"No Tom" said Mastema and held his arm out to stop him, "I think this is my fight."

Mastema walked towards them and as he did his skin hardened and began to sparkle in what dim light there was.

"What the fuck?" said the thin man before Mastema struck him in on the chin, the two fat men rushed at Mastema and thrust their knives into him but the blades did not piece his skin. The two men dropped their knives to the ground in disbelief then staggered back into the shadows speechless.

"And now my friend you are coming with me" Mastema said to the man on the step and he reached out a hand to help him up.

The poor man was still bewildered and confused but Mastema helped him back to the truck. There was no room for him in the driving cabin so he sat in the back with the shopping bags.

"Back to the farm I guess" said Savage, "Are you really sure that this guy is… your kind?"

"I am sure, we can sense one another and I recognise him."

"He doesn't seem to recognise you."

"I know and that worries me, his name is Theolus."

***

Back at Savage Farm, Savage and Mastema helped the man called Theolus into the house.

"He's drunk as a lord, and boy does he need a shower!" exclaimed Savage.

Together, Mastema and Savage washed and clothed the man using some of the new clothes that were bought for Mastema. They then laid him on a bed in one of the guest rooms. Savage and Mastema then went to the main room where Savage immediately made a home delivery order.

"We're going to need more food I think."

"We do not need food Tom, but it will comfort him hopefully."

"How about drink then? I think I need one."

After opening two bottles of beer, Savage sat down opposite Mastema.

"Theolus will be sleeping like a baby now, he'll not go catatonic will he?" added a concerned Savage

"His skin did not suggest that" replied Mastema who sounded worried and slightly overawed by the presence of the sleeping man called Theolus.

"Look Mastema, I'm finding this hard to believe. We find a homeless wino and you're now trying to tell me that he is an angel! What Heaven or God would allow such a thing to happen to him?"

"My thoughts precisely, this worries me too Tom but I know all too well about the wrath of Aenor... it is sad though to see Theolus in such a desperate state. Theolus is older than I am; he originates from what you call the Mediterranean continent now, from a country that was as civilised and well developed as Hibrasil."

"Then he may know what happened to Hibrasil?"

"Yes he may, I am hoping that he does. Theolus is the angelic that took me to Enolan, our name for Heaven."

"Look Mastema, I have to know if the both of you are ancient astronauts, of alien origin... this 'angel' thing is just too much for me to comprehend, surely you can understand that?"

"I do understand Tom and as far as I know, Theolus is not an alien and neither am I... I think it is time to take you to Enolan."

ENOLAN

Tom's bottle of beer tightened in his hand as Mastema began to tell him of what had happened to him after he had died on Lolar beach.

"I had imagined the steps on the beach; I wanted them to be steps that would take me back to my farmhouse but that could not happen. I stepped into the shining column of light of the portal, one of the many that can take you to Enolan. These portals open when the living veins between this world and the next sense that death is near, in an instant the angelic are notified if necessary and an appropriate angelic is sent. Sometimes these portals will take you straight to Enolan with no threat from the malevolent forces of the Dark Conscious but sometimes they can be very hazardous indeed. If you have lived an evil life then a Dark Portal would claim you. My journey to Enolan was peaceful and safe."

"You mentioned living veins, are these all around us?" Savage had to ask.

"Yes, invisible strands of life that float unseen around us, veins that touch us all, some will attach themselves to you, they will feed and influence you, both good and evil, the hidden world is more complicated than you think Tom."

"God, you're telling me, and these Dark Portals would take the dead straight to Hell if they deserved it?"

"That is what we assumed; there was no known 'Devil' at the time, only a Dark Conscious, no entity for which we had a name."

"No Lucifer then?"

"Not in my time... Lucifer was an angelic I was aware of, I knew of him and I knew that he been as concerned as I was about the suffering that humanity had to endure."

"Savage stood up and paced the floor, beer in hand.

"We thought that the Fallen Angel was you but I think that you are going to tell me that Lucifer was the first?"

"Correct Tom... as far as I know Lucifer was not evil, how could he be, he would not have been chosen for a portal to Enolan. How he became humanities 'Devil' completely baffles me, we shared the same beliefs, same concerns. One day though because of what happened to my family in Hibrasil, I confronted Aenor also... But I will come to that later."

"My God Mastema, this is completely mind-blowing, I have been recording this on my phone if that is okay with you?"

"Mastema looked at Savage's phone on the coffee table and remarked, "I know, you did the same when I told you about Hibrasil and I do not mind, you are a honest and trustworthy person Tom Savage, I would not stay here if you were not."

Savage sat down again and then asked, "So these portals are capable of taking you to Heaven?"

"Like I have said, some do only if you are worthy, think of them as a conduit that hungers for your very soul and if your soul is corrupt then you now know the alternative."

"They are like... black holes then, only on a much smaller scale?"

"Yes, sort of I guess but I am no scientist as I have stated earlier and they are much more than black holes Tom, they are a living organism that are part of a much higher consciousness."

"But surely God or Aenor would have explained all of this to you?"

Mastema laughed out loud, "Not so... what is that saying I read on the device known as a computer, 'God moves in mysterious ways' and so it was with us."

"Us?"

"The chosen, those that shine, the angelic, call us what you will."

"Not everybody is chosen then?"

"Not at all, the fact was that there were not enough of us to do the work that Aenor constantly required."

"You sound like... celestial nurses" exclaimed Savage who felt instantly proud of this sudden perception.

"That is a good way of putting it Tom; we were there to comfort the confused and the scared or the angry even, then to guide them through the portal whether it was safe or hazardous. I still think that I was chosen because I had been able to see the shining people. We all seemed to have some special quality; Theolus' qualities were wisdom and patience, I however, was not as patient he was as you will come to realise."

"So your journey through the portal was safe and painless then?"

"Completely, there was no threat from the Dark Conscious. We walked as if in a dream, the portal was full of trees and fields and birds that sang glorious songs as they flew around us... the portal seemed to be simply an extension of Hibrasil."

"So it had accessed your memories then?" remarked Savage who was trying his best to understand the seemingly impossible things that Mastema was telling him.

"You are very perceptive Tom and basically you have just described Enolan, a Heaven, a place that is based upon your memories."

Savage smiled smugly to himself, he was now completely enthralled by what Mastema was saying

"I was taken to a village by Theolus that was almost a carbon copy of my village of Lolar but not quite, it was much bigger, much more spacious and seemed more colourful. The birds in the sky seemed to be more exotic, the sea seemed to be a clearer, deeper blue, no storms raged anywhere, there was only a warm stillness, and the soft breeze in the air was soothing and calm with a luscious scent of exotic flowers.

Theolus walked me to my farmhouse and to my dreamlike amazement out stepped my father, mother and grandparents and tears instantly flooded my eyes. I stopped still in shock and cried without shame as if I were a young boy before I had become a true warrior. My family encircled me and held me, comforted me in my highly emotive state. I was then taken inside the farmhouse where a lavish meal was waiting on the table complete with a large barrel of Necal. Theolus stood at the door and did not enter, "Your time of acceptance has begun Mastema, enjoy the day, now and forever" he said then his shining figure disappeared in a wisp of light as he took to the air."

"You did not mention that he had wings" remarked Savage and he was thinking of stereotypical angels.

"Yes he could fly and I will come to that later too but we did not have the feathered wings as shown in the many illustrations I have since come across."

"No wings, but what then, how?"

"Pure light again Tom, a light that emanated from two points on our backs, this gave the balance and ability, the power of flight… I guess the light did give the impression of wings… I had made drawings of the angelic I had seen beside greatmama; I had drawn great white feathered wings too."

"And that angel had been Theolus?"

"Yes, I think that is why he came for me because I had seen him."

"And you met Aenor?" asked Savage and he could not believe that he was asking someone such a thing.

"Eventually I did… at least I think it was Aenor. After one cycle to the day of my ascension to Enolan, Theolus came to take me to Aenor. I did not have the power of flight yet so Theolus lifted me with great ease and we soared effortlessly over Lolar, across the sea and up into the multi-coloured clouds until we eventually descended into a place that was beyond belief.

The colours of the land were almost blinding but my eyes quickly adjusted. It was as if the whole world was made of a glass like substance, a substance that seemed to have a life of its own. This living glass reflected the life that moved around it… man, animals of every kind walked through this mirage as if it were a dream and of course I became to think that it indeed was all a dream. I became infused by a great feeling of calm and love, any worry and doubt I may have had vanished completely and I finally felt totally at peace with myself and the new world I now inhabited.

We walked along a wide white pathway that sparkled with a vibrancy that embraced our feet. We passed through luscious gardens full of multi-coloured flowers that defied description until we came to what seemed like a large wide doorway that was part of a gigantic white wall that seemed to stretch out to infinity across the landscape. We were about to enter the gardens of Enolan, the place where Aenor was known to reside.

Once inside I expected to panic as I knew the enormity of what was happening was too much for me but I surprisingly remained calm and composed.

"Fear not Mastema, you are about meet Aenor, you are about to become one of us."

We then entered a large hall that had beams of light shining through tall marble-like columns, it seemed like an enormous circular temple but I could not believe that I was expected to worship the Great Aenor face to face

"No, you are not expected to do that" said Theolus as if he had read my thoughts.

In the surrounding glittering light I saw a multitude of shining figures hovering in complete silence. Suddenly the light of the temple turned inward and pointed to a spot in front of me. The light began to move and twist and turn until it became a form that was at least fifty foot high, the outline of the figure was basically that of a man but as it shifted slowly the form showed female tendencies too…"

I AM AENOR
I AM ETERNITY
WELCOME MASTEMA
TO ETERNITY

Savage dropped his empty bottle to the floor, he wanted to say something but he could not, his mouth moved slightly but no words came from them..

"Yes Tom, I was standing before the God of this world."

Savage quickly opened another bottle of beer and passed one to Mastema, "I… I think my mind would have exploded!"

"I thought mine would too" replied Mastema, "but the feeling of immense love was too great, it is hard to explain but I will do my best."

"So God did not appear as a man or a woman… but as both?"

"Yes that is correct in a way Tom, it was hard to tell because of the moving light around Aenor, my guess was that He was more than man, that He came into being at the beginning of the universe, that He is in fact the accumulation of conscious that developed from the passing of life at the very start of things."

"Something that became aware?"

"Yes Tom; that is what I came to believe. Aenor has never mentioned his origin as far as I know; I think He or She thought that there was no need to do this."

"But He felt a need to worry about the world that created Him?"

"Initially I thought that Tom then after a few years my belief in Aenor began to wane."

"In what way?"

"I felt that He had the power to defeat the dark forces that pervaded the world of the living and to eradicate the suffering that I came to observe but He did not."

"You still became angelic then?"

"Yes of course, it would be a long time before these thoughts would pervade my mind. As I stood before Aenor, an intense beam of light which I believe emanated from His eyes, hit my body and I felt the light cut painlessly out of my back, He had given me my 'wings' so to speak. The whole thing was short and without any ceremonial pomp."

GO MASTEMA

FOLLOW THE WORDS OF THEOLUS
FOLLOW THE WAY OF AENOR

"Then Aenor was simply no longer there, the great hall seemed empty and vacant, He had moved away in his mysterious way. Theolus put his arm around my shoulder and we walked away from the temple....

"Go Mastema, fly back to Lolar, master this gift of flight as you will need it for the portals, you will need it for the work you will do. You are now truly angelic."

3

"I simply had to think it and the light was released from my back, this light did feel like wings but it was the power of thought that propelled them. Slowly I left the ground and headed up into the glorious colour of the clouds and I soared through them, up higher into the vast sky where the multi-coloured stars twinkled like they were welcoming me, it was a wonderful feeling, it almost felt like I could touch the stars if I wanted to as I glided past them like a bird. Then I wondered how I would ever find Lolar, and suddenly I felt as if I was being pushed in the direction I should go, like a homing pigeon I guess. Soon I descended by instinct and Lolar came into view. I circled around my farmhouse then gently dropped down to the ground in a beam of light.

My family came to greet me, there were so pleased and proud that I had been chosen by Aenor but they also knew that my afterlife was about to change."

"In what way?" interrupted Savage.

"It is hard to explain Tom, shortly after I had returned to Lolar, Theolus came again for me; he said that I was now to reside with the angelic, to be there for when I was needed. This time a portal shone down from above, glittering and moving like a thing alive, suddenly a great swirling hole opened in the side of it and we floated through it. Inside the portal everything seemed to be blue, like a gigantic blue vein that was throbbing and moving and we flew along it. Then another swirling doorway opened and once again we were in a gigantic hall which was circular and dome shaped and seemed to have a never-ending multitude of levels that gradually reached the top.

"This is Angelica" declared Theolus, "This is where the angelic reside. Your habitat is on the very highest level, follow me Mastema" and he began to float up through the dome."

"So that is where the word angel comes from then?" asked Savage.

"Yes, one would assume so; of course other communities would have different names for it."

"Were you never allowed to return to your Lolar in Heaven?"

"Oh yes, occasionally but Angelica was now my permanent place of residence, there was work to be done, constant work.

As I have said, my habitat was at the top level and when Theolus and I entered I was amazed at the size of the rooms within. Everything was white and shining and we walked through two such rooms that were obviously living and rest rooms to a wide curved balcony that looked out across Angelica. What I saw were more similar domes, towering trees, spacious gardens, blue pools and springs that stretched away as far as the eye could see. This was a truly a wondrous sight set under the most glittering of skies but what really amazed me were the blue strands of the portals that kept opening and closing, they did seem like living floating veins that were constantly touching and probing the multitude of white domes.

"The blue veins... portals opening up to take angelic to those that need their help. The same will happen to you soon Mastema, they will come for you and take you to the land of the living" said Theolus.

"They will take me to the living Lolar then so that I may see what happened to my beloved Meliah and my child that I have never seen?"

"I am afraid that you are not allowed to return to the place you came from" replied Theolus and there was a serious look to his face as he ssaid this.

"Why... why not?" I had to ask and for the first time for a very long time I felt a sudden anxious anger build within me.

"None know for certain, emotional attachment I would guess, there is so much work to be done that we need no distractions, you have wait for them here like your mother and father waited for you."

"But surely that is nonsense; if a portal can take me to the land of the living then surely I could go to Lolar?"

"You will be taken by the living veins for a purpose, once completed you will be returned back here... and a point to note is that not all portals are safe."

"So I cannot go to see my family in the living Lolar?" I asked, almost trembling with the anger I felt.

"No, it is forbidden. We wait for them to come to us."

What Theolus was saying did make me feel tense and frustrated but it was something I knew that I would just have to bear... and I did, until I could no longer."

"You broke the rules then?" asked Savage.

"Yes, but not immediately, it was after a few cycles of my angelic work.

My habitat was very comfortable, I became friends with my neighbouring angelic then eventually my first portal opened up for me on my balcony... I was sent to a battlefield in the northern lands, cold, ice, death everywhere and not all were brave warriors. I was to comfort a young soul who had been cruelly and mercilessly axed to death in vicious combat. The warrior was only a boy really, of about fourteen cycles and in death he was confused and terribly scared, I guided him safely to Enolan and found his family who welcomed him with open arms. A great sadness filled me for this poor soul, for his life had been cut short abruptly without any kind of mercy.

"But surely he was in a better place now?" interrupted Savage.

"Yes, but at what cost to his sanity, what I eventually came to realise is that the afterlife is full of tormented souls, some which never recuperate from traumatic death... some lose their minds and the will to continue."

"What happens to them then?" Savage had to ask.

"They simply cease to exist Tom, gone from any sort of known reality forever."

"Another existence then?"

"Who knows Tom, I doubt if even Aenor knows that. But this was my existence, my very reason for being. I was sent to battlefield after battlefield because of my warrior background, because of what had happened to me... and my sadness and frustration increased. Why did the living have to suffer like this? Why was the world of the living like Enolan? These questions came to torment me, and I came to crave the sight of my beloved Meliah more and more."

4

"But you could not," said Savage, "You could not go to see her?"

"Yes... or so I thought. I stupidly thought that I would be struck down by lightning or whatever... but it was now over five cycles since I had last spoken to and seen Meliah. I needed to see her, to talk with her, damn the 'rules' I thought with impudence. I felt that I was beginning to go mad with what I was witnessing, I needed her words, her wisdom or I was surely lost.

Then one night as I stood on my balcony observing the living veins coming for the angelic, I thought that I could not do this work anymore, the suffering of the dead and the living had become too much for me to bear. I thought that we had no control over the portals, that the only blue veins could open them once we had been selected but I was wrong... I began to plead to them this night, "Come to me, I need you, I need you" but no veins came. Then I triggered my light and floated up into the sky, "Please, I beg you" I called out and something stirred in the rainbow air... a portal swirling in front of me, inviting me to enter, "We can open them!" I said to myself and flew immediately inside the blue opening. I thought of living Lolar and the portal took me there, back to the real village I loved so much.

I was actually trembling as I descended. It was early evening and my cloak of invisibility had been automatically activated upon leaving the portal. The night was still, the sun setting beautifully on the sea horizon and as I stood in front of the door to my farmhouse it opened.

It was Meliah…

My heart began to beat like it was alive again.

Did she know that I was there, standing directly in front of her?

How?

I began to panic.

What will I say to her?

Meliah stepped toward me and I held out my arms to hold her.

But she walked right through me.

Of course she had not seen me.

Meliah walked slowly down to the cliff edge and I followed her. I knew that she had come to watch the sunset as we had done so many times together. I stood beside her. After the big red sun had had finally disappeared I heard her whisper to herself, "Oh Mastema, I still miss you my love."

"And I you" I said and I kissed her on the cheek, of course she did not hear or feel me and she turned and we walked back home. Again I became anxious, I was about to see my child for the first time, I did not even know whether I was a father to a boy or a girl."

"Wait, you said she walked right through you, did not feel your kiss?" asked Savage.

"That is right Tom, I was attached to a vein of a portal, and this gives us complete transparency for transference of souls, in the portal we have complete control over our bodily cells, density, size, but when unattached these powers are limited."

"Enough to survive an eternity on the moon though."

"Quite right Tom, walking through walls does not seem such a necessity now but I do miss the power of flight."

"The power of light that enables you to fly?"

"Yes, cruelly stripped away from me because I had broken the rules but I will come to that shortly.

I entered the farmhouse with Meliah who went straight to a bedroom to check on our sleeping child, "Sleep well dear Matta" she whispered gently, "Your father is forever watching over you."

And indeed I was and I saw that I had a son, a beautiful handsome boy. My heart seemed to grow so big inside of me that I thought that it would burst out of my chest. I also kissed Matta on the cheek and my tears fell onto his face, angelic tears that seemed to make his face glow bright in the light of the bedside lamp. I do not know if Meliah noticed this but I was not worried.

"Damn the rules, I do not care, I have a son and I have seen him!" I called out in the night and it seemed as if the whole farmhouse shook...

Then the vein tugged at me.

Tugged at my heart.

I was needed somewhere else, somewhere where someone had died. I knew that had to go, I had to help that soul get to Enolan but I vowed that I would return to see my wife and my son again. And I did return on a regular basis, not worrying about any such rules or anybody knowing what I was doing. I watched my son grow, watched him play, learn, laugh and I was filled with so much love when I did this and for a short time I was happy.

But then my anger at the suffering of the living returned and continued to grow inside of me, the joy of seeing my family somehow made it seem worse when I was called away to godforsaken battlefields where evil and bloodlust reigned supreme... I guess I could not understand how to balance my emotions and then one night as I emerged from the portal above my farmhouse, I sensed that something was wrong.

It was winter and the wind howled along the cliffs as if calling to the waves of the sea to crash louder. I do not know why I was filled with dread but my skin tingled uncomfortably. The farmhouse was silent as I entered except for the faint sound of sobbing coming from Matta's bedroom, he was now ten cycles, the time he should be Coming of Age as a warrior but it was not he who was crying, it was Meliah who was sitting beside his bed, "Please get well Matta, please do not leave me" she was whispering.

My blood began to pump loud through my veins, through my head as I approached my son's bed... I staggered back in horror when I saw his deathly white face.

"Your son is dying" a gentle voice behind me said. I turned and saw that it was Theolus.

"What are you doing here?" I said quite stupidly.

"Your son has contracted some sort of virulent virus; he has not long left dear Mastema."

"No... no!" I shouted, "He is only a young boy, he has a full life to live."

There were tears in Theolus' eyes as he held out a hand to comfort me.

"More suffering... for Meliah, I cannot take this anymore Theolus."

The sight of my dying son tipped me over the edge,

Damn you Aenor,

Damn your Enolan!

What about the living!

Do you delight in crushing my wife's heart?

I denounce you!

I curse your ignorance of this world.

My anger shook the farmhouse and I saw that Theolus was surprised and stunned by my anger. This was something that I had never discussed with him, something that I had kept to myself. My anger was all-consuming as the density of my body began to harden.

"No!" shouted Theolus, "You will reveal yourself."

"Do I care? I care not of Aenor, whose world is full of pain and constant heartbreak, damn you again Aenor, do you hear me!"

And just as I was about to fully solidify, the veins of the portal dragged me away…

Dragged me back to Angelica then through the gardens of Enolan and into His temple.

YOU HAVE DISOBEYED ME MASTEMA

YOU HAVE SOUGHT OUT YOUR LIVING FAMILY

YOU WERE PREPARING TO REVEAL YOURSELF TO THEM

"I wanted to touch my son that is all; I wanted to show them that life goes on. You are taking that away from him and the grief will tear my wife apart… you have ruined her life!"

I HAVE RUINED HER LIFE?

Replied Aenor and his voice rebounded around the gigantic hall with so much volume that I had to cover my ears.

"Yes you, you created the world of the living, you are responsible for all of it's suffering that I have had to witness for you."

YOU DO NOT UNDERSTAND MASTEMA

THERE HAS TO BE A BALANCE IN THE UNIVERSE

I HAVE NOT CREATED ANYTHING

I AM PART OF IT

I TRY TO MAKE LOVE SUPREME

THAT IS HOW THE WORLD OF THE LIVING WILL SURVIVE

"You lie!" I called out in grief and anger, "I think you know nothing of love, nothing of suffering… you have no dying son, how could you? I will leave here, go to my son and wife and I will try to comfort them… I am finished with you, go and do your own dirty work if you are able, see for yourself. You are a false god, a god with no heart, a god not worthy of those that believe in you!"

The great hall began to shake as if the walls were about to crumble and fall.

WHAT?

YOU DARE SAY SUCH WORDS TO ME!

TIME WILL CHANGE YOUR MIND I THINK

Suddenly my arms were held by the strength of two angelic either side of me. The massive amorphous figure of Aenor moved closer to me, his eyes growing larger, burning like two gigantic suns.

Beams of ultra bright light burst from the eyes of Aenor and pierced my chest and back.

I cried out in pain as the light was cut out from my back.

GO AWAY FROM ME MASTEMA

GO AND CONSIDER YOUR WORDS

The two angels lifted me out of the temple, high into the sky that was no longer rainbow coloured. The night was dark and dismal and full of anger.

I was floating in space.

Drifting away…

Until the eyes of Aenor appeared again.

ONLY THOSE THAT WANT TO HELP

ARE NEEDED HERE

ONLY LOVE WILL SAVE HUMANITY

Then that burst of light again…

Extreme power that sent me flying through a portal.

An immense force that propelled me without mercy, down to the mountains of Lunar where I crash-landed like a dying bird saved only by the hardness of my skin.

The rest you know Tom. This was my banishment then, not to Earth where I suppose I could have existed quite comfortably if I learned to ignore the continual eternal suffering but I was sent to a place devoid of life, a place to consider my words and my anger."

"You argued with God Mastema, people do that all of the time, have done for centuries."

"You have to remember that this was four thousand cycles ago, attitudes were different, even that of a God."

"Do you think that He simply forgot about you?"

"Possibly… I just do not know, from what I read and saw in that Complex, the workload of the Lord seems to have increased beyond imagination, it might have become unbearable even for Aenor."

"So you still think that the man sleeping it off in one of my rooms is someone called Theolus, an angel of God?"

"I know that it is he, we shall see how he is come the morning. Your attitude toward me seems to have changed though Tom?"

"In what way?"

"I think that maybe you believe in what I say now?"

Savage seemed a little confused for a moment then he smiled, "It is all so convincing, your vivid memories and heartfelt feelings… I am a military man though and I am still aware that these memories and emotions could have been implanted into your mind."

"For what reason?"

Savage was stumped by this simple yet honest reply.

"God… I just don't know."

"I think that you need to sleep Tom and rest, it has been another long day… for me too; revisiting these memories has taken their toll on me."

"I'm sure they have. Okay, we'll see what tomorrow brings, maybe we will learn what happened to your friend Theolus?"

"Maybe… and that is something I am now dreading."

NAMELESS

1

The next morning Doctor Corrigan was still in his car on the edge of Savage farm, out of sight in the shadow of trees. Corrigan had done what had been asked of him, he had followed Savage to the shopping mall and back and then had waited, another uncomfortable night in the car. Corrigan was rubbing his unshaven chin when he heard the voice.

WHAT HAVE YOU SEEN DOCTOR?

The doctor looked around, scouring both sides of the car.

Then into the car mirror...

At the eyes that were changing.

"I... I followed Savage yesterday. It was just a shopping trip, with someone who looked like him, his brother I think."

HIS BROTHER?

"It was not Gunn, Gunn's a black guy; I think he left in the black car. Like I said, this guy sort of looked like Savage, he had similar features. After the shopping mall they drove around Vegas for awhile and I followed them."

IS THAT ALL?

"Yes... but they stopped downtown, brought a man out from a back alley and took him back to the farm."

WHAT DID THIS MAN LOOK LIKE?

"Shabby looking, dirty looking with a overcoat, like a hobo, long silver hair, I think he was drunk or confused or something?"

SOMEONE WHO HAD GIVEN UP?

"Yes, you could say that, the guy looked like he did not have long left on this Earth" and Corrigan laughed at this.

THEY WERE GOOD SAMARITANS THEN?

"Fucking idiots more like, why help a stinking bum like that, I would have spat on the tramp."

INDEED

YOU HAVE DONE WELL

THERE IS NO NEED FOR YOU TO STAY HERE

"Thank you... thank you, I am pleased that I have served you."

Corrigan wiped his face and breathed out, the voice instilled a great fear inside him like he had never known; his hands were still shaking as he reached for the car keys in the ignition...

The cold steel of a gun nozzle was suddenly uncomfortable on the side of his head.

"Talking to your self doctor?"

It was Gunn.

"Get out, you're coming with me. I think the Major might be interested as to why you are parked beside his farm."

"I... have no idea the Major lives here, which Major?" Corrigan said unconvincingly.

"Don't play fucking games with me you creep, hurry up and get in my car and don't move a muscle unless I say so, understand?"

Gunn drove up to the farmhouse, never taking his eye or gun off Corrigan.

Mastema saw the dust from Gunn's car first in the distance; he then called out to Savage that it seemed that they had visitors.

"It's Ray" said Savage, "Just the guy I want to see."

When Mastema saw Corrigan step out of the car, he quickly changed his facial features to that of Savage's brother.

"What the Hell's going on Ray, what's Corrigan doing here?"

"I was thinking the same thing Tom, his parked car near your residence triggered my curiosity."

"I was just on my way to Vegas; I parked to check my bearings... why am I being treated like this, why are you pointing a gun at me?" pleaded Corrigan in the best bewildered voice he could muster.

"Bullshit" growled Gunn, "I think you've got some explaining to do creepface."

At that point Mastema joined them at the door.

"I see you've got other visitors Tom" observed Gunn immediately.

Savage was surprised at Mastema's appearance again but he understood why.

"This is my... brother John, Ray."

Gunn shook the hand of John Savage not realising who it really was, "Nice to finally meet you John, I've heard a lot about you."

Savage was keen to get everyone inside the farmhouse, Corrigan had just confirmed that they could be under some sort of surveillance, "Right, all let's get inside and find out what's going on here."

Gunn poked his gun hard in Corrigan's back and forced him to go into the house. They followed Savage to the kitchen at the back of the house where Savage knew they would be more secluded

"Okay Doc, what are you really doing here, are you spying on me?" asked Savage bluntly.

"I will report this, General Stobbs will hear about the way I am being treated, this is not normal behaviour."

"These are not normal times" interrupted Gunn, "And look at the state of you; you don't exactly look too normal yourself."

Corrigan smiled, he felt his mood changing, and he immediately became much bolder…"I think you have the angelic here, I think that you are shielding him."

"And just why would we help someone who was being held captive against his will, someone who was about to be tortured" Savage replied sarcastically. Corrigan's eyes darkened.

"That man is not your brother, I think he is the angelic known as Mastema and I will prove it!"

Suddenly, Corrigan reached for a large sharp kitchen knife and lunged at Mastema with it…

Two bullets hit Corrigan in the back and he collapsed instantly to the kitchen floor, Savage reached down to him.

"I… have to know…" Corrigan gasped as the face of Mastema changed back to normal.

"What the?" said Gunn in total disbelief looking at Mastema.

"Your time is over angelic… they are coming" Corrigan managed to say then his head dropped lifelessly to the cold hard floor.

"I… I thought he was going to kill your brother Tom."

"He wanted Mastema to reveal himself Ray; you were not to know that."

"You can do that Mastema, change your face?" asked Gunn still trembling from killing Corrigan.

"A trick of the light Ray" Mastema replied.

"A bloody good one too" said Gunn, "but not for Corrigan though."

Gunn shook his head, "There was something about that guy I did not trust, but I guess he did not deserve two bullets."

"You did what you thought best in a moment of crisis like a true warrior, nobody would blame you Ray" said Mastema with no sympathy for Corrigan.

"I ain't taking this to the Feds Tom." Gunn declared.

"We can't, it's too complicated and I think you're right, there was something not right about Corrigan."

"He was filled with darkness" added Mastema, "The Dark Conscious had consumed him; he was probably on the verge of madness, I think you may have done him a favour."

A sullen silence filled the room.

"I know a guy that can make Corrigan disappear or maybe he will make it look like a murder, y'know, Corrigan in the wrong place at the wrong time in Vegas."

"Bullets Ray" said Savage thoughtfully.

"Yeah right, I'm not thinking properly am I? Corrigan needs to disappear."

"And you too, I now think you need to disappear for awhile, a vacation maybe and I know just the place, I'll write it down for you."

Savage jotted the destination on a note pad and gave it to Gunn. It was Susan Eden's address in England and he also added... *Guard her Ray, she may be in danger.*

"Got it, look I'd like to stay around but I now have to drop Corrigan off at my buddy's place... fuck, how the Hell did this all happen?"

"Keep cool Ray, it will be fine, I will cover for you work wise, you've come down with a virus or something. Just remember what Mastema said, that guy had become a living Hell, you only had to look at him."

"Sure, you're right man, okay, I will need a blanket or something; there ain't much blood for you to clean up."

"Don't worry about that, you just focus on that new assignment I have just given you."

"Will do sir" was Gunn's quick reply, his army training had kicked in, he had regained his focus... until he saw the figure standing in the kitchen doorway.

"Who the fuck?" Gunn stammered.

"I... heard the sound of gunfire?"

Mastema and Savage turned to look at the man known as Theolus who was standing looking totally bewildered.

"Theolus!" Mastema called out.

"Theo... yes... I am called Theo, I think?"

"No, it is Theolus" replied Mastema instantly and with authority.

"I... know of no Theolus. Where am I?"

Savage took Theolus' arm and made him sit at the kitchen table, Gunn was still dumbfounded by the strange man with the long hair and beard he was now looking at.

Theolus down at the dead Corrigan on the floor and he became scared.

"You... have killed this man are you going to kill me" asked Theolus nervously.

"Okay guys, just who the fuck is this?" asked Gunn outright.

"His name is Theolus Ray but you do not have time to listen to his story I think" said Mastema.

"No, I bloody well haven't, you'll have to bring me up to speed with this guy later Tom."

"Sure, let's get the poor doctor into the car; you've got a body to dispose of and a plane to catch."

***

After Gunn had left, Savage returned and joined Mastema and Theolus at the kitchen table, "I don't know about you two but I need a drink again, another strong one."

"As I but maybe not Theolus I think."

"Please… please, I need a drink, I'm confused, please do not kill me!" pleaded Theolus and Savage noted that he did have a mild Mediterranean accent.

"Hey, nobody is going to kill you unless you are allergic to coffee and a good meal" replied Savage trying to add a bit of humour to the depressing mood that had invaded his home.

Savage made a pot of coffee then poured two large brandies for himself and Mastema. Theolus' hand shook as he drank the coffee. "You… you say you have food?"

"Micro pizza it is then" said Savage and he turned to the freezer.

Within minutes Theolus was gulping the hot food down like it was his last meal on Earth. Mastema was saddened by the sight of this wretched creature… "Dear Theolus, what in the world has happened to you?"

"I know no Theolus, I am Theo, I know only hunger and thirst… and pain… men beat me, laugh at me, call me despicable names… but you help me?"

"Sure bud; those guys back in the alley were scumbags but you're safe now with us."

"And who are you?"

"I'm Major Tom Savage, this is my farm and this is…"

"Mastema" Mastema interrupted, "I am angelic and you are too."

The slice of pizza dropped from Theolus' mouth, "Angelic… what is that?"

"Mastema thinks that you remind him of somebody, somebody called Theolus."

"But I… am Theo?"

"Yeah and that is too much of a coincidence I'm thinking" added Savage.

Mastema looked at Savage and smiled then turned to Theolus, "I will tell you things Theolus, maybe you will remember?"

Savage shook his head.

"I think it may be necessary that you remember, Corrigan said that 'they' are coming… I need access to a portal."

"And how is Theo… Theolus going to help you?" asked Savage.

"I lost the light that opens the portals remember, cruelly torn from my back, maybe Theolus still has his 'wings,' it may be my last chance to return to Enolan."

"That is what you want then?"

"It has always been what I have sought Tom, to see my wife and family again."

"Y'know, the angel cast out of Heaven is known as Lucifer, the Devil... in the back of my mind, in that bit reserved for surreal nightmares, I was worried that it was you, that you were in fact some clever demon or whatever and that all this was some demented trick or trial?"

"Lucifer is not the Devil!" interrupted Theolus and his voice suddenly sounded more authoritative, "He was cast out of Enolan but he is not the evil one..."

"You remember then?" declared Mastema and he suddenly sounded rejuvenated.

Then Theolus looked confused again, "No... it is something... I just know."

Mastema moved from his seat and went and held Theolus, "Dear Theolus, you are still in there, please try to remember."

Theolus returned to eating his pizza, he asked for more food without any sign of humility or shame. Savage and Mastema went to the kitchen widow for more privacy.

"Well, there's nothing wrong with his appetite then... hey, are you're sure that he's not Lucifer? I don't particularly want the Devil at my kitchen table."

Mastema laughed, "Neither would I Tom, no that is surely Theolus and he seems to know what happened to Lucifer... but how or why he has ended up like this is a mystery. I need his light Tom; I need him to open a portal to Enolan for me."

"I think the only thing he wants to open is a bottle of booze" said Savage and Mastema smiled again.

"He seems better now that he has eaten."

"I think you just need something to trigger his memory, y'know like..." and then Savage stopped talking, he was looking out of the window to where a man was standing, a man that was standing as still as a statue and staring straight at the farmhouse, "Who the fuck?"

Mastema saw the man too and his face became stern.

"I'm getting my gun, the cheeky fucker!" bawled Savage.

"No Tom, wait... he is probably only the first of many."

"Many who?"

"They that will come."

"I'll kill him for trespassing if I have to."

"Another will take his place Tom, then another, you will not be able to kill them all."

"I'll fucking try."

"No... we need to know their motive, we need to wait."

"I'll call the police then"

"They may come too Tom, you know what I am saying?"

"Yes… I think I do, still, this is my home and I'm not standing about waiting for more to come, I'm going to ask the fucker what he wants."

Savage stormed out of the kitchen and walked right up to the unwanted trespasser and stared him in the eye.

"What the fuck do you want? Get off my lawn!"

The silent man who was dressed simply in jeans and a green casual jacket did not reply, he just stared back at Savage with dark blank eyes that showed no emotion whatsoever. The man seemed like a robot that was standing waiting to be activated and this unnerved Savage.

"I don't know if you can hear me but I am going back into my house to get a gun and if you do not leave soon I will use it, understand?"

The man said nothing and Savage returned to the kitchen and saw that Theolus had joined Mastema at the window.

"They are… here" mumbled Theolus.

"Who are they?" asked an irate Savage.

"Those that are nameless."

"You do remember then?" stated Mastema.

"I… think I do" Theolus replied then he collapsed to the floor, Savage and Mastema realised that this was maybe too much for him too soon.

Savage and Mastema took Theolus back to the kitchen table and Savage poured him a large brandy. Theolus drank the brandy and his eyes seemed to clear, he looked at Mastema with some sort of recognition, "Is… it really you Mastema?"

"Yes my friend, I have returned. I was cast down to Lunar. This man is Major Tom Savage; he has helped me greatly here in the land of the living."

"And I… am Theolus… I am angelic!"

THE LAST ANGEL

1

This revelation by Theolus almost seemed too much for him, he became unsteady and confused again which prompted Savage to say, "Okay there Theolus, steady now, take another shot of brandy."

Theolus followed Savage's advice and his nerve seemed to steady somewhat, he looked at his hands.

"My hands, my fingers, they do not shake as much now."

"How long have you been like this?" asked Mastema.

"I... cannot remember... we lost control of the portals, lost the battle. We could not get back to Angelica... the Nameless sought us out, those of us that were trapped in the land of the living."

"And how did you end up here... in the city known as Las Vegas, why did you not go back to the country of your origin?"

"I did, many, many cycles ago... but I became lonely, scared so I wandered the world looking for others."

"And did you find what you sought?"

"Some... they were becoming confused, suspicious, they did not trust me... this was the power that Nameless now had. Eventually I came upon this land but it was the same story, the angelic were becoming hard to find. When I came to this place, something told me to stay; now I think I understand why."

"So there are no other angelic?" asked a worried Mastema.

"The last one I saw and spoke to was Lucifer, he was banished from Enolan like you... he wanted to fight, to find others but he told me that many had taken to the stars even though they knew that it was dangerous. They had no idea what was out there, how long could they exist as they looked for a new Enolan?"

"So you are telling me that Enolan no longer exists?"

"I... don't know Mastema" replied Theolus and his sadness was tangible.

"But you can access a portal surely?"

"I think I still can but as I have said, they are now much more dangerous, they are infested by the Dark Conscious, the dark light that can destroy us."

Mastema became thoughtful then asked, "Tell me what happened to Lucifer, why was he banished?"

"I do not know where he is now, maybe he tried to get to Enolan again but I think not... I really thought that I was the last angel."

"But why did he get banished, I have to know" stressed Mastema.

"You were not the first to feel the full wrath of Aenor and eventually all the angelic came to know why but initially the story of Lucifer was only spoken about in hushed whispers. You were not alone with your suffering and argument Mastema, Lucifer rose up against Aenor with a band of others but Aenor was too strong, Aenor is far older than any of us and thus far more powerful. All I know is that there was a struggle for power, the light clashed in Enolan like never before and Lucifer and his cohorts were cast out, not to Lunar like you but to the far reaches of the cosmos, Lucifer somehow made it back to Earth, I think he told me how but I cannot remember exactly."

"So he is the fucking Devil then!" burst in Savage, "He decided to take his wrath out on the living; on the place that Aenor created?"

"Aenor did not create this place or the universe, it created Him" stated Theolus and his voice was sounding more authoritative now.

"Sorry, sorry, I meant the place that Aenor presided over... I think."

"It is fine to be confused Tom Savage, Aenor did indeed preside over this world and I think that he did really care for what happened here."

"But not enough!" declared Mastema banging his fist down hard on the kitchen table.

"Oh He cared Mastema... eventually He devised a Great Plan, He sent His son to this world."

"The one called Jesus or Yeshua; I have read about this... I think I may have sown the seed for this idea at the time of my banishment" said Mastema calming down somewhat.

"It was the greatest of plans, the greatest of stories... to turn the cross of death into the cross of everlasting life and love. Over two thousand years ago He began the battle against Nameless with love... but I fear time eroded the message, people turned to Nameless like they had in the Old Testament not even realising it I suppose."

"So you think Aenor gave up the good fight then?"

"Like I have said, I just do not know, the modern world became ravaged by war and hatred, people still believe in Aenor and His son but if they knew the reality?"

"That Heaven does not exist anymore?" burst in Savage and his heart was beating loudly now, "But if there is no Heaven then where do all the dead souls go, surely not all of them go to this creature you call Nameless?"

"That is a profound question Tom Savage and I wish that I knew the answer... I think Nameless only takes what he needs, those that are similar to them, I fear the others are lost, maybe floating in confusion in some other dimension, maybe like those angelic that took to the stars they glide in a never-ending void."

Savage thought about his family members that had passed on and shuddered.

"I have to know whether Enolan exists or not, I have to know what happened to those souls and to my family!" shouted Mastema and he went to the kitchen window to vent his frustration, "Do you hear me Nameless, I HAVE TO KNOW! I curse you and your kind, damn you to whatever Hell you come from forever!!"

Mastema's head dropped and he began to cry uncontrollably. Savage had never seen Mastema show emotion like this and his body began to tremble. Savage went to Mastema and held him and as he did he noted that there were now more people standing in his garden, still staring mindlessly, still saying nothing. Savage turned back to Mastema, "Look buddy, we're here for you, we can work through this together... fuck those Nameless goons out there, those fucking lifeless statues, they're like sad rejects from some zombie b-movie; they don't scare me. I mean, what's their purpose, they're just standing there, are they going to stare us to death?"

"They will have a purpose Tom Savage" said Theolus ominously, "I don't think that Nameless is here yet but we will find out soon what they intend to do."

"But what can they do to you, you are both indestructible?"

"Not to the dark light, it can consume us as it has so many others."

"Okay then, we will fight them if we have to, I can understand that."

"I know what I want to do" said Mastema who had stopped sobbing and now seemed more resilient, "Could you open up a portal for me Theolus?"

"Yes, I think so, I think I still have the power deep within me but like I have stated, it will be far too dangerous, they will devour you in one way or another, long before you get to the shining gates of Enolan."

"What does he mean Mastema?" asked Savage.

"The portals are strange places Tom; I have told you this before. They are capable of feeding off your memories and this means that they can be safe but if infected by the Dark Conscious, the journey through them can be perilous and..."

"Fatal" said a stern Theolus. "Do not attempt it; let the two of us try to rebuild here... even reveal ourselves to the living, like you did on Lunar Mastema."

"And do you think Nameless will allow such a thing, I think not."

"I think it is worth a try" said Savage not quite believing that they intended to let the world know that there was an afterlife and angels really did exist.

"This could be worth a try, remember though that I have already done this, exposed myself to the living and I was secretly incarcerated" said Mastema, "But I will do this only after I have tried to reach Enolan, I owe it to my family."

2

"I can see that you are resolute Mastema and that I am not going to be able to talk you out of this. If we are going to open a portal then we need to do it while it is light, while their strength is weaker, come the dark night they will be more powerful."

"And you will not come with me Theolus?"

"No, I think I will stay to guard the portal."

"But by yourself will be a hard task?"

"Hey, I'm here y'know and I could rustle up a cavalry if necessary" interrupted Savage.

"Your courage is virtuous Tom Savage and I thank you for it, it is good to know that I am not alone."

"If only I had my golden sword" lamented Mastema but it is now long gone with Hibrasil."

"Hey, Theolus, do you know what happened to Hibrasil?" asked Savage at the mention of the mythical island.

"Not exactly, the story I heard was that there was some cataclysmic earthquake under the sea that sucked the island beneath the waves... I was so saddened when I heard the news, I do know that the angelic did all they could that day for those that needed their help."

Mastema was visibly shaken by Theolus' revelation, he was obviously imagining the horror his descendants would have suffered, "And you dear Theolus, were you not there?" he said as tears began to fall freely from his eyes as he thought about all the family he never got the chance to meet.

"It was about a thousand cycles before the coming of the Christ child if I remember rightly, I was on the other side of the globe when it happened, all I know that it was quick and completely devastating."

"My sword, the family I never knew, devoured by the sea..." mumbled Mastema looking to the floor.

"Nature is and always has been cruel; it is unpredictable even to this day."

"And so is the nature of Aenor, do you have a sword Tom?" asked Mastema suddenly.

The question caught Savage slightly off guard; "A sword? No... no but I have a large hunting knife and a sharp axe; I'll go and get them."

"Yes please, time is now running out" said Mastema as he looked at the silent crowd outside that was growing increasingly in numbers.

Savage returned wearing a green military style jacket, he was carrying a knife and an axe but he also had a rifle and a .44 Magnum handgun which was strapped inside a brown shoulder holster. He offered Mastema the rifle first, "Thank you Tom but you keep the firearms, I am more comfortable with a sharp blade."

"Suits me fine, if those zombies step out of line then they can taste the bullets of this Magnum" replied Savage and he also looked at the growing silent crowd, "Make my day punks!"

"We need to try and open a portal now Mastema" said Theolus with urgency.

It was late afternoon when Savage, Mastema and Theolus stepped out from the kitchen into the surrounding garden that stretched to the fields owned by Savage. Mastema was wearing the leather jacket that Savage had bought him but not the 'I ain't no angel' hat, he thought that maybe the sentiment was not what he wanted to convey now.

The silent trespassers did not move or show any sort of awareness or emotion. Theolus looked at them with concern, "In a few more hours it will be darker and their power will be stronger then."

"Why don't I just shoot them all now?" declared Savage, "They have no right to be on my land, it will be like shooting fish in a barrel."

"Could you do that Tom Savage," replied Theolus, "Could you kill unarmed innocent people?"

"But you said that they are evil and that they will try to stop you opening a portal?"

"Yes, they may belong to Nameless and they may be driven by him this day but so far they have done nothing."

"They creep me out just standing there staring like the undead from some horror movie."

"They probably do not realise what they are doing."

"Then why are they here?" asked a frustrated Savage.

WE ARE HERE TO OBSERVE

The crowd called out in unison and for the first time Savage realised just how many there was, "My God, they stretch right around the house!"

OUR STRENGTH IS IN NUMBERS

"That means shit to me, get off my property!"

YOUR CONCERN IS NOTED MORTAL

BUT IMMATERIAL

"What the fuck do you want, whoever you are?"

I AM NAMELESS

I AM ETERNAL

"He is here" Mastema whispered to Savage and Theolus, then to the staring crowd he shouted, "So you have come to stop me accessing a portal Nameless one?"

ON THE CONTRARY
I AM HERE TO MAKE SURE THAT A PORTAL
IS OPENED FOR YOU
WE KNOW THAT THEOLUS IS WEAK
HE HAS PLEASURED US FOR SO LONG
HE HAS BEEN AMUSEMENT FOR US
WE THOUGHT HE WAS THE LAST OF HIS KIND

"So you see that he is not now but you have still not explained why you want a portal to open for me?"

SO THAT YOU CAN SEE FOR YOURSELF
THAT ENOLAN DOES NOT EXIST

"You said that to me in the army complex but I defy you, I will see with my own eyes the truth."

GOOD
GOOD
OPEN YOUR PORTAL THEN THEOLUS
DO IT WITH MY BLESSING

Savage looked to Theolus then to Mastema, "This sounds wrong guys; it's as if that thing wants you to go inside the portal?"

"I mean what I said Tom, I have to see myself. Can you still do it Theolus; can you still open a portal?"

Theolus smiled, "I will try my best friend."

Theolus closed his eyes then lowered his head; it was as if he had gone instantly into some sort of a deep trance.

Suddenly there was a flickering of light behind him, a sparkling, crackling light that spread out behind him as if it were two large wings.

"My God, they do look like wings" said an astonished Savage looking at the light that was illuminating his farmhouse.

Then Theolus lifted his head to the sky and opened out his arms and called out, "Great Aenor, hear me, grant me access to Enolan one more time!"

Suddenly a thick bolt of blinding light descended from the sky, a column of energy that hit the ground directly in front of them and a swirling wind whistled around it almost like screeching trumpets heralding its arrival.

"You did it Theolus!" exclaimed Mastema.

"Go now Mastema, I will keep it open for as long as I can."

Mastema kissed Theolus gently on the cheek; a round twirling doorway had opened in the side of the wall of light for Mastema to enter through.

"Stay with Theolus Tom" Mastema said to Savage, "Stay and watch over your farmhouse" then he turned and walked into the portal but just as the spinning doorway was about to shut behind him, Savage jumped through it and joined Mastema.

"What... are you doing Tom, no living person has ever entered a portal to Enolan!" exclaimed Mastema and he was clearly worried by what Savage had done.

Savage looked shaken, he was breathless and disorientated. A blue glow had surrounded him as if it were analysing an unknown entity but Savage was resolute, "There has to be a first for everything Mastema, you of all people should know that."

"But why, why have you done this Tom?"

Savage breathed out heavily as if preparing his thoughts, "Well I thought that you might need a helping hand after what you have told me about these portals... but there is another reason and I think you know what it is."

Mastema smiled, "Yes Tom, I think I do."

"I have to know Mastema, I have to know the truth."

WHEN ANGELS DIE

1

Inside the portal, the day was dark, what appeared to be black clouds dotted the sky like large floating bruises. Savage looked around this new place, not in wonder but in obvious disappointment, "Well, it is not what I was expecting Mastema, looks like there is a storm brewing."

"Those are not storm clouds Tom; those are the mark of the Dark Conscious, infestations on the portal."

Mastema touched Savage's arm and shoulder, "You seem solid and sturdy, how do you feel?"

"I feel fine I think, my skin is kind of tingling though and that blue glow around me is fading but other than that I feel normal."

"Portal energy, I was not sure how it would react to living tissue, I thought you might have been torn asunder?" replied Mastema and he was not smiling.

Suddenly, spots of rain began to fall gently onto their heads.

"See, I told you it was going to rain, what now?" asked Savage of Mastema.

Mastema looked to either side then back to the front of them.

"This way, we walk this way Tom."

"How do you know which way to go?"

"I have not lost my angelic sense; it seems to be guiding me."

"Oh, the homing pigeon again?"

"That is right Tom."

And as the pair walked on, the desolate rain followed them.

Soon grey shapes formed in the distance, shapes that became the outline of buildings and as the rain eased, the buildings became visible.

"Do you recognise this place Tom?" asked Mastema.

"No, I was hoping you would; trust us to find shelter just as the rain is stopping."

The nearer they got to the buildings, the more defined the buildings became.

"Wait, I think I know now" said Savage and as soon as he said this a young girl appeared suddenly in front of them.

"Where have you been Tom, I have been looking all over for you, mother said that the barbeque is nearly ready" said the little girl who was dressed in a light yellow summer dress that had frilly white trimmings.

The girl's hair was golden and tied back in pigtails and her large round eyes were as blue as any of the seven seas.

"Do you know this girl Tom?" asked Mastema but Savage had froze and he was as white as a ghost.

"It… can't be… it's Sally… my sister!" stuttered Savage in disbelief.

"Of course I am silly, and who is your friend?"

"I am Mastema young one."

"Well you can come to the barbeque too, there's plenty to eat."

"Where are we Tom?"

They were standing in front of a large white house that looked like it had been built in the thirties, "This is White Palms Mastema… and that house there is owned by a friend of my father. But we were staying at a house near the beach, it was the summer, we were on vacation."

Suddenly the sun appeared from behind one of the dark clouds and the temperature increased instantly.

"Oh goody, that nasty rain has gone, come on I can smell delicious food" shouted Sally and she ran into the large house that was now fully defined.

The house was large and three tiered with the thin windows of an attic at the top. The house looked like it belonged in an Edward Hopper painting and there were no people on the surrounding streets.

Savage did not move.

"I… I don't think I can."

"Are you are expecting to see your parents, is that it?"

"Yes… I think it is."

"But they are not dead."

"No, they live in White Palms now but not here."

"Then if your parents are here then it is not them, it will only be what you remember."

"So we have gone back in time?"

"No, it is the portal; it has accessed your memory, it is capable of that."

"But I do not want to be part of this memory" stammered Savage, he was now shaking as he talked.

"We do not have to go inside Tom, we can walk on by" said Mastema and as he did he caressed the side of Savage's head, "I will access your thoughts Tom, it may help us understand" and as he did, tears began to flow down Savage's cheek…

They were in the house; Mastema could smell the food that had been cooked on the barbeque. The music of a vinyl record playing filled the air. It was 1992 and Tom Savage was seven years old, his sister Sally was five. It was late afternoon and people had eaten their fill and were now relaxing, some dancing to a band known as U2.

Suddenly the sky darkened and the mood of the party changed.

"Damn, it looks like that storm is going to hit us after all" said Savage's father, "Okay gang, I think we better get back to our beach shack before the weather worsens."

Tom's mother rounded up her children, Sally, Tom and his brother John and they said their goodbyes to their hosts and as soon as they got to the car the weather did indeed worsen... heavy rain, a threatening wind that hinted at a possible hurricane.

"Jeez, don't those weather guys ever get it wrong, it's the summer for Christsakes" shouted Savage's father when they were all seated comfortably in the car.

Savage was sitting in the middle on the back seat and his sister Sally was sitting to the right of him.

"Check that the door next to Sally is locked Tom okay" said Savage's mother as they drove away in the now pounding rain... but Tom was messing about with John and ignored his mother's request.

"Right you bunch of Savages, it won't take long" declared Savage's father.

"Please be careful love, the storm is picking up now" replied Savage's mother and lightning crackled brightly across the sky above them.

Their beach house was indeed not far as Savage's father had said but as they drove down the wood enclosed road toward it, the storm increased dramatically. Thunder roared above them and the lightning became more intense and regular.

"It's just at the end of this road" said Savage's father and he pushed his foot down harder on the pedal.

"You're going too fast!" shouted Savage's mother and as she looked at Savage's father, a bolt of lightning struck a tree to the right of them and immediately caught fire. In an instant Savage's father swerved the car to the left by instinct.

Sally's small hand went to grip the door handle in a moment of panic...

And she flew out of the car like rag doll in the wind.

The car smashed into the first tree ahead of them.

Savage and the rest of his family were bruised, bloody and broken but nobody inside the car had been killed...

Only poor Sally, whose neck had snapped as she had hit the hard road.

The only thing Mastema could see and hear was the screams of Savage's mother...

Mastema withdrew his hand from Savage's head, "I am so sorry Tom" was the only thing he could say.

"She died... and it was my fault, I did not push the door lock down."

"It was not your fault Tom, it was fate, Sally may have died inside the car."

"No, no, it was me, I was not listening to mother."

It was obvious to Mastema that Savage had blamed himself all of his life for what had happened to Sally. Savage began to cry, "She was only…"

"She would have went to Enolan, one of the angelic would have taken her… she will be there, waiting for you."

Savage dried his eyes, "But… that little girl, is it not her?"

"I do not think so Tom, this is not Enolan; she is just a manifestation of how you remember her."

"Then where the fuck are we?" growled an irritable Savage who was now obviously emotionally unstable.

"The portal Tom, remember it is capable of playing games with us."

"Some fucking demented game… but why?"

"It is just your memories Tom, we have to be aware and remember this" said Mastema and as they looked to the house that now seemed to be very sinister, the girl called Sally came rushing towards them with a silver tray in both of her hands.

On the tray were burgers and sausages with large dollops of red tomato sauce.

"Come on you two slowcoaches, I have brought you some food" and this Sally smiled as she said this.

"Do not eat the food Tom!"

"Do you think that I am foolish Mastema, I have no appetite anyway?"

"But I brought this for you" said Sally and her large eyes saddened.

And then her face whitened.

And her eyes and mouth darkened grotesquely.

In a zigzag pattern.

Mastema and Savage stepped back from the thing in front of them.

"Vaagen" Mastema gasped in horror, "That food… the meat is human flesh!"

Savage felt sick at the gruesome sight of his sister Sally, he kicked the tray from her hands sending the monstrous meat flying, "Get away you evil bitch, you're not my sister!" he shouted at the top of his voice.

The thing called Sally became afraid and cried and she suddenly looked human again, "I'm telling mom about you… you're a monster!"

"You're the fucking monster, creature, Vaagen, whatever the fuck you are!" shouted Savage and as Sally ran back into the house crying, Savage started to run down the empty street. Mastema followed quickly behind, "Tom, Tom wait, slow down!"

Eventually Savage stopped head down between his knees, retching as if trying to make himself sick. Mastema was soon with him, "You're telling me that cooked meat was… human!"

"It is the way of the Vaagen, that meat would have been the flesh of man."

"My father?"

"You should not think this Tom."

"But it could have been or maybe my mother even! Let's eat our parents shall we?" and Savage began to laugh but it was the manic laugh of someone who had just been touched by madness.

"This is your Hell Tom; we have to find your Heaven."

2

As Mastema and Savage walked away from that eerie 'Hopper' house, Savage kept looking back; Mastema knew that he was looking out for his sister.

They were still in some sort of suburbia but Savage was not sure where they were now. Eventually the predominately white buildings gave way to wide open fields.

"Where are we now Mastema?" Savage asked and Mastema sensed that Savage was tired; it seemed as if they had been walking for some time. Day had turned to night and as they came upon a wide oak tree they stopped underneath it, the branches of the tree seemed to stretch up to the stars.

"You need to rest Tom, regain your strength, sit beneath this tree and rest against it."

Without saying anything, Savage sat down against the tree and Mastema joined him.

"I know this has been a strain for you Tom, it always is for mortals new to the portal."

"You said I was the first?"

"The first living mortal Tom, you now know what these portals are capable of, they are living organisms feeding off your soul... this will take its toll on you, not physically so much but mentally, you have to be aware of this."

"Oh I am now; I assure you, my little sister turning up like that... then suddenly looking like she was part of some mad evil Halloween party is something I am not going to forget in a hurry."

"The Dark Conscious Tom, it will torment as much as it can, basically to try and break your spirit initially."

"And why does it do that?"

"Because it enjoys it" was Mastema's cold reply.

Savage's eyelids did indeed feel heavy and Mastema knew it.

"Rest and sleep Tom Savage it will give me time to get my bearings."

"So we are lost?"

"Not lost, just adrift."

And those were the last words Savage heard as he drifted away into a deep sleep…

And he was drifting…

Or at least the ship he was on was.

His body was aching and painful, blood and bruises covered his arms.

He was in the hold of the ship and all was dark and misty.

A sickly smell pervaded the air.

"Do not worry my friend Arna, once this heavy fog clears, the fleet will find us."

It was Mastema and he too was covered in blood. In the mists of a sudden fog, their ship had become detached from the fleet and lost. In this confusion, three Vaagen ships had surrounded them. Sudden images invaded Savage's mind…

Swords cutting into flesh.

Axes, spears being thrown.

Then ropes and nets.

They were outnumbered.

And eventually captured.

Like fishes to be gutted without mercy.

"We will not have time my brother; I have seen these misty conditions like these before and they can last for hours."

It was Savage who was now talking as Arna, he was describing the doldrums, "It could last for days, weeks even; we do not have the time."

"Then we will fight them to the death, with our bare hands" declared Mastema.

Suddenly the door to the hold opened and the vicious white faces of the Vaagen appeared, they brutally killed some of the men near to the door then approached Mastema and Arna whose hands were tied tight. Both men tried to resist and fight but they were battered unconscious.

When they awoke they were tied against the main mast beneath the vile blood stained human flesh of the Vaagen sails. Directly in front of them was a large iron drum in which hot coals were burning.

"No… no, not this memory" called out Mastema who now realised that this was a dream… a nightmare.

Savage turned to Mastema and asked "What do you mean, what is going to happen?"

"It is a dream Tom; remember that, a dream… dreams happen in the portal and they are just dreams, it is not really happening. You need to wake up now Tom!"

Suddenly without warning, a large knife pierced Savage's stomach and warm blood from the deep cut flowed down his legs, he was then cut free from the mast and taken to the smoking iron drum.

Savage was tied to the rotating rack and cooked alive as he was dying.

Savage screamed in pain...

Mastema screamed in agony...

"No, no, not again" and then Mastema lost conscious.

It was the smell of burnt flesh that made Mastema wake up, human flesh that was being forced into his mouth.

"Eat... eat" was all the vile Vaagen could say, their voices sounding like that of a demon.

"Please wake up Tom" muttered Mastema, "Please..." and a thick sickness filled his mouth then spilled down to the blood soaked deck. Mastema knew what was going to happen... from out of the rising mist came the ships of Hibrasil, the Water Guard. It was the Vaagen who were now outnumbered and doomed but the ships had come to late to save Arna... to save Savage.

"Wake up Tom, you have to wake up!"

Mastema shook Tom; he knew that if he did not regain conscious then the horrific death he had experienced in his sleep would become a reality.

Eventually Savage's eyes opened slowly, "Have... I died?"

Mastema hugged him with both arms, "No, you are still here my friend."

"Are you sure that I am not dead?"

"I think the dark tentacles would have claimed you, dragged you away if you were dead."

"It... seemed so real. I felt the knife cut into my stomach, felt the heat of that damned cooker, I could even smell the salt sea air, strange how that was my last memory."

"It was strange that you were dreaming my memory" said Mastema.

"That really happened?"

"Yes, the Vaagen are truly evil, they believe that if they eat their enemy then they consume their souls... but I was saved by the lifting of the heavy mist and I did have my revenge, a blood lust consumed me that day and I severed the heads of those that had killed my friend Arna."

The stress of the dream had fatigued Mastema and Savage so much that they were soon sleeping again but there were no more nightmares for them. When Mastema awoke he was worried, he knew that there could be more terrors in store for them, this was no blue portal anymore; this was a portal to Hell.

But he was determined to carry on, to find out what had happened to his Heaven.

THE LAST CHURCH

The day shimmered brightly to life. Savage opened his eyes lazily, hoping that the horrors of his nightmare had evaporated from his mind.

"Some dream" he muttered to Mastema who was standing at the start of a pathway that led down a gradual slope to a group of houses that were all painted white.

Savage stepped out of the cool shade of the large oak tree and looked up towards the sky, "A nice clear blue sky, I still find those dark spots unsettling though" then he joined Mastema, "I don't recall this pathway?"

"Nor do I but it is a path I feel we should follow."

At the bottom of the hill the pair walked cautiously through the wide streets. They were aware of the people that watched them, people that stood silent as they passed; people with jet black eyes.

"Careful Tom, I fear they may be the Dark Conscious."

"I've still got my Magnum gun, which is just itching to be used."

"Hopefully it will not come to that."

"But if they are Dark Conscious like you said Mastema; why are they are they not doing anything?"

"Remember what Nameless said, that he wanted me to be here."

"Yes I do and that is what is worrying me."

After walking a few blocks in what now seemed a surreal setting, Savage had to make an observation, "Y'know Mastema, I think this place is White Palms still."

""The white houses?"

"Yes, it is noted for that, so what are we doing, just going around in circles?"

Savage was suddenly agitated again.

"Life is a circle Tom, you are born, you live you die then you are born again, you live…"

"Let's just leave it there Mastema" Savage interrupted as Mastema's description of life was surely going to irritate him.

"Of course Tom" said Mastema smiling.

At this point they turned into another street that led down to a coastal road; they could see the sea, hear the gentle crashing of the waves in the distance and feel a soft breeze that seemed to pull them towards the beach.

Like two eager boys with buckets and spades, the pace of Mastema and Savage quickened

"The attraction of the seaside never wanes, it will forever more remind me of home" remarked Mastema.

"I'm a desert boy myself" replied Savage, "and it is something I always desire, the air, the view, that feeling of a horizon beckoning to you, the ocean inviting you to cross it."

When they reached the coastal road, they looked right and left.

"Left will take us to the town centre if I remember rightly" said Savage and Mastema had his eye on something else now.

"And right will take us to a church Tom."

A few yards away to the right of them was a set of old stone steps that led up a hill to a small white church that had palm trees either side of it.

"A sight for sore eyes is it not Tom, come I feel the need to pray."

"Me too, maybe we should pray for a way out of here?" said Tom who had now noticed a group of silent people who obviously seemed to be following them. The pair ascended the steep stairway.

It was not a large church and it was completely white. At the front of the church above the main entrance was a large cross but the cross was not painted white, it was an old wooden cross, big enough to hold a crucified man and this cross seemed to be stained and marked with blood.

"The cross of Christ!" stuttered Savage.

"A representation more likely" replied Mastema.

"It sure stands out."

"I think it is meant to."

While Savage and Mastema gazed up thoughtfully at the cross, a man in faded blue overalls shuffled from the left side of the church with a wide plank of wood which he laid onto an outdoor table which was obviously a workbench.

Savage and Mastema turned in surprise as the man said to the, "Greetings friends, we don't get many visitors here so glad to see you both."

The man's skin was well-tanned and of a light brownish colour and his hair was shoulder length and white, in some ways he reminded Savage of Theolus. The man somehow looked old and young at the same time and as he began to smooth the wood with a plane he added, "Feel free to look around... I rebuilt this place; it's all my own work."

"That's real cool old-timer, it's a real nice piece of handiwork" remarked savage.

The man became thoughtful, "It's my trade, I'm a carpenter, always have been."

"The large brown cross adds a nice touch to this building" said Mastema.

"Yes, I thought so too. Feel free to have a walk around, the fields are a lovely sight at the back there."

"Yes, yes we will; thank you" replied Mastema and he and Savage made their way around the church. They noted that that there were even small stained-glass windows on the sides of the church, all of which glistened brightly in the intense sunlight.

"Wonder if that guy made those too?" remarked Savage.

"I would imagine he did Tom, it is a fine restoration."

At the back of the church they looked out across the vast fields.

"My God; that is impossible" gasped Savage suddenly.

"Not impossible Tom, improbable more likely I would think."

"Whatever, but I have never seen anything like it."

Stretching out in the fields as far as the eye could see were white crosses in the ground. Their number seemed countless and when they reached the horizon they became the horizon.

"That's one helluva graveyard but who's buried here, soldiers?"

Mastema's face became serious, "Soldiers of a different kind I fear."

Savage was puzzled by this statement as they returned to the front of the church. The man in the blue overalls stopped smoothing the wood when he saw them, "A glorious sight isn't it but like I said they get no visitors, nobody lays flowers there, just me."

"Who are those guys, I mean who are buried there?" asked Savage and Mastema turned and laid an arm on him. The old man looked confused by this question then eventually answered, "The fallen, those that fell, those that have found final peace I hope" and a solitary tear fell from the old man's eyes, "Well, I better get back to work, there is more to bury… I do wish that I knew their names."

"More?" queried Savage in surprise.

"Quiet Tom, come with me" said Mastema then turned and entered the church.

Somehow the inside of the church seemed much larger than was suggested by the outside building, blue light filled the church from the stained glass windows and highlighted the altar next to the vestry.

The altar table was wide and on it in front of a large silver cross lay a white figure.

"What is that, it looks like a statue?" commented Savage.

Mastema did not reply, he just walked slowly and silently down the aisle towards the altar and Savage was compelled to follow.

At the statuesque figure, Mastema reached out a hand and touched its shoulder; it was as if a sudden sadness had suddenly consumed him. Savage reached out his hand too and as he touched the hand of the statue he noticed that the other hand was laid flat across its stomach.

"Why do you look sad Mastema, I mean it is only a statue isn't it, it's made of marble?"

Mastema looked to Savage with tear filled eyes, "Not marble Tom."

"What do you mean?"

Mastema looked around the church; the only other door was to the left of them. Mastema went to the door and opened it,

"Wait, that's just the vestry or something isn't it?"

Mastema entered and Savage cautiously followed him. At first it was completely dark inside then slowly the room lit up as if motion sensors had detected their movement.

But it was not a room.

"Dear Aenor!" cried out Mastema in disbelief.

"What the?" added an astonished Savage

They were now standing outside but the sky was white and grey not blue as it had been, what they were looking at made them both speechless… white statues in rows that stretched out to another horizon. These statues had not been lovingly carved though; they looked like they had been frozen in the throes of death… some were hanging by a black rope that stretched up to the dark clouds above them, some were crucified, some lay on the floor, obviously the victims of some fatal struggle and some just looked that they had collapsed and died suddenly.

"What the Hell is this place Mastema? Is that workshop guy some sick fanatical sculptor?"

"Not a sculptor Tom, remember that he said he was a carpenter" said Mastema who had begun to walk through the gruesome looking statues.

"Well whoever made these must have been one twisted bastard, that's for sure, I mean they must be angels, look some of them look like they have wings."

Some of the angels did indeed have that crackling light spreading from their backs and now it looked like frozen ice that would crack if you touched it.

Savage noted that Mastema no longer looked sad; it was a fiece anger that now burned in his eyes… his skin began to harden.

"Hey, are you okay Mastema, your skin is beginning to look like diamond?"

"I… think we need to return to Theolus and your farm" Mastema said coldly.

"I hoped you were going to say that but how do we do it from here, it's like a maze?"

"The end of this aisle Tom and we need to go now."

"I can't see the end; why not go back into the church?"

"This way Tom, I think I see something in the distance that is not right."

"Your eyesight is better than mine but I think we should maybe talk to that guy outside the church, he might be able to help us?"

"He cannot help us now I fear… be on your guard Tom; the forces of darkness are near."

"I hear you my friend, and whether this is Heaven or Hell or Timbuktoo, I still have my trusty Magnum."

The wary pair made their way through the row of macabre statues until they came to a statue that seemed to be crawling, this statue was not fully white, and flesh coloured patches covered parts of its body… Mastema's mouth opened wide in disgust as he gasped, "Theolus, dear Aenor, it is Theolus!"

"Yes, you are right angelic… the one you call Theolus is dead."

Mastema and Savage turned to face the emotionless deep dull voice…

It was the Vaagen known to Mastema as Redface.

"I think we have unfinished business angelic, have we not?" he said and his words spat from his mouth like a deadly venom.

Redface was wearing no armour, he held no weapons, and he was fully naked and completely white except for his red face and red hands. He looked at his hands and declared, "This is not paint Mastema; this is the blood of the angelic" and looking around he added "and this place is the Enolan you so desperately seek."

"Nooo…" Mastema cried out and his anguished voice echoed hollowly around them.

Mastema withdrew his axe from his belt and hurled it with the force of a hurricane but Redface managed to side step it with lightning speed that was preternatural, the blade of the axe just cutting his side, thick dark blood flowed slowly from the cut…

"Still using crude weapons angelic?" Redface said touching his blood and tasting it, "Yes they do hurt and we can die again in this portal but I know that you were banished and have lost your light, your hard skin will not protect you from the power that I can wield."

Savage knew that Redface's focus was solely on Mastema, it was as if Savage was insignificant to Redface, slowly he crept to the side and then behind a statue. Savage began to reach for his gun inside his jacket…

"Human flea!" Redface called out and a blast of black light burst from his eyes and hit Savage on his chest, sending back towards the cross of a crucified angel… Savage slumped down beaten and his eyes closed slowly with the pain.

"You will make a tasty meal mortal" grinned Redface and his head turned back unnaturally to look at Mastema who was now charging at Redface with the hunting knife Savage had given him. Redface just laughed and the same black light hit Mastema full force and sent him hurling back to the ground beside Theolus. The skin of Mastema began to change; white patches began to replace the hard diamond of his skin.

Redface began to walk slowly towards his two victims, grinning like a madman who had just killed someone…

"I will light a fire angelic I will enjoy my feast this day."

"Not today tomato-face" said a trembling voice behind him, "I think you have underestimated the strength of humanity."

It was Savage and his skin was covered in multiple dark patches, his Magnum .44 was pointed directly at Redface.

"You said that you could cease to exist in this in this portal, well make my day punk!"

Before the beams of darkness could burst from Redface's eyes, the bullet of the Magnum pierced his forehead causing little ripples of dark blood to trickle into his eyes. Redface stood as still as the statues around him, his eyes gazed blood-filled and lifelessly at Savage... there was no thought, no reaction, he was finally truly dead in every sense of the word, the entity known as Redface no longer existed. The empty body of Redface dropped backwards to the ground in front of Mastema and slowly began to disintegrate until there was nothing left but a pile of grey dust as if he had been a vampire that had been consumed by the light of the sun.

Savage stumbled toward Mastema, holding is chest...

"Mastema, Mastema, c'mon buddy, we've got to get the Hell out of this place, I don't know how but we have to try."

Suddenly a voice said, "I know how Tom Savage, take hold of Mastema, take him back, I will open the portal."

It was Theolus but he sounded weak like he did not have much time left.

"We... we thought you were dead?"

"I am ceasing to exist... too much dark light now crawls through my body like a hungry poisonous snake, I fought to keep the portal open for you."

"Those bastards... are they still there then?"

"No, I defeated them all; you will find grey dust on your farm... but there were too many of them. I will die soon and I want to die here with my brethren."

"I... don't know if I can lift Mastema, I feel so weak myself?" replied Savage and a inner panic began to grip him.

"You were right Tom Savage, that red faced creature underestimated your strength, he was saving his main thrust of dark light for Mastema... lift him Tom, look his skin is no longer hard, his body is lighter now. Take him through the doorway; take him to your home to live once again."

Theolus waved his hand as best he could and a swirling doorway opened before them. Savage gripped Theolus' hand tightly but did not know what to say, he hardly knew this man, this angelic who was thousands of years old and tears filled his heavy eye.

"Go quickly Tom Savage before the Dark Conscious return."

Savage tried to lift Mastema but he could not so he began to drag him through the doorway, Theolus was now looking down the aisle of the frozen angelic to where a host of Vaagen had emerged...

"Go and live!" were the last words Savage heard as he pulled the lifeless body of Mastema through the sparkling blue light.

WHEN ANGELS CRY

AN EPILOGUE

As soon as Savage had managed to drag Mastema's body through the portal opening, he collapsed onto the soft grass of his garden beside the angel that he had just saved. Savage was exhausted, where he had been, what he had seen, no living mortal had ever witnessed and this had been too much for him, he knew this but he had to try and remain strong somehow. Savage looked at his hands and the dark patches that covered them and wondered if he was now scarred for life. Savage then looked at Mastema but Mastema was not moving, instead of dark patches on his skin, there were white patches. Savage hoped that Mastema had not ceased to exist, he hoped that maybe he had at least gone catatonic, the deep sleep from which he could awake at some point.

Savage's head dropped back to the ground and he stared up to the clear night sky and looked at the comforting shining stars of his real world and while he did, he thought about what he had just experienced, what he had witnessed... his long dead sister, who he had missed so much throughout his life, he then thought about the abomination that had brought him the human meat to eat.

Savage then thought about the horrific nightmare of being cooked alive by the creatures known as the Vaagen.

Then the strange man at the white church.

Who was he?

Did that man bury all those dead angels?

And the white angels that had been killed, crucified, hung...

All now lifeless statues.

Was that to be Mastema's fate?

Savage sat up, the blue portal that had stretched up beyond the sky was now gone and there were grey patches of dust all around his garden just as Theolus had said... no more silent staring stationary people with black blank eyes, Theolus had vanquished them all but had paid the ultimate price for doing so.

And then Savage thought, *where did all those people come from, how did they get to the farm? Surely they would now be 'missing people' possibly reported to the local police, maybe they had hired taxis to get to the farm which means that they could be possibly traced here... maybe they were loners though, vagrants, criminals on the run?*

Savage knew that he was worrying too much, there was no way that he would considered as a mass murderer, as soon as it was light and if he felt strong enough to do so, he would clean up any remaining grey dust that had not been blown away by the night wind. Savage's main priority was to look after his friend Mastema and he dearly hoped that he would recuperate from the deadly dark rays of the evil Redface... he began to pray, "Dear Lord, I really do not know where you are but I believe in you now, please show compassion to your fallen angel who risked everything to see his family again. Maybe this world needs someone like him now, someone to give us all hope. Please God; please let my friend Mastema live."

"I... am your friend Tom Savage."

It was Mastema, his eyes were open and he was smiling.

"Mastema, you're back!"

"Yes, we made it back dear Tom."

Savage stood up and helped Mastema to his feet who was still extremely weak and wobbled in Savage's arms as he held him.

"I believe you saved my life, it must have been a miracle."

"A .44 Magnum with a bit of guts miracle, that bastard Redface got what he deserved."

"I am glad Tom, revenge does indeed taste sweet even though I have waited thousands of years to experience it again... but what of Theolus, had his soul expired, could you not get him out of the portal?"

"Theolus still lived, his final act was opening a doorway for us but he did not want to come through Mastema" Savages' face saddened as he said this, "He knew that he was dying, he wanted to stay where he was."

"He would have felt that he was near to home, I would have done the same I think."

"Home?"

"I think that was Enolan Tom; that was Heaven."

"But... there was nobody there, just white statues."

"Dead angelic Tom."

"But where was everybody else?" asked Savage not believing what he was about to say, "Where was God?"

"That is what I want to know, I believe that it was the last church, I believe that caretaker may have the answer."

"But he was just a gravedigger, the guy that was burying the angels behind the church?"

"I think he was more than that Tom"

"He was the carpenter that rebuilt the church?"

"Yes... he was a carpenter."

Savage suddenly realised what Mastema was implying and his head began to spin in shock, surely it could not be?

"I have to go back" said Mastema, "I have to somehow open a portal again" he declared and his now diamond eyes shone brightly with a renewed vigour.

"You cannot though, you said yourself that you have lost the light."

Mastema became silent and his head dropped, "Then the road to Enolan is finally closed."

Suddenly Savage thought about Susan Eden.

"Maybe it is not closed Mastema, maybe there is still a way."

EDEN'S DREAM

Susan Eden was sitting in her conservatory enjoying a large glass of red wine when her phone rang, it was late and she had just been thinking about the strange dreams of the previous night, she did not know that her life was about to become even stranger.

It was not a phone call she was expecting, it was Ray Gunn and he had just landed at Newcastle airport. Gunn did not explain to Eden over the phone why he was in the north east of England but he said that he would find a hotel and they could get together in the morning if that was possible.

"No way Ray" Eden replied to this, "I've got spare rooms here at home so get your butt into a taxi and get here, you have my address yes?"

"Sure Sue, be there as soon as I can and thanks."

Within half an hour or so, Gunn was knocking on Eden's door. After big hugs Eden took Gunn to her conservatory at the back of the house, it was a warm clear night and the moon was full.

"I have just been sitting here looking at the moon and stars, having a glass of wine."

Music was playing quietly in the background, a play-list of Bryan Ferry songs and No Reason or Rhyme caressed the air, "Can I get you a drink Ray?" Eden asked.

"Sure, wine will be fine but a beer if you've got one would be better Sue?"

Eden came back with a bottle of Guinness then as she refilled her glass of wine, she looked at Gunn and was a bit mystified.

"What... what are you doing here Ray?" Eden asked bluntly.

"Tom asked me to come here a few days ago, there was little bit of business to attend to first though" and he breathed out heavily after saying this.

"But why?"

Gunn told Eden about what had happened at Savage's farm, how he had shot Corrigan because he thought that he was going to kill Savage's brother, he also mentioned the mysterious man called Theolus but he concluded by saying that he was there to protect her in whatever way he could.

"From who, from what?"

"That Corrigan was consumed by something Sue; I saw it with my own eyes."

"Consumed by what?"

"I... really don't know, the fucking Devil I think, Corrigan wanted to kill Mastema I know that for sure."

"So you think I am in danger because I am carrying Mastema's child, is that it?"

"Yes, that's what Tom thinks Sue."

"And what do you think Ray?"

"Again, I don't know, I'm just pleased to be out of the country."

"I can understand that, but it may be a wasted journey for you as I have been told that I am not pregnant."

"What!" exclaimed Gunn and he nearly choked on his pint of Guinness.

"I have been told that it is a phantom pregnancy."

"But, I can see a small bump there" Gunn said looking at Eden's slightly inflated stomach.

"It happens in phantom pregnancies; the body adjusts to the baby it thinks is there."

"Fuck me Sue... I'm sorry, swearing again, I just don't know what to say, I guess I'm sorry."

Eden laughed, "Don't be sorry Ray, there are no complications now; did Mastema know that I thought that I was pregnant?"

"Not that I know?"

"Good, good..."

"You were not going to tell him then?"

"I couldn't see the point, how could I, he did not exist as far as the security forces were concerned."

"I see... but he's with Tom now, God knows what is going to happen next?"

Eden looked to the stars again then to the moon, "It seems like an eternity now since we were up there amongst the stars, on another world that contained the greatest secret of mankind... you're right, we have no idea of what will happen next. Y'know, last night I had the strangest series of dreams, about Tom and Mastema, they were somewhere but it was not this world, of that I am sure. I saw a little girl that I felt was Tom's sister then her face changed into a grotesque white and red mask. I was then on an old wooden ship that seemed to be covered completely in blood and it had huge sails made of human flesh. Tom was killed and cooked and eaten but somehow it was not Tom. I was then looking at a small white church and the old guy that had built it... and then there were dead angels, white like marble statues, then an evil man appeared with a red and white face and red hands... dark rays from his eyes killed Tom and Mastema. I woke up sweating; it felt like there was no hope left in the world."

Eden was shaking, she drank more wine.

"Jesus Sue, have you been having more dreams, nightmares like this?"

"No not really, some strange dreams but none as vivid and as real this one."

It was quite late now and both Eden and Gunn were tired.

"Can I get you another beer Ray?" Eden finally asked Gunn.

"No thanks Sue, I think I'll hit the sack if you don't mind, we can talk about this tomorrow if you want?"

"Sure, I'm a bit tired myself. Y'know, I'm glad you're here Ray, I feel that I have somebody to talk to now, someone I can confide in, someone who has seen the unbelievable like me, c'mon, I'll show you to your room."

***

It did not take Eden long to fall asleep and it soon became evident that her strange dreams had not quite finished with her.

"Mama... mama."

A baby crying somewhere.

Eden was running frantically through the house.

Looking for the baby.

Then she was in the garden, then amongst the trees.

Even on the moon...

Jumping, bounding across the silver soil

of the moon's quiet surface.

She was outside of the moon-base

Looking toward the light of the domes.

She had no spacesuit.

She was completely naked.

Suddenly pain, searing pain...

In her stomach.

Eden falls to the ground.

And her stomach begins to move, begins to expand.

Something inside her stomach was trying to burst out.

Then it cut through her skin

And she began to scream...

Eden woke up completely covered in sweat and immediately checked her bed for blood.

"A dream... a dream that's all" Eden whispered to herself then she went to the bathroom to bathe her face. Before getting back into bed, Eden changed the wet sheets and hoped that she had not disturbed Gunn's sleep.

Back in bed Eden began to pray that she did not dream again but her prayers went unheard.

But this time the dreams were gentle...
Gently moving in her stomach
Like the small lilting waves of an ocean
As her stomach expands...
She can feel tiny hands, tiny feet
pushing softly at her skin...
Pushing down between her legs.
But there is no pain.
No blood.
Only the sound of a young baby's lungs.
Eden feels like she is floating
Bathed in the most glorious light ever.
A light she holds and caresses
And loves...

Eventually there was a gentle knocking on Eden's bedroom door.

"Sue... Sue, are you alright?"

"I am Ray, please come in."

Gunn opened the door slowly and was immediately aware of the sparkling light within.

"I... I thought that I heard a baby crying?"

"You did Ray."

Gunn's tired eyes began to widen in disbelief as he looked toward Eden who was holding a small baby, a baby that had light emanating from behind it.

"That's... impossible!"

"Nothing is impossible in this world Ray, I know that now."

THE FALLEN ANGEL

1

Lucifer Heylel looked out across the New York skyline at the sparkling multicoloured blinking lights that heralded the start of night. Lucifer liked his modern Manhattan penthouse but like all the other dwelling places he owned throughout the world he could not call it home, home was still buried in the dim and distant past, a past that still haunted him when it wanted to.

Lately the past had been trying to resurface and this puzzled, intrigued and irritated Lucifer, he had been experiencing strange dreams and dreaming was something he did not usually do or indeed did not remember and he thought that these dreams were triggering his latent nostalgia.

Lucifer was standing completely naked as he looked through the large wide window admiring the view before him. The sun was setting on a cloudless clear day and its vibrant red orange rays seemed to caress the tall buildings as it descended amongst them. The pulsating night life would soon come alive and this night he wanted to join it, to merge with it, to forget the unwanted memories that were being forced to emerge.

His desire to kill had to be satisfied.

Lucifer had spent the afternoon having sex with a lady from one the agencies that he trusted. The lady was beautiful as was expected, tall with dark brown hair and the most perfect body. She was a New Yorker and although she tried to sound like a high-class business woman sometimes her accent would betray her roots.

"Hey Lucky, are you going to stand there like God's gift to woman or are you coming back to bed, we have unfinished business or should I say you have unfinished business" called the naked lady from the bedroom door.

Whenever women asked what his name was Lucifer would say that it was Lucky, he had a reason for this but he never told them, there was no point because they would never believe him unless he revealed his true self to them. Lucifer turned toward the sultry woman, indeed they did have unfinished business because Lucifer had not climaxed during their hours of lovemaking, it was something he could never do now, something that had been taken from him by the heat of the sun. It did mean however, hours of satisfaction for the women he chose, he could make love for hours, for days, weeks even and no angelic sperm would leave his penis, a penis that had almost unlimited growth. When Lucifer made love to women, it was something they would never forget and for Lucifer it was still a highly enjoyable erotic experience as he brought the women to unimaginable heights of ecstasy. Sex for Lucifer was a way to forget.

This night though, it was more than sex he craved, he knew that he needed a victim. Lucifer casually thought about the woman in his bedroom and what he could do to her but the woman was basically a good woman trapped in an unfortunate profession, she was not evil, he knew this because he had touched her head and had accessed her memories and thoughts, this was an angelic trait that had survived his banishment. Lucifer only killed those that followed and worshipped Nameless and this night would be no different. Lucifer pondered what he would do as he watched the first stars appear in the darkening electric blue sky... he would have sex for two hours, then he would have dinner delivered and then he would walk the nearby streets until the opportunity for death presented itself. Evil is never far away in the city when the sun goes down and that is why he preferred to reside in the city rather than the countryside sometimes, of course there was evil in small, isolated places but the city was the large breeding ground. The city was the place of money, power, sex and debauchery, the place where every type of ungodly sin could be found, the place where the morals of God no longer existed. The city therefore was the ideal place for the work and wants of Lucifer.

After the satisfied lady left with a much fuller purse, Lucifer decided to have lobster for dinner. Seafood was always a delicacy for Lucifer probably because he had been born in the desert and he could have eaten more even though he did not even have to eat. The lady had been delicious too and Lucifer had been tempted to ask her to stay the night but his urge for mortal death was too overpowering, he knew that the New Yorker had left a richer, happier person and this pleased him.

After Lucifer showered in the large mirrored bathroom, he admired his ever youthful body – he was tall, lithe and muscular, like a modern day sportsman he always thought. Lucifer's straight brown hair had been shoulder length for years but now he preferred it short cut at the back and sides and long on top which would always be combed back over his head, he knew it was a thirties style and indeed he had worn it this was since that era and he found it amusing to know that this style was now very much back in fashion.

Like his hair, Lucifer's eyes were a deep brown with a complex pattern that glowed with an inner beauty, another angelic trait he replicated with effective precision. Every now and then he would add tattoo designs to his body but would discard them when he became bored with them. Lucifer knew that his bodily appearance was desirable to both men and women but he also knew that if they knew what he really looked like this would not be the case, like all angelic he had the ability to change his appearance and he was eternally grateful that this gift of light had not been taken by the sun. Again this was a memory that he did not want to think about at the moment.

After drying himself, Lucifer went to his computer desk and browsed through his list of wanted criminals, known drug dealers, seedy pimps and other undesirables. Lucifer's database of these reprobates was immense and he had a list for just about every city in the world, over the years, compiling these lists had become something of a hobby for him, an enjoyable activity that appealed to him as a predator.

After staring at the screen for some time, Lucifer decided that he could not be bothered to choose this night, he decided that he would jut walk and let fate decide his hand.

Lucifer dressed in a black suit and plain white shirt, the only luxury he allowed himself apart from his antique silver wristwatch were a pair of large diamond cufflinks which he knew would attract nefarious people.

As Lucifer left the ground floor entrance to the building, he tipped the doorman Max as usual. Lucifer liked Max, he trusted Max and he knew that his salary was not that great so every year, no matter where Lucifer was in the world, he would return and give Max a huge monetary bonus and many gifts for his large family for which Max was eternally grateful.

As Lucifer walked the streets of Manhattan, he breathed in the city air, it was a scent that always rejuvenated him, a smell that was vibrant with the energy of life and tonight he knew that the scent of death would be an added ingredient.

As Lucifer passed a Catholic church, he was tempted to go inside but he knew that he would linger there too long, he had always found churches lovely places to sit and contemplate, he never confessed his sins though as he never wanted God to forgive him. The church he was passing though reminded him of the small white church of his recent dreams, he suddenly realised that this small church probably existed somewhere in the world and that meant that it was calling to him, it meant that he would have to seek it out and find out why.

Deep in thought now, Lucifer wandered deep into the city and soon he was standing at the entrance to Retroz nightclub. *Perfect* he thought as it was a nightclub he liked, a nightclub that played music from different eras on varying nights and tonight it was the seventies.

Once inside the club, Lucifer took a seat at one of the bars on the upper level and surveyed the scene. Multicoloured strobe lights scoured the dance floor and Lucifer noted that many people had indeed bothered to dress in clothes from the era – tonight it was flared trousers and jeans, flowery paisley shirts, bright colours, girls with flowers in their hair but it was also the era of punk rock ad the so-called new wave so leather studded jackets and safety pins were in abundance. It really was a vibrant scene, a 'happening' as Lucifer seemed to remember and he smiled broadly as he drank his large vodka.

Lucifer noticed that his smile had seemed to attract the attention of a man standing at the side of the bar. This thin gaunt looking man was dressed in a large shabby green coat and was wearing a yellow t-shirt that displayed the Beatles Sgt. Peppers album and the slogan 'All You Need is Love' but it was the man's eyes that drew Lucifer to him, deep sunken dark eyes with aura of malcontent about them.

Lucifer stood up from his stool and walked past the man and went to the Gents room that was two doors down from where the man was standing.

Lucifer pretended to relieve himself then as he washed his hands he listened to the song Sympathy for the Devil by The Rolling Stones that was being piped into the room. Lucifer liked the music of The Rolling Stones and had met them on various occasions in clubs in London during their early days and he was convinced that the song now playing had been inspired by him. Again he smiled at this thought and as he dried his hands he noticed that the thin man from the bar was now standing beside him.

"I was just admiring your cufflinks man; I think they're pretty cool."

Lucifer kept smiling.

"But I thought that you might prefer a different kind of 'ice'?"

The man was a petty drug-dealer and drug-dealers were among Lucifer's favourite victims, they were abhorrent people that made a living from other people's misery, they were people that preyed on the vulnerable and the weak without any feeling of remorse.

"Yes, I could be interested" said Lucifer looking around the men's room to check that they were alone.

"Don't worry, we can conduct our business in here" said the man as he pointed to one of the wide invalid cubicles.

"Please step into my office sir" he said with a grin that displayed gold and silver capped teeth. After the man had shut the door, he sat down onto the toilet seat and reached inside his jacket pockets but Lucifer stopped him, "Before I check your merchandise, I thought you could check mine" he said looking down between his legs.

"Oh, you're the business with pleasure sort, cool, but it will cost you more."

"Money is of no consequence to me but you are" growled Lucifer as he loosened his trouser zip to reveal his penis.

"Wow man, now that is impressive, you might get reduced rates for that" the evil man slobbered as he took Lucifer's penis into his mouth. Lucifer held the man's head as he probed the man's mouth. Lucifer had been right about the man, he was evil through and through and had even killed two people, two murders he had managed to get away with but tonight, justice would finally be served to him.

Lucifer was not particularly aroused by the man's mouth; it had been a ruse that had enabled him to access the man's thoughts. Lucifer's penis grew larger inside the man's mouth causing the man both pain and pleasure, "I do hope that you are enjoying yourself" said Lucifer looking down at the man who was now red in the face and sweating, "because the taste of me will be the last thing you will taste in this world."

Lucifer increased his grip on the man's head and thrust his throbbing penis further down the man's throat then he increased the size even more and suddenly their was cold fear in the man's eyes and he struggled to break free but Lucifer was too strong... garbled pleas for help and to stop were ignored by Lucifer as he pushed deeper and deeper down the man's throat.

The man could no longer breathe, his eyes became bloated and began to bulge out of their deep sockets and it was then that Lucifer revealed his true appearance to the dying man...

The thin man stopped struggling.

Fear became disbelief then disbelief became insanity as the man looked at the black and charred creature that was choking him to death.

Burnt red eyes stared mercilessly at their prey, red eyes that were now burning deep into the man's soul.

The man stopped struggling suddenly and slumped down to the toilet floor, "May your soul burn in Hell for all eternity" said Lucifer who had reverted his image back to normal. He zipped up his trousers and went to wash his hands. Another man entered the men's room and noticed with alarm the dead man that was lying on the cubicle floor.

"He looks a little blue and cold, I think he may have a bit too much ice" said Lucifer casually, "I will inform the management" he added but of course he never did, instead he left Retroz and headed for another club. What Lucifer needed now was sex.

2

Lucifer found what he wanted in a back alley, another unfortunate lady of the night but it was what he needed, perhaps now he would be able to have a restful night's sleep without having to go catatonic. Unfortunately it was not the case though as the dream of the little white church with the old wooden cross returned and this time it was more vivid than the night before.

This time there were angels in the dream.

Dead angels

White marble statues
Statues frozen in the throes of death
Angels crucified
Angels hung with black rope
Angels gripped by deadly despair.

Lucifer rolled uncomfortably on his king sized bed but he did not wake. The carpenter that had built the church was now making coffins in which to bury the angelic.

"We need to talk" he said to Lucifer as he began to dig another grave.

"Why do we need to talk, who are you?"

"I am a carpenter and I have much work to do but he needs your help."

"Who… who needs my help?"

"Come to me and I will tell you."

And then the voice faded.

The church faded.

And the last thing Lucifer saw in his sleep was a field full of white crosses and a place name… The Field of the Fallen.

***

As soon as Lucifer was awake he went straight to his computer and searched The Field of the Fallen. Many pictures and places came up but he persevered until he found what he wanted, the small white church from his dreams, a church that was situated on the west coast of America in California, in a town called White Palms.

Lucifer felt the need for coffee, he made himself a pot and took it to the veranda of his penthouse to sit and ponder what to do next.

Lucifer had always been an impulsive person, a man who reacted by instinct but this time he decided that he would think before flying to California. For some reason he thought that it might be some sort of trap. The only real enemy he was aware of was an entity known as Nameless but he had thought that they had reached some sort of agreement the last time that they had met.

Lucifer always thought that it humorous that he was the one that was thought of as the Devil, he understood why and that was rooted in the past but he suspected Nameless as the reason for the continuing decline in the angelic leaving him to be one of the last angels. Nameless had foolishly said that Lucifer was doing his work but Lucifer had disagreed venomously, claiming that he was ridding the world of the living evil. Nameless had just laughed at this saying that Lucifer was misguided, twisted and delusional, stating that Lucifer was as evil as those he killed and like any murderer he would be damned forever. The last thing

Lucifer could remember about Nameless was the echo of his sick laughter that rippled with a multitude of voices.

Lucifer sipped his coffee; again those past thoughts began to bubble up inside him and for the first time in years he said, "Come… come to me, I need to remember" and as the warm rays of the sun caressed his naked body, a small boy in the desert city of Meccus ran through the market…

3

The boy had stolen fruit – apples, date palms, a coconut even… his wide pockets were so full of nuts that they were leaving an unwanted trail for the fat fruitier that was hastily trying to follow him.

"Come back you little thief, I will have your guts made into headbands you young scoundrel you!" he growled but the young boy was too fast, too knowledgeable of his environment, he knew all the quick escape routes and soon he evaporated amongst the packed crowd like a needle that had fell into a haystack.

The exhausted fat man gave up the chase, wiping his forehead and shaking his fist frantically in the air at the little phantom who was now nowhere to be seen, "Next time I will be ready for you and your fingers will be cut from your hands!" but the boy did not hear him, he was already heading for his house with his much needed ill-gotten gains.

The narrow streets on part of the perimeter of Meccus were vast and intertwining like a giant compact maze or a snake that was in the process of encircling the city so that it could crush its heart.

The young boy lived in the poorest part of Meccus, a district known as Shakas. He lived there with his parents, both of whom were struggling but for different reasons – his mother suffered from severe ill-health and every day her condition seemed to deteriorate. His father worked as a building labourer, long hours and the poorest of wages meant that the family was constantly struggling to survive, the boy had become a thief due to necessity.

As the boy neared his ramshackle home which was basically three small rooms, two rooms for sleeping and a kitchen come living room, the lack of prosperity of the area became abundantly clear: beggars, homeless people, petty criminals and prostitutes filled the cramped streets, it was the proverbial den of iniquity from which there seemed no escape for the unfortunate that lived there, a blot on the magnificence of Meccus.

As the young boy turned into the dusty street on which he lived, he noticed a man sitting beside the door to his house, a man he had never seen before and somebody who seemed to be not of Meccus. The man was wearing a long robe with a hood that covered most of his face. This man did not seem like a beggar and yet the boy sensed a sadness about him. The young boy did not enter his house straight away and the hooded man spoke to him with a gentle voice, "You do well for your family little Lucifer, your parents are very proud of you."

"You… you know my name?" replied young Lucifer and suddenly he was scared, was this man an agent of the fruit merchant? But if he was, why was he sitting so placidly and calm before him?

"Yes I do, I am here for your mother, and she has not long left in this world. Go to her and say your goodbyes because tonight she will be with Yahweh in Heaven."

Tears suddenly filled Lucifer's eyes, "No… no, you lie!" he cried, "You know nothing of Heaven" and he sprinted into his home, straight to his mother's room where she lay on the bed, gasping pitifully for her breath.

"Lu… cifer… I am so glad that you are home."

"Mother, I saw a man, he said…"

"Said what dear son?"

"No… nothing… look, I have fresh fruit and nuts for you."

"Oh that is lovely my son but you must be careful, you know what they do to young thieves these days."

Lucifer held up both hands and opened them out, "Look, ten fingers mother, they do not call me 'Lucky' for nothing."

Lucifer's mother began to laugh but this was cut short by a vicious rasping cough that seemed to drain what little colour there was from her thin cheeks. Lucifer had never seen his mother look so pale and frail and this worried him greatly.

"I need to sleep now son" she said weakly, "I do not know what time your father will be back from his work but he will really enjoy the fruit that you have brought home."

It was late when Lucifer's father returned from his work and the first thing he heard was the sound of his son crying at the side of his mother's bed, his mother had died peacefully in her sleep.

"It… is alright father; the man said she would be with God in Heaven this night."

Lucifer's father stood as a statue, a statue that was soiled and unclean, exhausted from the long days work, his head slumped as he muttered, "The Goddess of Death has claimed her then… she… struggled so hard for us…"

Then finally he began to sob and Lucifer went to him, they held each other tight in grief and their small home in Meccus seemed to fade away.

As soon as he was old enough, Lucifer joined his father on the building sites of Meccus, hard tasking work that made him physically stronger and he kept their bellies well-fed with his highly developed art of thievery. Lucifer knew that to survive he had to remain strong; his father was now struggling to keep up his work load and regularly received the studded strap from the taskmaster which usually resulted in Lucifer receiving the same for intervening.

"Do not worry my son, I can take it, I just have to keep working" his father would say.

"There is no need for them to beat you father; you have worked hard for Meccus all these years."

"Yes I have, and what have I to show for it?" his father replied, and then he looked at Lucifer who was also bleeding from the lash, "I have you my beautiful son and I am so grateful for that."

Lucifer hugged his now frail father; both were covered in sweat, a sweat that was tainted with their blood. Lucifer swore that they would not be beaten again.

A year later, Lucifer's father's strength had dwindled greatly. Lucifer begged his father to stay at home saying that he would steal more to supplement their income but his father declined, "If I have to die it will be with dignity, I will die paying my way" he said, like Lucifer, his father was stubborn and proud.

Eventually, Lucifer's father paid the price for that stubbornness. Both men were working at a construction site that was busy building yet another temple to the king and queen of Meccus, they had been given the task of carrying buckets of hot black oil into the temple for the immense roof. This black tar-like substance was poured into two metal buckets and was carried by a heavy wooden beam across the shoulder. Lucifer was glad that he had been given the same task as this meant he could keep an eye on his father.

As the day drew on, Lucifer's father became visibly weaker and slower and Lucifer knew that the taskmaster had noticed this. The taskmaster was a cruel brute of a man; he looked more like a warrior than a labour supervisor.

Near the end of their lengthy shift, Lucifer's father slipped, causing the oil from one of his buckets to splatter on the wooden platform to the temple. Lucifer was directly behind him with his load of boiling tar.

"You bloody old fool" shouted the taskmaster as he wiped small spots of black oil from his sandals. The enraged man then reached for his leather strap.

This time Lucifer was not going to let the man beat his father. Just as the taskmaster was about to lash his father, Lucifer swung his bucket, sending the hot tar all over the taskmaster's body. Smouldering oil from the other bucket splashed onto Lucifer's legs and feet but he was not bothered, he was enjoying the sight of the evil man screaming in pain... the taskmaster looked like a living lump of molten tar and as he screamed louder, Lucifer smiled, he knew that this vile man would never beat anther worker. Lucifer's excuse would be that he had tripped on the long leather strap of the taskmaster so it was in fact the taskmaster's own fault for what had happened, he knew that the building security leader would not believe this but at least it would be some form of defence for his actions.

Shock and silence apart from the cries of the taskmaster surrounded the entrance to the temple... and in the vacuum of that stillness, Lucifer noticed a hooded man watching from the shadows of the temple. Unbelievably it was the same man that Lucifer had spoken to the night his mother had died – the same shining blue eyes, the same beard, the same cloak. And the man smiled and nodded... Lucifer looked down to his stomach, a sharp wide blade had cut through it from his back and blood was gushing before him like a cruel fountain. They had not waited for Lucifer's excuse, an armed security guard had seen what Lucifer had done and had decided to take immediate lethal action.

Lucifer dropped to his knees and the buckets of black oil merged with the sand. The last thing Lucifer saw was his father coming toward him, eyes full of tears, shaking like he was about to collapse.

5

A blinding blue light surrounded Lucifer and his father and as they stood up together they looked around and noticed that the temple and Meccus had disappeared.

"Walk with me" said a voice behind them. It was the hooded man with the blue eyes.

"We are to go to the goddess of death?" asked Lucifer's bewildered father.

"There is no goddess, only one God. Come now, someone is waiting for you."

The three men began to walk slowly through the pulsating vein of the portal and Lucifer marvelled at the beauty and colour of it, he had just died but he had never felt more alive.

At the end of the portal they noticed a transparent shadow in the distance, it was Lucifer's mother. Both Lucifer and his father ran to her and the light in the portal changed, a bright sky full of coloured clouds and birds appeared above them.

"I have waited so long for you, come with me to rejoice" said Lucifer's mother who was now youthful and beautiful again.

6

The three of them lived as a family again in a habitat that constantly filled Lucifer with wonder and love. Their plight and grim circumstances in Meccus was now a thing of the past, a memory that they no longer wanted to endure. The family now led a serene and joyful afterlife but deep inside, Lucifer was restless, the young roguish scamp that terrorised shops and the market place began to yearn for excitement and eventually he was given the chance to fulfil this desire.

"Join us Lucifer, become one of us and work for Yahweh" said the hooded man to him one day.

"Work for Yahweh? I have felt His love in this wondrous land but I have never seen Him."

"Then come with me, Yahweh awaits you, you have been chosen."

The hooded man opened his arms and a great sparkling light burst from behind him, a bright light that formed the shape of wings.

"You... can fly?" gasped Lucifer.

"Yes and you will too soon, the power of Yahweh is great and mighty."

The hooded man took Lucifer to that glorious place in Heaven where Yahweh was known to reside. For once the garrulous mischievous Lucifer was struck dumb as the entity known as Yahweh appeared before him as a living mass of light.

WELCOME LUCIFER

THE ANGELIC HAVE NEED OF YOU

That is all that Yahweh said to Lucifer then he was hit by a warm blinding light that consumed him completely. All at once he understood the true power of love and before he was overcome by this new revelation, the hooded man took Lucifer to Angelica, the place of the angels where he could rest and recuperate before his work as an angelic began.

7

For years, Lucifer worked tirelessly for the angelic and the people he guided safely through the portals had usually lived in similar circumstances to him... gradually though, Lucifer began to question why cruelty and evil still existed in the land of the living.

Then one day it was as if something suddenly snapped inside of him, and that something forced him to go to Yahweh and voice his opinion, Lucifer was worried about what Yahweh's reaction would be but he felt compelled to have his say, he was still the mischievous boy from Meccus who was not afraid of confrontation.

But what at first was only intended to be discussion soon escalated into a vicious argument that shook the Temple of Angels. Other angelic had gathered to offer Lucifer their support but Yahweh was in no mood for a debate. Lucifer stated that he and his followers would take up residence in the land of the living and work to eradicate evil and suffering permanently.

YOU ARE NOT PERMITTED TO DO THIS

was the last booming words Lucifer and his band of rebels heard.

A light of imaginable force burst forth from Yahweh's eyes and hit Lucifer and his companions… within an instant they were expelled from Heaven to the surrounding universe, each heading in separate directions, Lucifer headed in the direction of the sun.

The ethereal body of Lucifer was travelling at a speed he could never imagine, his mind was in shock but instinctively he knew that he had to harden his skin or the approaching sun would devour his angelic body totally.

The diamond like body of Lucifer eventually slowed down and became part of a vortex that orbited the sun. Heat as intense as the deepest depths of Hell began to melt Lucifer's hardened skin and for the first time since he had ascended to Heaven, Lucifer felt pain and fear. Lucifer's hard skin became black and charred and his features changed, he did not know it but he now looked deformed and demonesque.

Lucifer tried to open the light of his wings but like his skin they were burnt and scarred and could not help him escape from the mighty clutch of the sun. In that instant Lucifer realised that he could not bear an eternity of so much mental and physical pain, he had to go catatonic, a form of suspended animation that would prevent him from going mad but before he did he shouted his final goodbyes to his parents and angelic companions and hoped that his words would travel on the winds of space to them.

8

Time became immaterial for Lucifer in his catatonic state, dreams came and went, reality came and went and then nothing but darkness and numbness. The great giant burned before him with contempt and disregard for the living entity that flew around it like an irritating fly.

Solar flares burst and spat persistently on the surface of the sun as the years of Lucifer became a blur then as Lucifer neared one such violent flare it suddenly and inexplicitly exploded with such force and venom that the body of Lucifer was freed from its incarcerating orbit. The power of this massive solar flare sent the black body of Lucifer hurtling through the vast emptiness of space again. Lucifer's body flew past Mercury; then

Venus and the catatonic Lucifer had no idea what was happening to him. As luck would have it for the man once nicknamed Lucky, Lucifer's speeding body began to slow down.

His body was nearing Earth.

As Lucifer entered the blue planet's atmosphere, gravity grabbed hold of him like a greedy giant and increased the speed of his descent. Lucifer hurtled like a speeding comet towards a landmass that was unknown to him, his body crashed through a canopy of tall trees causing an instant forest fire then his body smashed along the ground until it came to a standstill near the edge of a quiet jungle stream.

It was the start of a monsoon that awakened Lucifer from his death-like slumber, the feel of cool life revitalising water on his battered skin. Lucifer's red eyes opened like long shut trapdoors and surveyed the tropical scene that surrounded him...

Where am I?

Who am I?

Lucifer could not remember who he was; his mind knew that it would be too traumatic for him, so it had shut down its memory banks because it knew that he could go instantly insane. Lucifer felt no pain but the muscles in his body felt weak and stiff and awkward like a machine that had rusted from years of neglect.

Lucifer crawled nearer to the nearby stream to taste the enticing water but when he saw his distorted reflection in the rain splattered stream, he recoiled in abject horror...

What... what am I? ...who is this red eyed demon that stares back at me?

Lucifer staggered backwards, his mind reeling from what he had just seen and when he came to the stump of a thick tree, he sat down against it and tried to remember who he was.

Lucifer closed his eyes and went into a dream-like state and eventually after many days, images began to flash through his mind... gradually his life returned to him like an intricate puzzle, piece by piece...

I am angelic.

The angel who had argued...

I am Lucifer, the fallen angel.

Lucifer lost count of the weeks he sat beneath the rump of that tree, memories just kept flowing through his mind like the illustrations of a book that he had to see to the end and then one day when the rain finally stopped, he decided to walk into the jungle behind him to explore and find out where he was. Lucifer had remembered that he had the power of flight but he was frightened to open the light, worried that the sun had burnt this most precious gift of his like it had his appearance.

Stumbling through the dense jungle foliage, Lucifer eventually came to a clearing that suggested the evidence of life... crude wooden huts and mud habitats that suggested a primitive culture but nobody was to be seen. Looking through the sprawling village, Lucifer saw a large wooden building in the distance that seemed big enough to hold all that lived here and here a disgusting and gruesome sight greeted his eyes, this place was surrounded by decapitated and decaying heads that were crudely stuck on sharpened wooden spikes, dead eyes still open in horror.

As Lucifer neared this sickly building, he heard a slow dull chant inside that set a cold deep chill course throughout his body. Whatever was happening inside this wooden structure, Lucifer sensed that it was most likely evil and primitive and a forgotten urge compelled him to go inside.

Lucifer stood quietly in one of the corners next to the doorway, his charred black skin made him virtually unseen; he had forgotten in that moment that he had the ability to bend his light and turn invisible.

It seemed like all the residents of the village were inside this giant hut which Lucifer now definitely thought of as some kind of a temple. Men women and children were sitting quietly chanting and swaying on the straw covered floor oblivious to the dark entity behind them. These people had straight black hair and a dark brown skin and wore little in the way of clothing; in fact the women were virtually fully naked. They wore beads and bracelets made from small coloured stones and necklaces made of small bones that included human teeth.

At the far end of this crude temple, two torches burned behind a deep pit with a thick wooden pole across it. Inside this pit a fire was burning, its smoke circling around the top of the hut and escaping through whatever airway it could find. The sound of the chant increased and from a side entrance two of the tribesmen entered holding a small girl who did not look of the same tribe. Lucifer guessed that she had been captured from a rival tribe and that this girl was going to be roasted on top of the open fire.

The young girl struggled and screamed but to no avail, the two men holding her were too strong for her. As they neared the burning pit, Lucifer began to get angry fuelled by his pity for the girl.

I cannot allow this.

I cannot watch such a thing.

And as Lucifer thought this, the dark light opened from his back giving the impression of black spiky wings. Lucifer flew across the surprised seated villagers until he stood before the two men and the girl. The villagers stood up instantly in terror and backed away toward the temple doorway.

The two men began to shake and released their grip on the girl; their mouths open wide in shock.

"Dialo!" they stuttered but they did not dare move.

"What are you doing?" bellowed Lucifer, "Do you intend to cook and eat this poor girl? This is something I will not allow... be gone from me you vile things, be gone!"

The men and the villagers did obviously not understand the tongue of Lucifer but fear made them all react, they sped from the temple as fast as they could all shouting "Dialo!"

Like the two men had, the girl stood before Lucifer in frozen terror.

"Come with me young one" said Lucifer quietly and he grabbed the girl gently and flew out of the temple, far up above the tightly knit canopy of trees where he spotted plumes of smoke miles away in the distance.

"Your village?" he asked the girl but she did not understand or react, she was in some kind of shock, in awe of being in the sky with the birds. Lucifer flew to the smoke and encircled the village from a great height. Like an eagle he noted that the markings on the bodies of the tribe below were similar to that of the markings on the girl.

It has to be her people he thought and he then flew swiftly down to the centre of the village and the reaction to the sight of him was the same as the other tribe, the people recoiled in terror.

Lucifer released the girl gently on the ground and looked around at the stunned frightened faces... the girl ran to them shouting "Dialo, Dialo!" and this immediately angered Lucifer as his kind deed had not been recognised.

"Yes, look at Dialo... but I am not evil!" he called out to them, then he took to the air again, straight up into the clear blue sky and as he did he thought of home, of Meccus. Lucifer had no idea of the location of Meccus from where he was but he closed his eyes and envisaged the great city and suddenly a direction came to him, the instinct of a bird which all angelic had would guide him.

10

Lucifer soared over land and sea until he came to the great deserts that surrounded Meccus. In the distance the city glowed like a beautiful mirage, like a tropical island surrounded by miles and miles of flat sand that eventually reached the feet of tall jagged mountains.

As Lucifer approached Meccus, it was apparent just how much it had changed, it was now much bigger, bigger statues and temples in the same vein as the one's he and his father had helped construct dominated the city.

Lucifer flew around the city from a great height and surveyed the changes below with much intrigue; to any casual observer he must have looked like an eagle circling for prey.

How long was I held by the cruel grip of the sun? Lucifer pondered, *it must have taken hundreds of years to make these changes to Meccus.*

Then as Lucifer glided in the hot still air, he noticed a large crowd below in one of the open public spaces. Three men with their hands tied were kneeling on a sturdy wooden platform; their heads were bowed in front of three strong muscular men who held heavy curved swords that reflected the light of the sun like ominous beacons.

Execution! Lucifer thought, *my people have not outgrown their primitive laws* and again he became agitated and angry.

"So you still do the work of a devil, then I will show you a devil!" Lucifer cried out then he descended with great speed widening the dark light from his back as he alighted on the execution platform.

The crowd gasped at the sight of Lucifer calling out "Devilah, Devilah!"

The three executioners tightened their grip on their swords.

"Yes, I am the Devil, fear me!" Lucifer called out and as he did his skin hardened making his appearance even more demonesque, he then flew at the executioners with great speed and with his diamond sharp hands he cut and ripped their heads from their bodies before they could jump to escape from the platform. The crowd screamed and panicked and ran in any direction they could.

Lucifer then went to the three men who backed away from him in terror. Lucifer freed their tied hands.

"Yes, fear me and do no more evil or I will find you and I will execute you myself!"

The shocked men ran for their lives, confused as to why they had been saved and Lucifer looked at the heads he had just decapitated. He knew not why the men were being executed, perhaps he had been wrong saving them but the memory of what had happened to him in Meccus had prompted his action. Evil was still prevalent in the land of the living and he vowed that he would seek it out and destroy it; the love of Yahweh had no place in his heart now.

Lucifer flew to the mountains in the distance and took shelter in the first cave he came to. He looked at his hard black hands that now were covered in fresh blood, at his black body that was gnarled and molten... he had forgot that he had the angelic ability to change his appearance, the magical light that could also conjure up whatever clothing he desired. Lucifer thought about what he had looked like before the ravenous flames of the sun had forged him into a demon and his appearance became as it was before his banishment.

Lucifer stood naked at the mouth of the cave and shouted out to the world…

"I will be the Devil… and when the Devil's work is needed, I will do it!"

A red hooded cloak formed in the air and covered his smooth muscular body, a snake slithered towards his feet and a sudden wind whipped around him as if worshipping him and that made him smile.

WHITE PALMS

This memory of his life had flashed through Lucifer's mind in an instant, there was so much more but he now wanted the vivid images to stop, one could only endure ecstasy and pain in staggered doses.

Lucifer sipped his coffee then decided that it was time to seek out the white church of his dreams; he would go to White Palms. The dreams, the resurgence of memories were more than just coincidence he felt, maybe the answer then lay in California.

Lucifer went to his bedroom and dressed in something casual, white t-shirt, blue jeans with a thin brown leather jacket and classic Ray-Ban sunglasses for the west coast sun, of course all these clothes could be conjured up by his control of light but he always preferred the feel of real garments. Lucifer then went back to the balcony and opened out the dark light of his black wings and took to the sky.

Lucifer flew as fast as he could which was that of a speeding bullet. The land of America below became a blur and soon dawn beckoned over the Pacific coast.

As Lucifer approached White Palms he began to scan the area for the Field of the Fallen and on a deserted hill that ascended up from the beach he spotted the white church.

It was early morning in White Palms and the yellow sun was shimmering over the ocean like a giant beacon that was welcoming the day as it had always done. Lucifer could not see anyone about but he still deployed his cloak of invisibility as he alighted to the ground in front of the church. Double checking that he was alone he became visible, for Lucifer this process had become natural over the years.

The church was exactly the same as the church from his dreams except the brown cross above the door was much smaller. Lucifer walked to the back of the church to where the graveyard was situated, the Field of the Fallen, gravestones and burial grounds with simple wooden crosses dedicated to military personnel who had fallen in battle from the Civil War up to one or two from the first World War. There were not the endless white crosses from his dreams here he noted, here was a graveyard that was overgrown and neglected, burial places that had not been cared for or visited for years.

Lucifer went back to the front of the church and called out, "Hello; is anybody there?" but there was no reply. Lucifer then entered the church and felt an instant peacefulness; it had been sometime since he had visited a church he realised. The morning light was cutting beautifully through the painted windows as he walked towards the altar which displayed a solitary large silver cross. This was a church that few came to he concluded, it was the Field of the Forgotten not just the Fallen he mused.

"Why have you brought me here, who needs my help?" he said towards the cross. Lucifer looked around the church, there was no answer to his question but did he really expect one?

"The dreams, the memories... do you taunt me then!"

I THINK YOU TAUNT YOURSELF

Lucifer turned to see an old woman sitting at the back of the church. The woman was dressed in the style of the fifties and was wearing wide angular sunglasses from that period.

"And who are you old woman, what do you know of me?" Lucifer asked and he almost spat out his words with frustration.

I KNOW EVERYTHING OF YOU

The woman smiled.

"Nameless... you take the guise of an old woman, why?"

SHE WAS NEAR

SHE SAW YOU FLYING IN THE SKY

LIKE A PATHETIC BIRD

"She is one of you?"

SHE ALWAYS HAS BEEN

"So it was you who brought me here, why?"

NOT ME

I WANT TO KNOW

"This is not your concern."

YOU ARE ALWAYS MY CONCERN

WE WORK TOGETHER

"I work for myself, not you... not anybody."

NOT EVEN THE GOD KNOWN AS YAHWEH?

Not even Him, why should I? We do not exactly see eye to eye."

BUT WE DO

"No we do not, do not tempt me again Nameless."

ME TEMPTING THE DEVIL

THAT IS STRANGE

IS IT NOT?

"It is strange that I am here, talking to an old woman."

YOU ARE AT A CROSSROADS

I THINK

"I am at a church; that is all."

CHURCHES ARE CROSSROADS

"You know why I am here?"

Suddenly the old woman stood up as if in trance…

BE CAREFUL WHICH PATH YOU CHOOSE

LORD LUCIFER

And then the woman turned and ambled awkwardly out of the church leaving Lucifer with his troubled thoughts, he turned again to the silver cross.

"You have deserted this world and I curse you for that, there is only one pathway for me, the one I walked for an eternity."

***

Outside of the church, Lucifer breathed in the fresh salty air and a cool sea breeze caressed him, he had confronted his dream and nothing had come from it, *a wasted journey?* he thought but before he left White Palms he thought that he would take a relaxing stroll along the soft sands of the beach, he thought that it might help clear his thoughts.

And just as he was about to descend the steep stone steps towards the beach below, a voice behind him asked.

"I hope you enjoyed your visit, there is not much to see but the church still stands and that is the main thing I guess."

Lucifer turned to look at an old man in battered weather worn denim overalls.

"And who are you, another Nameless voice?"

"I… am just the man who looks after the church, nobody comes here much anymore. I just look after it, repairs, cleaning; it gives me something to do."

"Then you have done a good job old man, the church and graveyard are well kept considering."

"Thank you… I'm sorry, I don't know your name" and the old man reached out his hand.

"My name is Lu…Lucky" and Lucifer took the old man's hand but was puzzled that he could not easily access his thoughts, nothing much was in his mind, just the church, the graveyard and the silver cross.

"That is a good name I like that; maybe you will bring luck to this church?"

"The church is lucky having you" replied Lucifer, "and you have not told me your name."

"Oh my name is of no concern to a gentleman like you… some days my memory plays tricks on me, some days I don't even remember my name" said the old man and this was followed by a chesty laugh that suggested a lifetime of too many cigarettes, "Enjoy the day sir, it is all we have."

"Yes quite so, it is all we have."

Lucifer turned to walk down the steps then he heard the words…

"You are not the last!"

Lucifer froze and contemplated what he had just heard and when he turned to look back, the old man was no longer there.

PART TWO

—

THE FIRST ANGEL

THE OUTLOOK HOTEL

You are not the last! The words echoed throughout Lucifer's mind with an ominous refrain. Lucifer looked at the small white church that was glowing brightly in the Californian sun and considered where the old man had gone. The man was a sort of caretaker, working to upkeep the church in his retirement. The man had most likely wandered off to tender to the graves at the rear of the church, a task that was clearly getting the better of him but at least he tried.

Lucifer thought about his walk along the soft sandy beaches of White Palms that had been interrupted by the intriguing words of the old caretaker, maybe he should just ignore them, the man probably meant that Lucifer would not be the last visitor to the seemingly redundant church… but his voice had sounded different, Lucifer was sure of this, it was a voice from the past, from over two thousand years ago.

Surely not, I am imagining things, my memory playing tricks on me again, or the sight of the cross?

Lucifer decided that his walk could wait, why not: he had all the time in the world after all. He went to find the old man.

The caretaker was at the rear of the church in the Field of the Fallen, tending to some flowers at the grave of a soldier. Lucifer went to him; the man did not turn to look at him but continued to prune the flowerbed of the strangling weeds.

"I see you have returned Mr. Lucky; I thought that you were going to enjoy a stroll along our lovely coast"

"I want to know what you meant by 'You are not the last?'

"Did I say that, I don't recall?"

The old caretaker stood up gingerly and breathed out, "I think maybe I am getting too old for this job, don't think my knees will take much more."

"Yes, you did say that I was not the last."

The caretaker looked puzzled, "I'm sorry, maybe I meant… that you would not be the last visitor, we get so few these days, the fallen here belong to a forgotten generation, a time gone by, that is why the church is so neglected."

"Why is it neglected?"

"I don't know, there hasn't been a priest here for years, guess it's the way things are going in this world today."

"Indeed."

"Do you have family here?"

"No, I was just curious; I saw the church from the coast road."

"You out for a stroll then, I see no car down there."

"Yes, I like to walk and think, a time to remember."

"Good for you, walking is the best form of exercise, especially at my age… funny, there was another guy here yesterday with no car, no family here."

Lucifer became instantly thoughtful and curious, was it just a coincidence? "Did this man want anything?"

"Want anything?"

"I was just wondering why he was here?"

"Curious like you I guess, this church is very old, y'know, he had a similar way about him."

"Similar, in what way?"

"Similar in the way he spoke, the look in his eyes."

"You seem very observant my friend, do you happen to remember what his name was?"

"He didn't say, just asked questions about the church like you."

"Did he say where he was from?"

"Now you are worrying me sonny, you're not the cops are you?"

Lucifer laughed, "No, no, I am not the cops, but I do believe in justice."

"Justice… does that exist anymore?" and the old man looked around at the multitude of graves.

"Could this man be staying in White Palms then?" Lucifer asked, trying to get the man to focus again.

"Well if he was, a hotel within walking distance would be the Outlook Hotel which is just down the road apiece… nice place, art décor period."

"Thank you, I need a place to stay tonight" said Lucifer and these words lit a curiosity in the caretaker's eyes, "Oh, one last thing maybe, what did this man look like?"

"Well I said that he had a similar look to his eyes as yours, that sparkling brightness but he was a rough looking man."

"In what way?"

"Black hair, close shaven beard, big head with a large brow above deep set brown eyes. His body was solid and muscular... he almost looked Neanderthal to me, a bit like Mr. Hyde from the horror movies y'know? But the funny thing was, he spoke ever so gently and politely which was completely at odds with his appearance."

"Judge not a man by his appearance" said Lucifer thoughtfully and his own true appearance flashed through his mind.

"Quite so, quiet so, my father always said that to me. Well, time for a break I think, gonna brew up a pot of coffee, care for a cup with me young fella?"

"Thank you but no, I think I will continue with my walk."

Lucifer pulled out his large wallet and took out a wad of one hundred dollar notes, "Here, for your kindness and information" he said to the old caretaker.

"Hey, no need for that much, we get by, but there is a donation box inside the church."

Lucifer stuffed the money inside the man's top pocket, "Then you put it in."

Lucifer turned to leave but once again the old man had to say something.

"If you do stay in the Outlook, watch out for the Widow mind."

Lucifer turned and the caretaker was smiling.

"Widow?"

"The hotel ghost... a young couple were killed on their wedding night at the hotel in the early thirties, they say she waits there for the return of her husband, they reckon his body was dumped in the sea."

"Sounds sad and gruesome" reflected Lucifer.

"Sure was, poor kids on their wedding day, somebody there will tell you the full story I'm sure."

"Yes, I suppose every hotel like every castle has a ghost maybe" and Lucifer became immediately thoughtful for a moment, "that sort of thing is good for business."

The caretaker began to laugh, "Sure is, but if I were you I would keep away from the honeymoon suite."

"Ghosts are of no concern to me, we will all become ghosts one day" said Lucifer as he began to walk down the steps to the coastal road. The old man watched him go and as he did he whispered to himself, "I think you're right sonny, I think you're right."

***

As Lucifer walked along the wide coastal road, he admired the Californian sea view. Maybe he had been in New York too long he thought; he had flown to White Palms from Manhattan because of the recurring dreams of the white church so why not enjoy his visit? The mystery of the dreams had not been resolved so it made sense to stay in White Palms until there was some sort of conclusion. Lucifer liked mysteries; it made his eternal life more interesting.

The old caretaker had said 'walking distance' and soon The Outlook Hotel came into view. Facing the sea and it's blue horizon, Lucifer realised that the caretaker's description of a thirties style art décor hotel had indeed been correct. The main building which seemed to be four storey's high was flanked by two circular smaller towers which were only three storey's high. The rooms in the main building all seemed to have their own private verandas and these verandas stretched around the building. The building was primarily white with blue linage and on top of the building in blue capital letters was the name THE OUTLOOK. Palm trees at the front of the hotel added an exotic touch to what seemed a very enticing hotel. *Much better than those many plain structures I have stayed in* thought Lucifer as he approached the main doors.

After Lucifer had completed the signing in formalities at the reception desk, the young lady seemed a little surprised by Lucifer's lack of baggage "No luggage sir?" she enquired.

"No, I am travelling light it seems, I was not expecting to stay in White Palms but circumstances have changed."

"Of course, I am sure that you will not be disappointed by what White Palms has to offer" replied the receptionist, blushing slightly because she had suddenly realised that her question may have been a little personal.

"I hope so" grinned Lucifer because he liked the look of this young lady, "now could you show me to my room please?"

Lucifer had asked for the most expensive suite and was given the rooms on the top floor next to the Honeymoon Suite; both apartments looked out toward the sea. Lucifer was generous with his tip for the young man who had taken him to the suite and the man was surprised and delighted considering that there had been no bags for him to carry. Lucifer gave him an order for the best cigars and Champagne that the hotel had. The suite was known as the Mariner's Suite which was named after a famous sea captain who had stayed there after retiring.

The suite was spacious which delighted Lucifer and the interior design was in keeping with the art décor style of the building, thirties, forties, fifties design elements were all prevalent, Lucifer saw that there was even a real ship's anchor on the veranda which he assumed was a small homage to the sea captain. Inside the suite there were basically four large rooms, a bedroom, adjoining bathroom, a reception and private room and all the rooms except the bathroom opened out onto the veranda. Lucifer walked through the main reception room and stepped out onto the wide balcony. Again Lucifer looked out towards the sea and took in the view. To the left of him he saw the beginnings of White Palms; to the right was the road back to the church and here the buildings along the coastal road became sparse, these buildings were probably holiday dwellings or retirement homes thought Lucifer.

On the veranda next to the large anchor was a table with two chairs and in the corner an unopened sun umbrella. Before sitting at the table the doorbell rang and it was the young porter with Lucifer's order, Davidoff Winston Churchill cigars and three bottles of Moete Chandon Champagne. Two of the bottles he placed in the fridge in the kitchenette and the other bottle he placed in a silver ice bucket then asked, "Where would you like your Champagne sir?"

"On that balcony, I feel the need to watch the waves of the sea" replied Lucifer.

"Indeed sir, a wonderful sight from here."

"From anywhere" Lucifer instantly replied

"Can I get you some sun lotion?" asked the porter, a sensible question because he knew that Lucifer had no luggage.

"No, I will purchase what I need tomorrow; the sun and my skin are well acquainted."

Lucifer laughed but the young porter was puzzled by his words.

"Sure sir; will that be all?"

"For now yes" said Lucifer and again he gave the young man a generous tip.

Back on the veranda, Lucifer cut the end of one of the cigars with the silver clipper provided in the box and poured himself a glass of Champagne; he did not bother opening the sun umbrella. As he lit the cigar he relaxed back into the comfortable chair and gazed out at the sea. Lucifer lazily rolled the cigar around his fingers and enjoyed the thick plumes of smoke that flowed smoothly from his mouth and as he sat there his thoughts began to drift... back to another time, another place... suddenly German Stukas and English Spitfires were flying through the skies in the distance, engaged in deadly dogfights. Lucifer laughed, the name of Churchill on the cigar had evoked memories of World War Two, the bloody conflict that had claimed so many souls, young and old.

As the smoke trails and the planes faded from Lucifer's mind, other images and memories took their place. Consummate evil had festered and thrived throughout that period, culminating in one the worst atrocities known to mankind, the Nazi's abominable Final Solution that was implemented in their evil death camps. It was as if the time of Nameless was at hand, a time for Nameless to revel in the depths of humanities despair, a time for Nameless to feed dark temptation to the multitude that were susceptible to it. One such man was Adolf Hitler, Lucifer was convinced that at some point Nameless had possessed him, driving him to do the unthinkable. Many times had Lucifer thought about killing Hitler during that period but he always concluded that he should not, who was he to alter the fate of mankind, he was not a god? Such an act would weigh heavily on his shoulders if the assignation had lead to some sort of venomous backlash from the Nazi hierarchy, an even greater evil if that was possible might take Hitler's place, Nameless might make sure of that. No, mankind had to solve it's own problems, Lucifer would deal with evil at it's grass roots as he had done for hundreds of years, It was this decision that had prompted him to visit one of the death camps he had heard about during his war travels… Auschwitz.

Lucifer followed the trail of the Jewish people to the railroads and travelled with them on the top of the train to their deadly destination. When he arrived at Auschwitz, he could not believe what he witnessed, Lucifer thought that he had seen it all throughout his second life on Earth, mass sacrifices, torture, war, horror of every kind but the way in which the Nazis were controlling their genocide was truly reaching new depths of evil… cold, calculated mass murder in concentration camps that were nothing more than human abattoirs, people thinking that they were being taken for a shower were being gassed to death instead. At the same time these poor unfortunate people were being starved and worked to death and when selected, executed in the name of Aryan supremacy.

Walking slowly around Auschwitz, invisible to all, Lucifer noted that in some ways it resembled a small village, there was a grocery, a hairdresser, a bar for the German soldiers, recreational sports facilities, a small cinema and theatre and even a brothel in which Jewish women were forced to perform immoral and degrading acts of sexual gratification and perversion. It was late at night, streetlamps lit the narrow roadways in this most evil of places as Lucifer approached the red brick house which was the camp brothel. Two soldiers were standing in front of six new female arrivals to the camp and the higher ranking officer spoke first.

"This one I think, I will take this one to my private quarters."

This man was small and overweight, a man not particularly suitable for combat but suitable for what was required at Auschwitz. Lucifer could hear his heart beating faster after he had made his choice, a young girl with fair hair who was too young and innocent for what lay ahead of her this night.

Lucifer followed the man and the pitiful girl and as they entered the officer's room, he entered with them.

Slowly the man took off his uniform jacket, he then went to the young girl who was now white faced and shaking uncontrollably with fear.

"Good… good, this is your first time, I will fuck you where you stand, in your shabby clothes first" the vile officer said and the side of his mouth began to dribble with saliva as his rate of breathing increased. The girl tried to scream but the man held her mouth tight.

"No, no noise, we do not want to wake the rest of the camp do we? You can scream later with pleasure" and he laughed at his own words as he pushed the girl up against the wall of his room.

"I feel your fear young Jewish and it excites me, tonight you will know how good a German fucks and tomorrow night, if there is a tomorrow night for you, you will want me to do the same to you again."

The officer now had his hand around the girl's throat as he took out his small erect penis but just as he was about to put it through the girl's under garments, Lucifer grabbed it tightly.

"How does it feel Nazi scum?" a voice from seemingly nowhere said.

The man stumbled back in pain. Lucifer then grabbed the man by the neck and increased his grip on the man's penis. The girl standing behind them was confused and scared and could not move; fear had frozen her limbs at the strange sight before her.

Lucifer wanted to tear the man apart but he was aware of what that would do to the girl's state of mind, also there would be reprisals, they would somehow think that the girl was responsible for the officer's gruesome death. Lucifer listened to the man's heart again and could hear that it was about to burst open with fear… Lucifer dropped his cloak of invisibility and revealed his true sunburnt appearance.

"My God… the Devil!" was all the astounded man could mutter just before his heart stopped beating. The officer slumped to the floor and Lucifer turned to towards the girl, his red eyes burning in his black molten face… the girl fainted, it had been all too much for her, she had expected evil in the camp but not to meet the Devil face to face!

Lucifer grabbed a sheet from the bed and wrapped it gently around the girl, he had decided to intervene this night; he had decided that he would save the young girl. Lucifer needed a housekeeper for his lonely mansion in Scotland and this girl would be given the opportunity to be a housekeeper for him.

Lucifer flew with the girl who was still unconscious, away from Auschwitz until he reached the outskirts of Berlin; it was now nearly dawn and he found what he wanted, a deserted woodcutter's cabin in the forest. Lucifer laid the girl gently on a small bed, reverted to his human image and waited for the light of the sun to awaken the girl.

Lucifer was seated beside the bed on a makeshift wooden stool when the girl woke up… at first she screamed when the terrors of the night came to mind but Lucifer gently grabbed her.

"Ssh my pretty, you have had a bad dream; that is all."

The girl's deep blue eyes were now wide open as she peered frantically around her new surroundings for any sign of the beast that had walked toward her in the officer's room, "Where... am I? Who are you?" she asked then her heartbeat increased, "You... you are the Devil, aren't you? Keep away from me!"

Lucifer laughed quietly, "Do I look like the Devil?"

The girl seemed confused suddenly, "No... no but..."

"I know that you have questions, and so do I, what is your name girl?"

"I... am Elize Montel."

"Good, I am Lu... Mr. Heylel, people call me Lucky and I think you have had a lucky escape, don't you?"

"But, how?"

"That can wait Elize Montel, I will explain everything later, there is coffee here, tins of beans and spam for breakfast, the name on this woodcutter's cabin suggests that he has most likely been taken by the Nazis. I want to take you to Scotland with me, would you like that Elize?"

Scotland seemed a million miles away to the girl but she knew that she would be safe from the Nazis there and this was a question she would never have expected to be asked but she tried to compose herself, "Why... yes, of course, both my parents are... dead now."

The girl burst into tears, instigated by her sudden strange new circumstances and the painful memory of what had happened to her parents and Lucifer hugged her immediately, "Now, now, I understand your sadness Elize and your safety and wellbeing is my main concern now, life has to go on and you will be safe in Scotland, no matter what happens."

Lucifer lit the fire in the small stove and filled the kettle from the water pump outside then placed the kettle on one of the hotplates, "Right, I want you to stay here, wait for me, I should not be long, there is somebody I want to see in Berlin."

* * *

The war between England and Germany was at its peak now; Lucifer guessed that Hitler was most likely at his headquarters in Berlin, overseeing military operations.

Lucifer knew where the army headquarters building was as he had been there before but Hitler and his henchmen were parading through Paris at the time, he knew where Hitler's private room was and he went straight to it and entered unseen. Lucifer's hunch had proven to be correct; Hitler was in deep conversation with two of his Generals over a large folded out map on his wide executive table. Lucifer's rage increased as he watched the little corporal descend into an enormous tantrum.

"No… no… no!" Hitler repeated with fury, "Get out, get out, you incompetent donkeys, you know nothing of war!" he shouted and both of his clenched fists thrashed through the air. The two Generals picked up their brown leather folders and left the room like two frustrated sheep. Hitler went to the drinks cabinet and poured himself a large Schnapps, mumbling wildly to himself as he did.

"You seem a little flustered" said Lucifer behind Hitler but he remained invisible. Hitler turned in surprise, his hand tight on the glass he was holding, he looked around the room but nobody was there.

"That is right, you cannot see me, I am the voice of your conscience" whispered Lucifer. Again Hitler said nothing, his eyes rolled around his head and up to the ceiling as he took a large drink from his glass of Schnapps and Lucifer noticed that his hand was shaking. Hitler's face contorted into a manic grin, "My conscience? I have no conscience; you are just a thought that wastes my precious time."

Lucifer had decided not to kill Hitler; that oath about mortal affairs was just too strong to break, however there was another tact that he could employ and that was what a cat would do to a mouse that it had caught.

"I am more than just a thought; I am the one who will take you to the edge of insanity, you will pay for your acts of evil, one way or another."

Hitler was so seriously agitated; he went to a drawer in his desk and took out a box full of various pills and shoved a handful of them into his mouth then hastily swallowed them with the Schnapps. Hitler was sweating profusely now; his eyes were swollen and bloodshot as he looked around the room.

"Still her conscience?" he said sounding like a pitiful patient in some mental health asylum.

"Oh yes, very much so, I have been here for hundreds of years."

Hitler's eyes now took on a look of fear, Lucifer knew that it was time to reveal himself, *surely it will send the madman over the edge* he thought, *taunting this evil man is immense fun.*

Lucifer slowly shed his cloak of invisibility and Hitler began to shake in revulsion. Lucifer stood before him black and burnt as if all the fires of Hell had consumed him. Black light was crackling from his back and his red eyes stared intensely at the man known as Adolf Hitler. Hitler screamed like a young boy who had just awoken because of a nightmare and sped out of the room shouting, "Guards, guards, save me… the Devil himself has come for me!"

Lucifer laughed at this sight and his laughter echoed around the spacious room as he listened to the nearby chaos but now it was time to leave the German High Command, it was time to get back to Elize and as he flew high in the sky away from the city of Berlin to the woodcutter's cabin, he looked forward to seeing Herr Hitler again one day.

As Lucifer alighted in front of the wood cabin door he changed his appearance, the only way he could access the black light for flight was when he appeared as he truly looked and that sight was not for Elize.

Lucifer opened the door to find Elize sweeping the floor, she had washed the dishes and had tidied the cabin but Lucifer suspected that this work had been done to help forget her nervous tension.

"There is no need to that Elize; we go from this miserable shack now."

Elize looked scared and Lucifer saw it in her eyes, not surprising he thought as she had seen him for a moment in his true state, he knew that what he was about to reveal to her would be a lot for her to comprehend but her mind was young and open to what the world had to offer.

Lucifer had revealed himself to mortals down the centuries both male and female, he had even nearly taken a mortal wife once which was another painful memory so he only confided in people he felt he could trust, people that worked for him and he had decided that there was something Elize could do for him.

Elize was shaking, "Where do we go now, do you intend to take me to Hell?" she blurted out but Lucifer was sympathetic to her words.

"My dear young one, I know that you are scared, that you think that you may have flown through the night with a demon... but you flew away from Hell remember and remember that I have saved you from certain death. There are things I will tell you but not here, I said I would take you somewhere where you will be safe from Nazi persecution."

"To Scotland then?"

"Yes, to a mansion I own, a place called View Ness."

***

This was simply an offer Elize could not refuse; she fought to put the memory of Lucifer's true appearance and what he really might be to the back of her mind... and the fact that she had flown through the night sky was a wondrous thought, hard to believe but it had happened and this being called Lucky had saved her life. Elize had to trust him, what other option did she have?

"Is that a smile I see little one? Do you want to come with me to the beautiful hills that surround Loch Ness?"

"Yes... yes I do" Elize stuttered as if destiny had suddenly taken her by the hand.

"Good, good, a better life awaits you now but only if you want it, you are not my prisoner, you are my special guest and you will be able to leave any time you want to, to come and go as you please" said Lucifer and suddenly he realised that he had fallen in love with the young French girl called Elize but not as a lover, more as a fatherly figure.

"Now to access my light for flight, I have to be in my true state but the light has the power to make me invisible to mortal eyes so when I disappear do not be alarmed, I will then hold you as I did last night and we will take to the sky like two birds.

"I... will not be scared" said a brave Elize but Lucifer could see that she was trembling again.

"You must close your eyes Elize if the journey becomes too much for you, but flying is a wonderful feeling, try to enjoy it, I am sure that you will want to do it again and remember, you will always be safe with me, I give you my word."

Soon, they were high above Berlin heading to the coast and the North Sea of the United Kingdom and Elize kept her eyes open, she was flying like a bird or maybe she was in some fairy tale or Wendy with Peter Pan heading towards Neverland. Elize wanted to fly with Lucifer forever.

***

The moon was full and welcoming and the man in the moon seemed to be smiling like never before as they finally reached Loch Ness. Lucifer glided down gently to a large grey stone mansion that was partly obscured by thick bushy trees. Lucifer placed Elize in front of a large wooden double door then reappeared before her in his normal guise.

"This is View Ness young Elize, a place where all your worries can be forgotten."

Lucifer was standing before a large marble statue of an angel that was next to the main doors, the angel was looking up to the sky, arms outstretched as if pleading for heavenly guidance. Lucifer grabbed the statue and moved it carefully to the side revealing a small metal box that contained a key to the doors. Elize marvelled at the strength of Lucifer and asked, "Is that a statue of you?"

Lucifer smiled as he mused, "Yes, I suppose it could be."

Once inside the vast View Ness, Lucifer took Elize to the main reception room where a fire was prepared and ready in the large ornate black marble fireplace.

"I have a grounds-man and housekeeper that live in a self-contained cottage not far from here, they always keep View Ness ready for me as it is one of my favourite habitats, the couple are called Jim and Joan McTaggart and I known them for years."

"And they do not question your youthful appearance?"

"You are sharp my little one... I have touched both their minds, my appearance has changed over the years so what they see is not what you see."

"So they do not suspect your true identity?"

"They do not, at least I think they do not" replied Lucifer and this made him laugh, "Maybe I will reveal the truth to them one day?"

Lucifer then turned and lit the fire and said to Elize, "Have a seat before the fireplace and I will get us something to drink, a brandy for me and a glass of wine for you, I think you are old enough."

"I am nearly seventeen... well, sixteen and a half" Elize said trying to sound older.

Lucifer laughed again.

As the thick logs on the fire began to burn brightly, Lucifer returned with the drinks and noticed that Elize was staring at the framed painting above the fireplace.

"It's beautiful."

"Yes it is, Raphael's, Portrait of a Young Man, stolen by the Nazis and I have stolen it from them. Do you like paintings?"

"Yes... yes" Elize said quite excitedly, "my ambition has always been to be an artist."

"Then that is what you shall be, if you like it here."

"Oh, I think I will like it here!"

"Good, then we shall drink to that."

Lucifer raised his glass to her and smiled, he felt so glad that he had saved the life of this girl.

"I love art" Lucifer suddenly said, "Here at View Ness in the underground vault is my main collection, some of which I have bought but some I must confess I have stolen, mainly from the Nazis after I had found out about what they were doing."

"So you will return them after the war?" asked Elize and Lucifer smiled that mischievous smile of his, "Maybe... maybe. From now on, you are in charge of my collection, my library is full of books about art and I will ask Jim to ready an art studio for you, a room at the top of View Ness for the light and the scenery, there are great views of the loch from the top floors."

Elize's broad smile filled Lucifer's heart with joy, "You will meet Jim and Joan tomorrow and I will tell them to make all the arrangements."

"But who will you say I am?"

"The daughter of my friend in France whom I am shielding from the Nazis and the horrors of the war there, they will like that, they will take you into their hearts and treat you like the daughter they lost" then before Elize could ask any questions about what he just said, he asked, "And now you shall tell me more about yourself."

"We lived in an apartment in Paris; my father was a bank clerk…"

Tears formed in the eyes of Elize as her head drooped in sadness, "My father was helping fellow Jews to escape then one night they came for him but he resisted and was shot… my mother went to him and she was shot too… both in front of me… I was taken; they said that I could be used in the camps."

Now the tears flowed freely from Elize's eyes and she began to shake again.

"There there little one, they will be in Heaven now, let that thought comfort you. Now we concentrate on the living and your new life here at View Ness."

Lucifer's memory of View Ness and Elize slowly faded; disturbed by a presence he suddenly felt, a figure to the right of him.

THE WIDOW

Standing on the veranda of the next suite was a woman with flame red hair, she was dressed in a floral patterned brown dress that seemed perfect for the art décor surroundings.

The bright moon and stars above the Pacific made the woman's jewellery sparkle as she stood in silence, staring out to sea. Lucifer felt compelled to speak to her, pleased that he now had company.

"Good evening, it is a lovely night isn't it?"

The woman turned as if in a dream, it was as if she had not noticed Lucifer sitting at the table. The woman smiled but there seemed to be a sadness to the smile.

"Yes, it is lovely" the woman replied then turned to look again at the gentle waves rolling towards the shore.

"The sea is so quiet tonight, so peaceful" Lucifer noted

"Like the lull before the storm" replied the woman and this time there was an urgency to her voice as if she had suddenly remembered something

"Forgive me; my name is Heylel, Lu… Lucky Heylel."

"Lucky? That is an unusual name, and do you feel lucky tonight Mr. Heylel?"

"Oh yes, all of the time" said Lucifer smiling.

"Then you have been surely blessed… my name is Mary Myers" replied the woman and she seemed to stutter as she said this

"And is Mary Myers alone tonight or does she have a partner or husband that will soon join us underneath these beautiful stars?"

"I… have a husband but he is not here at the moment, I am waiting for him."

"May I join you on your balcony?" asked Lucifer who felt suddenly drawn to this woman of mystery, "I will order more Champagne when your husband arrives."

"Yes… yes you may, it seems to have been some time since I have talked with someone."

Lucifer noticed that the verandas were joined by small almost unnoticeable gates, obviously something that helped the cleaning staff of the hotel. Lucifer went to the kitchenette for another of the large Champagne bottles and with the one from the ice bucket he joined the woman on her veranda. There was a table similar to Lucifer's apartment and as he put the bottles and his glass on it he said, "I'm sorry but it seems I have forgot to bring another glass."

"It seems a long time since I drank Champagne, do not worry I will get a glass" replied Mary Myers.

Lucifer opened the new bottle and when Mary Myers returned he poured out two large glassfuls.

"To this night I think" toasted Lucifer and Mary replied, "Yes this night… but not the sea."

It was an odd remark but this only intrigued Lucifer more, "The sea can be cruel but tonight it is like a gentle giant, at peace with the world."

Mary Myers did not say anything just looked out again across the still ocean.

"You say that you are waiting for your husband?"

Mary Myers began to tremble; it was as if she finding it hard to breathe suddenly. Lucifer held her hand to comfort her…

And then they were in the bedroom

A large four-poster bed

Flowers, cards, Champagne

A dance record playing the latest jazz

This was the bridal suite

And Mary Myers had just been married…

Her husband Jack opened the Champagne, "Well, we did it, we tied the knot and that money is safe and untraceable, it's going to be easy street from now on babe."

Mary Myers lounged back on the sumptuous bed against the giant pillows and sipped her drink and as her hand rubbed sensually against the soft silk sheets there was a knock on the Bridal Suite door.

"Did you order anything Mary, any supper?"

"No?"

"Must be more Champagne then" said Jack grinning widely.

At the door Jack asked who it was before he opened it.

"Room service for Mr. and Mrs. Myers sir."

Myers opened the door and a gun nozzle greeted his face.

"Evening Jack; thought we'd just drop by to say congratulations."

Five men, smartly dressed in suits and hats entered the room, "Where's your wife Jack?" growled the man with the gun.

"Look, she had nothing to do with it Sam... the money is safe, we thought the time was right to get married, I was going to contact the boss about the money, you know that man."

"I only know what I am told Jack, you know that and I only do what I am told to do... that's your mistake I think."

"But..."

"No buts, you're coming with us Jack, you can tell it to the boss."

"What about Mary?" asked the trembling Myers and at that point his wife entered from the bedroom.

"Who is it hun?" she asked then she saw the gun...

"It's okay babe, just business, I gotta go and speak to someone, you stay here, I won't be long."

"Oh, she'll stay here" said the man called Sam and he nodded to three of the men who then went and stood beside Mary, "These boys here will take good care of your wife, keep her entertained, so you've nothing to worry about Jack... now move, the boss don't like to be kept waiting on his yacht."

The two men and Myers left the room and as soon as they closed the door Mary Myers raced to the bedroom, but she had been too slow, one of the remaining men had his foot wedged in the doorway.

"That's really unsociable of you Mrs. Myers; the least you could do is offer us a drink."

Mary Myers went and sat on the bed; two of the men went to the drinks cabinet while the other one remained in the room and drank Champagne.

Time ticked slowly for Mary Myers, she lost track of how long her husband had been gone from the hotel then suddenly the phone beside the bed rang but it was the man who picked it up, "That will be for me I think" he said grinning and she noticed that one of his front teeth was missing. The man put the phone down.

"Well, it looks like it has all been sorted" he said and the two other men joined him at the bedroom door.

It was brutal.

Mary Myers was repeatedly raped, her mouth gagged so she could not scream. She tried to fight but the three men were too strong. She was badly beaten throughout her hellish ordeal and when the last man was finished with her she was stabbed to death and left like a limp bloody rag doll on her wedding bed.

The men hastily left the room and exited the hotel in secret by a back entrance.

Jack Myers was never seen again, he was wanted in connection with the death of his wife but his mutilated body was swimming with the fishes in the Pacific Ocean.

Lucifer withdrew his hand. The widow of Jack Myers was dead; Mary Myers was a 'ghost.' Lucifer had met many dead souls over the years, he knew that the touch of their reborn skin was the same as any mortal but like his skin it could control and reflect the light, Mary Myers could disappear at any time but she did not, she was aware that Lucifer had accessed her mind.

"You know who I am then Mr. Heylel... but I could not access your thoughts?"

"I was once angelic; you do not have that power over me."

"An angel? Then you have come to tell me that Jack is never coming back to me?"

An acute sadness filled Lucifer, "I fear not, a portal would have claimed him I think. The puzzle is why you are still here; was there no light, no portal, no angel for you at the end?"

"I do not remember, all I know is that I have waited here for Jack every night since."

"Even when living mortals have stayed here?"

"Yes... I watched them, so happy, so in love. I watched them making love, I even joined with some of them unseen but they thought that they were imagining it, like a fantasy, a sexual dream."

"I feel so sorry for you Mary Myers, but there is nothing I can do for you, the only portal I could open for you would probably be a doorway to Hell."

Mary Myers leaned over the table toward Lucifer, "Then maybe you could simply kiss me, I have been so lonely for so many years now."

Lucifer's lips caressed the lips of Mary Myers and then he gently lifted her up from her chair and took her to the bridal bed.

"Tonight I will be your husband, you will enjoy the night you never had with him" and Lucifer's appearance changed to that of Jack Myers, fully naked and wanting. Mary Myers clothes disappeared as if they had never existed and Lucifer kissed her again, it had been some time since he had made love to one of the living dead.

THE ROUGH LOOKING MAN

The next morning, Mary Myers was no longer there. Lucifer went to the veranda then to his own room, he was ravenous for breakfast.

***

The breakfast room was situated at the back of the hotel and looked out over the swimming pool where a few of the guests were enjoying a late morning swim.

Lucifer was informed that the breakfast room was about to close shortly and that the luncheon room would open thereafter.

"Good, I will have breakfast then lunch then."

The hotel waiter looked slightly puzzled then smiled, "Of course sir, what can I get you?"

"I will have bacon and scrambled eggs with fried tomatoes and a large pot of coffee; then I will have steak in your lunch room."

Watching the swimmers while he waited for his breakfast, Lucifer thought about Mary Myers, he wondered why she had not been there when he awoke. *Where do lonely ghosts go?* he wondered then he imagined her walking along the beach or simply window shopping in White Palms. What he did find curious though was why a portal had not opened for her, of course he knew that this had happened to so many and he concluded that her love for her husband had simply been too strong so somehow she had managed to stay Earthbound, continually waiting for her husband to emerge from the sea. Lucifer knew though that it was never going to happen and given the background of her husband, he was now probably in the realm of Nameless, or maybe he had misjudged him, *Not all thieves are evil* he thought and this made him smile...

"You are right Lucifer, not all thieves are evil; you are living proof of that are you not?" said a deep gentle voice behind Lucifer, who turned quickly, surprised that someone had seemingly read his thoughts.

Standing before Lucifer was a smartly dressed man in a brown stripy suit. The man was not tall but he was thick set and muscular, his hair was black and shoulder length and combed back and his broad chin was dark even though he had clearly shaven. This was the 'rough looking man' that had been mentioned at the white church. Lucifer looked directly into the man's eyes which were the most beautiful blue, they sparkled and shone and seemed to dance with the reflection of the swimming pool water in them, these were eyes that could easily bewitch anyone even though they were set in a fearsome face mused Lucifer. This was certainly the man that had been described as Mr. Hyde.

"I know who you are" said Lucifer blatantly, "You are the angelic known as Alphar, the first angel and this is a great honour for me to finally meet you."

"Quite so Lucifer and I have heard so much about you that I find it somewhat of an honour to meet you too."

"Do not believe all you hear Alphar" replied Lucifer and this made him laugh out loud, "Please take a seat, I have ordered coffee."

"Coffee will be good... strange how our bodies do not need such things and yet we find comfort in eating and drinking."

"We are just trying to remember I think; a link to our mortal selves of old."

"And I think you are right" replied Alphar as he sat down at the table.

"I am impressed that you read my mind without touching me" stated Lucifer, "But then you are somewhat older than me."

Alphar suddenly seemed to stare beyond Lucifer, up to the sky above the outdoor pool, "I was one of the first to walk upright, one of the first to make tools for hunting, one of the first to create fire, how many years ago now I seem to have forgotten, we did not have clocks then" and this time it was Alphar who laughed, "Sometimes I still long for that life you know, it was so simple, so easy to understand."

"I heard that you turned your back on Yahweh, that you deliberately made yourself Earthbound?"

"To help the needy Lucifer, in the poorest parts of the globe... and I heard that you were banished for arguing with the entity you call Yahweh's beliefs?"

"Not his belief, more so his non-action, I ended up in orbit around the sun, burnt beyond recognition in my hard catatonic state."

"But you managed to survive and return though, how so?"

"A gigantic solar flare sent me crashing back here... unfortunately mortals have seen my true appearance, they call me the Devil because of that."

"You cannot blame them, mortal existence is naïve."

Lucifer laughed, "An understatement if there ever was one Alphar... but I enjoy being the Devil when it suits me."

"I have heard that you seek out evil, that you enjoy eradicating it?"

"I do, it is the one thing I exist for now I think."

The waiter brought Lucifer's large breakfast and Lucifer barked, "Another plate, I shall share this meal with my friend."

"That is not necessary" protested Alphar.

"No it is not but I will not eat alone when I am with company."

Another large plate was brought and the two new friends heartily tucked into the food, they were now the only people in the breakfast room.

After they had eaten, the two angelic looked at each other and it was Alphar who spoke first, "This is no coincidence, the two of us here in this hotel, in this place called White Palms?"

"That is what I was thinking my friend."

"You dreamt of the white church then?"

"Yes... I was compelled to come here and you?"

"There are no angelic that I know of now, you are the first one I have seen for a very long time and yes, I have been to the church, spoken to the caretaker... and I fear Heaven as we know it may have fallen."

Lucifer's face became stern, "Fallen to Nameless?"

"Perhaps, I do not know, but something has happened; I feel it."

"Can you open a portal to Heaven?" asked Lucifer.

"No, that is the one thing that was taken from me when I decided to stay on Earth, when I shunned Yahweh and Heaven."

"Your punishment then, for defiance."

"And you, I guess that your doorway is blocked too?"

"Yes... I have tried to open a portal in the past but nothing happens, not even a doorway to the realm of Nameless."

"Not high on my 'places I want to visit' list I think" joked Alphar and this made Lucifer laugh.

"So what now Alphar, what happens next, do we simply let Nameless take control of this world of the living but what would life be like then?"

"Chaotic and cruel... Nameless is an entity that is as old as Yahweh itself, it feeds on evil, his kingdom both living and dead would grow until it had totally consumed this world called Earth."

"And then?"

"And then other worlds, other realities, this is just the start of this dark cancer."

"So we are just to wait and watch as evil takes over the world, what can we do; where do we go from here"

"I have sensed something this morning, a new light, something unknown to me... I suggest we go to church."

A GATHERING OF ANGELS

Lucifer and Alphar took a walk, back along the coastal road towards the white church on the hill. The Church of the Fallen was quiet as it had been when both men were last there but Alphar could hear voices inside.

"There are people inside the church Lucifer."

"I heard them, maybe worshippers?"

"Perhaps... but one is angelic... and another, that new light that is different."

"Let us see then, it will be interesting to meet yet another angelic."

Lucifer and Alphar entered the church quietly and saw three men and a woman who was holding a baby, one of the men was looking at them.

"Your angelic scent is strong gentlemen... I thought that I was the last angel."

The man who spoke was Mastema and he was with Tom Savage, Ray Gunn, Susan Eden and her child Matta, all of who turned when they heard his words.

Lucifer and Alphar walked slowly down the aisle to the surprised group and it was Alphar who replied to Mastema.

"I fear we are the last, it seems like fate has drawn us all here this day."

"Not fate" replied Mastema, "It is this church that has brought us together."

"Quite so" was Alphar's simple reply.

Ray Gunn was instinctively worried and wary, "Just wait a minute Mastema, who are these two guys, they could be agents of Nameless… I mean they look like Dr, Jeykll and Mr. Hyde or maybe the Beast from X-Men!"

"I am Alphar and this is Lucifer" was Aphar's cool reply.

"Man, you must be shitting me, the real fallen angel!" cried out Gunn and he produced a hand gun from within his coat and pointed it straight at Lucifer, his hand shaking at the thought that he might be about to shoot the Devil.

"No Ray" said Mastema but Lucifer was angered by the action of Gunn and Lucifer immediately turned into his hardened burnt state… Gunn, Savage and Eden recoiled instantly in horror, Eden trying to shield her son from the terrifying sight in front of them. Lucifer had seemed to grow in size and the black light from his back was crackling behind him like two large wings that darkened the light inside the church… Lucifer's burning red eyes stared intensely at Gunn.

"You dare point a weapon at me in this sacred house mortal, do you know who I am?"

"Yes, I fucking do and I don't fucking believe it!"

Gunn was scared and his hand tightened on the trigger of the gun sending a bullet towards Lucifer which immediately bounced off his black skin and ricocheted through one of the painted windows. Lucifer reached towards Gunn but Mastema stepped between them and took the shaking weapon from Gunn's trembling hand.

"No Ray, you are jumping to some terrible conclusion."

"But… he's the fucking Devil, the one that we thought that you were, the fallen fucking angel for Christsakes!"

Mastema still had no real concept of the Devil on Earth, all he knew was Nameless, he knew of Lucifer and that like himself he had been banished from Enolan for openly arguing with Aenor.

"Yes he was banished like me but that does not make him evil."

Lucifer noticed the fear in Eden's eyes at what she was looking at so he reverted back to his human appearance.

"Wise words Mastema and it is understandable why the mortal reacted so" said Alphar gently in an attempt to calm the situation down.

Mastema introduced Savage, Gunn and Eden to Lucifer and Alphar, "And this is my son Matta" he finally added.

"Ah, the new light I sensed... this has never happened before" said Alphar and he caressed the head of the baby Matta who was still held tightly by a shaking Eden, "There is no need to worry Susan Eden, I think that we are all here for the same reason."

"Yes, I think we are" replied Mastema who then began to tell the two other angelic the story of his banishment and his eventual return to Earth. Mastema told them about Theolus and how they had entered the portal in search of Enolan, he told them that the church they were in was the same church where the angelic were being buried and that they had come with the hope that the light of his son could somehow open the portal once more. Mastema still had to know where all the souls of Enolan were, he was not ready to accept that Nameless had destroyed or claimed them all.

"We do need to find out" said Alphar, "I need to know what happened to Yahweh or Aenor as you call Him... and I do think the new light of your son might be able to help us."

DARKNESS AND LIGHT

Alphar, Lucifer and Mastema stepped aside for a moment to discuss their plan of action. Savage and Gunn were understandably annoyed to be left out of the discussion but it was a chance to talk to Eden.

"Are you okay with this Susan? Whatever they are talking about could mean danger for Matta" said Savage.

"I will agree with whatever Mastema decides, Matta is his son too."

"I think that we should get the Hell out of this church Tom" said Gunn, "All of this is way beyond the likes of mere mortals like us."

"I agree Ray but we are part of this now, we have been since the moment Mastema walked towards us on the moon... I have been in that portal Ray, I have seen things no man or mortal should ever see... what they are about to do could mean the very survival of humanity as we know it! You are free to go Ray, you know that."

"I'm still a member of the security forces Tom, and that means I'm still responsible for looking after your sorry ass."

"I appreciate that Ray" and this brought a welcome smile to the three mortals as the three angelic approached them, again it was Alphar who took the initiative and addressed Savage.

"We think that you three mortals should leave now as there is no telling what might happen here."

"Funny, we have just been discussing that" replied Savage."

"That's right Mr. Hyde but no dice, we are staying" interrupted Gunn, "You might be thousands of years older than us but that does not give you the right to order us around!"

"I am millions of years older than you" replied Alphar and Gunn's jaw nearly hit the floor, "and I do admire your resilience... so be it, we will now try and access the portal, with your permission that is Susan Eden?"

"Of course, do what you must, as long as no harm comes to my son."

"All we need to do is touch the head of your son, channel his light through us... we hope it will activate the dormant portal light within us,"

The three angels took the baby Matta to the altar table and laid him beneath the large metal cross. Together they gently touched his head and then went into a trancelike state as if they were praying...

Bright light sparkled from the baby Matta and slowly surged through the arms of the angelic until their whole bodies were glowing like three living torches. Savage, Gunn and Eden had to shield their eyes as the light consumed the church.

"It has worked" said Mastema, "This is now the church of the angelic, the remnants of Enolan!"

The three mortals looked around and marvelled at the dancing shimmering beauty of the church.

"You mean that we are now in Heaven?" gasped Eden.

"What is left of it darling" replied Mastema, "But do not be deceived, dark forces now lurk here."

The swirling light inside the church suddenly began to fade and dark figures began to move in the shadows, crawling like slithery phantoms across the walls and floors...

YOU ARE SO RIGHT MASTEMA

BUT 'DARK FORCES'

DO YOU HAVE TO BE SO MELODRAMATIC?

The three angelic stepped in front of the three mortals who were now instinctively shielding the baby Matta on the altar.

THREE ANGELIC

AND ANOTHER

AN INFANT THAT REALLY INTRIGUES ME

"Keep your fucking hands off my son!" spat Eden to the moving shadows surrounding them and she quickly took hold of her son.

A MORTAL WITH SPIRIT

I LIKE THAT

HER SOUL WILL BE A JOY TO CONSUME

"Keep your vile claws away from her" shouted a defiant Mastema and the creeping shadows pace quickened.

YOU MANAGED TO ESCAPE FROM HERE LAST TIME

AND THOSE THAT FAILED ME HAVE PAID THE PRICE

THIS TIME MASTEMA YOU WILL NOT BE SO LUCKY!

"Are you referring to me somehow, I have been known as Lucky you know?"

AH MY FRIEND LUCIFER

I ASSUME THAT YOU ARE HERE

TO FINALLY JOIN FORCES WITH ME?

"I am not your friend dark one and I am here because you threaten the balance of my world."

BUT THIS WORLD IS DESTINED TO BECOME MINE NOW

AND NOW THAT YAHWEH HAS GONE

THAT MEANS THAT THERE WILL BE MORE PREY FOR YOU

AND I DO KNOW

HOW MUCH YOU ENJOY KILLING MY DEAR LUCIFER...

"And just where has Yahweh gone?" interrupted Alphar.

I KNOW YOU

THE OLDEST ANGELIC

AND THE WEAKEST

SHUNNED BY YAHWEH

BECAUSE OF YOUR WEAKNESS

"You are wrong evil one, I am perhaps the strongest, time builds strength within us, you should know that."

YES I DO

AND REMEMBER

I AM MUCH OLDER THAN YOU

AS OLD AS TIME ITSELF

AS OLD AS YAHWEH

SO BEWARE

APE THAT WALKS

"I have never been scared of you and I never will be."

I THInK YAHWEH WAS

THAT IS WHY HE HAS DEPARTED

AND WITH HIM GONE

DEFEATING THE ANGELIC WAS EASY...

There was a pause in the discussion as a beam of light from the church doorway sought out the darkness within, the light made the moving shadows squirm away to the dim corners of the building... everyone and everything seemed to hold their breath for a moment...

"The Father has gone but the Son remains. My father was never afraid of you Nameless, in fact He pitied you and those that followed you... He has gone to spread His word to new worlds throughout this magnificent universe."

From this light in the doorway stepped an old man in blue overalls.

"Who… the fuck is that?" exclaimed a stunned Gunn.

"My God, it is the carpenter, the caretaker who rebuilt this church" replied Savage.

"You're telling me an old carpenter is going to save our skin?"

"I think that he is more than just a carpenter Ray, he said Yahweh is his father!"

As Savage and Gunn gawped at the old man his appearance began to change, standing before them now was a young man with tanned skin, shoulder length brown hair and a short beard dressed in pure white gleaming robes.

"It is Yeshua" declared Lucifer enthusiastically, "It is some time since we last conversed Son of Yahweh."

Eden began to tremble as she held her son, "My God… my God" was all she could repeat but Nameless was unimpressed.

THE SAVIOUR OF THE WORLD

WHO HIDES IN A SMALL CHURCH

WHY DID YOU NOT LEAVE WITH YAHWEH?

"I built this church with my bare hands and when you began to destroy the angelic, I took the souls of Heaven into myself, they are safe within me, within these walls."

SAFE?

HERE?

And suddenly the walls of the church exploded and shattered revealing a foreboding barren landscape full of white blood stained crosses amongst dark crawling bodies…

GAZE UPON YOUR KINGDOM FALSE PRINCE

SEE WHAT REMAINS OF YOUR LOYAL ANGELIC

"I know; I buried them" said Yeshua and his face was sad and reflective.

YOU STILL HAVE NOT ANSWERED ME

WHY DO YOU REMAIN HERE?

ARE YOU HERE TO TRY AND DESTROY ME?

"I am here to save you" was Yeshua's simple yet surprising reply.

Nameless began to laugh, so hard and ear-splitting that the mortals had to cover their ears.

YOU AMUSE ME

NO ONE IS TO BE SAVED

THIS IS THE DAY

I WILL CONSUME THE LAST OF THE ANGELIC

I WILL CONSUME YOU

AND THE SOULS

THAT HIDE WITHIN YOU

THE DAWN OF A NEW EXISTENCE IS NIGH

"Then show yourself Nameless, I think it is you that always hides."

Again, booming laughter reverberated around the remains of the church and in the corner to the left of the crushed altar, a large form began to take shape... a human figure, thirty feet high or more that appeared to be made of glass, a transparent skin that revealed moving human forms within it, swimming and squirming in some twisted state of agony and ecstasy. It was a vile vision that transfixed those that looked upon it. In some ways it was hypnotic, a sight that was somehow darkly erotic and tempting to the eyes that were foolish enough to continue to gaze upon it.

YOU CAN SEE THAT MY SOULS ARE CONTENT
THEY ENJOY BEING PART OF ME

"They are mislead and trapped, imprisoned souls, they will never be at peace within you" declared Yeshua and his voice had taken on a much bolder tone.

THEY DO NOT SEEK YOUR BORING WAY OF LIFE
THEY NEVER DID
I GIVE THEM WHAT THEY WANT
THEY DO WHAT THEY ENJOY
WHAT YOU AND YOUR ANGELIC WILL ENJOY

Nameless waved his large hands before him and writhing figures began to move from him across the ruins of the floor towards the angelic and the mortals and Yeshua. Susan Eden wanted to run but the dark figures moved too fast and soon they had hold of her legs.

Lucifer became hard and black, dark crackling energy from his back surged towards the creatures.

Savage and Gunn fired their guns like madmen but their bullets simply passed through their gruesome adversaries with no effect whatsoever.

The angelic and the mortals were slowly being consumed...

Yeshua spread his arms wide and light from Lucifer, Mastema and Alphar flowed towards him.

"Come to me, be one with me, my kingdom forgives you!"

And this time it was His voice that boomed throughout the fallen church as a light as bright as the brightest sun shone directly at Nameless...

YOU WASTE YOUR TIME SAVIOUR
YOU HAVE WAITED TOO LONG TO TAKE ACTION
MY...
MY STRENGTH IS SUPREME
I GIVE THEM THE HELL THEY WANT
THEY...
WILL...
NEVER...

LEAVE...

ME...

But slowly the creatures of Nameless became confused, as if they were scared, as if a new awareness had suddenly struck them... they began to shrink, their dark forms began to circle in the air until they became small orbs of floating light... that began to drift like wary animals towards Yeshua and his open glowing arms.

NO

THEY DARE NOT!

Screamed Nameless but more and more orbs fled from his body... which began to shrink in size.

More and more...

Smaller and smaller.

And the voice of Nameless became weak and faint, almost pathetic sounding...

NO

THIS IS NOT POSSIBLE!!

"Love is possible, forgiveness is possible" stated Yeshua and his voice was once more calm and soothing in the swirling chaos before him.

The light from Yeshua filled the broken church like a giant sun rising above it.

"You were right nameless, this is the dawn of a new day!" cried out Yeshua as he watched the entity known as Nameless shrink ever smaller before him. Nameless fought and raged as a multitude of orbs continued to leave his glass-like form faster than the speed of light, until Nameless appeared as a transparent shell, he was now as small as a young boy...

When the last orb left his shaking body, his form shattered like a broken mirror.

There were no more dark crawling shapes, no threatening shadows...

Just Yeshua, still standing with his arms outstretched, an angelic light pulsating all around him.

"What... has happened?" muttered Susan Eden as if in a dream, still holding her baby Matta tight.

"Love has conquered all" answered Mastema.

Yeshua walked slowly towards the stunned mortals and angelic, he seemed larger to them but that was just probably a trick of the gleaming light and their admiring imagination.

"The gates of Heaven are open again" said Yeshua smiling, "and I could not have achieved this without the added power of your combined light my beloved angelic!"

"And the dead angelic?" asked Alphar and Yeshua's face became suddenly sullen and sad.

"Their souls maybe gone forever, only my Father was capable of making mortals angelic."

"There could be another way" replied Mastema looking at his son Matta... and this made him think of his wife and family in Enolan.

Yeshua smiled again, he had read Mastema's thoughts.

"You are welcome here any time Mastema as both Alphar and Lucifer are."

Then Yeshua looked at Savage, Gunn, Eden and the baby Matta and said, "Your time will come but not now... I think a spell of forgetfulness will be beneficial for you all."

And they did understand.

The waves of the Pacific crashed in the distance. They were all back in the solid reality of White Palms. Mastema, Eden and Gunn were the first to leave the shattered church and as Mastema said his goodbyes to Alphar and Lucifer he concluded, "Their memory of this great day will fade slowly, by the time we get home, today will be a mystery to them... and what of you two, what plans do you have now?"

"There is still mortal evil to seek out" replied a resolute Lucifer, "And I can only pray that Yeshua has not been tricked!"

"And there is still disease, oppression and poverty to overcome" added Alphar, "but first, I think we need to rebuild this shattered place, the place where the last church saved the world."

ACKNOWLEDGEMENTS

—

Many thanks to Paul O'Brien, Nigel Johnson, John and Miriam Smith, Pauline Averre, Tony Barrel, Julie 'Apples'Bramley, Lesley Fyfe, Teresa Whitaker, Glenna G Hale, Stephen Hubber, Colin Liddle, Steve and Jacqui Nanson for their continual encouraging support.

1 – Oscar Wilde. Lady Windermere's Fan.
2 – David Bowie. Space Oddity.
3 – The Wrong Reality. Richard Valanga.
4 – The Shining. Stephen King.
5 – The Wild One. Marlon Brando.
6 – The paintings of Edward Hopper.
7 – U2
8 – Bryan ferry. No Reason or Rhyme.
9 – The Beatles. Sgt. Peppers Lonely Hearts Club Band.
10 – The Rolling Stones. Sympathy For The Devil.
11 – Dr. Jeykll and Mr. Hyde. Robert Louis Stevenson.
12 – Raphael. Portrait of a Young Man.

RICHARD VALANGA

THE WRONG REALITY

Running to save the life of his son, Ryan Walker and the Reverend Daniel McGovern are transported to another reality by an enigmatic blue ripple that suddenly appears on the Tyne Bridge.

For Walker, this reality provides everything he has ever desired except for the complications caused by the death of his ex-wife.

For the Reverend, the other reality is absolute Hell, a Hell that is tearing his vulnerable soul apart.

Murder, blackmail, dark eroticism and a dangerous religion threaten the sanity of the two men but there is a way back to their own reality, a possible window of opportunity that could enable them to return...

The problem is; will they realise this in time as both men are slowly being consumed by their alternate personalities.

'The author's talent for writing engaging tales of the paranormal is second to none.'

'The Wrong Reality for the real world...'
'Richard Valanga's **talented and imaginative** writing style is so suited to the supernatural genre and this together with a mix of horror and dark eroticism, **"The Wrong Reality" is proof of his superb eclectic ability to engage his readers in a truly alternative world.'**

'Excellent read; nostalgia, horror and mystery.'
'The whole theory of one's world being turned on its head is both fascinating and terrifying. **Richard has hit the mark once again.**'

'**SUPERnatural** - Another **thought provoking** novel from this north eastern writer.'

'**Not like run of the mill sci fi** - Haven't read a lot of science fiction but this had a believable storyline, plausible characters, **couldn't put it down until I'd reached the end.**'

RICHARD VALANGA
COLOSSEUM

In the theatre of death only evil reigns supreme.

During the Festival of Death in Rome, four American art students go missing. One of the students is eventually found dead, horribly mutilated as if by wild beasts inside the Colosseum.

One year later, Nick Thorn is sent by the New Sanctuary to help the father of one of the missing students, a desperate man who is still looking for his daughter.

The New Sanctuary believes that Thorn has a psychic ability, a 'special gift' that could help him; Thorn however has always denied such a thing, claiming it to be pure nonsense and probably the product of an overactive imagination instigated by his drinking problem.

Shortly after Thorn arrives in Rome, the Festival of Death begins again and another of the missing students is gruesomely murdered. It is now a race against time to find the other two.

Can Thorn find and save the remaining two students or will Mania the Roman Goddess of Death succeed in devouring their souls and satisfy the blood lust of her followers?

RICHARDVALANGA
COMPLEX HEAVEN

Set in the North East of England, Complex Heaven is a psychological supernatural thriller that tells the story of a troubled soul tormented by the anguish of his distraught son. Called back from the Afterlife, father of two Richard; is concerned about the mental welfare of his youngest son JJ. There is a suspicion that somehow JJ is connected to the death of a young girl called Rose in Washington. The mystery however, is much more complicated as Richard finally confronts the evil that has been preying on his family for generations. A suffering that forces Richard back to the world of the living; where the answers to some of the darkest moments of his life are waiting.

'Complex and gripping.'
'I read this book in two sittings, very difficult to put it down. The characters are well developed and the plot twists and turns as it snakes to a dramatic conclusion. I heard through the grapevine that there is a sequel coming soon, it can't be too soon for me.'

'Brilliant, creepy and compelling!'
'I really enjoyed this **brilliant**, psychological supernatural book. **Totally unique** and wholly original I can't recommend this book enough!'

'Emotional rollercoaster I want to ride again!'
'When I started reading this book it brought forward so many emotions I had kept locked away. **It captured me right from the start and I couldn't put it down until I had finished!!** I would definitely recommend it.'

'Gripping'
'I started reading the sample to this book and could not tear myself away. I love the style, subject and setting. I have received my own copy of the book this morning and cannot wait to continue reading.'
'A resonating read for fans of the paranormal. Excellent!
'Profoundly thought-provoking and so descriptive at times I found myself there! An intense journey - but an enjoyable one. Would highly recommend.'
'A gripping read.''Complex Heaven is **imaginative and original in style and content. Definitely a must read.'**

RICHARD VALANGA
COMPLEX HELL

'It's present-day Sunderland and a mysterious manuscript is discovered in the house of an evil spirit, leading the unwary reader to a tale of the sixties in North East England, where not everything is quite as it seems. Forbidden love, loss and a lifetime of pure evil lie in store for whoever dares turn the ageing pages further.

In Devils Wood House the memory of the missing girl, Rose, waits desperately. Unfortunately, for her, time is not on her side. Can her soul be saved or will the child be lost forever?'

"Richard Valanga writes about the Afterlife like nobody else today, he's the 21st-century Dante of the North." – Tony Barrell, The Sunday Times

'Unique and interesting, thought-provoking, original and creative, it certainly is a tale that will stay in my mind.'

'Creepy paranormal read.'
'The author has a **wonderful and unique writing style** that draws you in instantly. "Complex Hell" is a wholly original take on the afterlife and quite believable too.'

'The author Richard Valanga writes like a poet and has a brilliant and impressive imagination to match.'

'A good read, good memories and pretty good musical taste…'
Once again Richard **Valanga excels in not only scaring the reader to death, but evokes fond memories of a time when things were simpler**, when mobile phones and computers were still in the imagination of Science Fiction writers! I feel sure Mr Valanga actually uses the typewriter mentioned in the first chapter! A good read; good memories and pretty good musical taste for something undead. **Richard writes like a man possessed**...because I think he probably is!

'A very good read.'
'This book was **a very good read, great concept**. Scary, but engaging; **I was compelled to keep reading.'**

RICHARD VALANGA
COMPLEX SHADOWS

Fleeing Devils Wood House in Washington with a car full of ill-gotten riches; a father and his son check into the Seaburn Hotel on the Sunderland coast.

With them is the father's old manuscript which is his account of what he experienced in the jungles of Burma during World War Two. Where there is war there is immense evil, a breeding ground for dark supernatural forces that once encountered will change your life forever.

This book is the third in the Complex Series and helps explain why one family becomes entangled with and haunted by the malevolent Dark Conscious.

'**A great read!!**'

I really enjoyed reading this creepy, ghostly and at times scary book. You could truly feel how passionate the author was about his personal and emotional memories during the first half of the story. The whole storyline comes together flawlessly at the end and was certainly quite emotional. **Richard Valanga is a highly talented and imaginative author and I highly recommend this wholly original book**.....it really is a frightening thought that the dead do walk our streets!!

'**Richard Valanga's amazing book Complex Shadows is not for the weak- hearted.**'

'The past can be intense and in this supernatural and extremely dark thriller that takes place in the north east of England (Sunderland to be exact) he adds more to this 'one of a kind' read that will have you captive from the start with great visions of the harshness and ugly events of Burma during World War Two to the Shadows of the Past which most of us can relate to.

The attention to detail in this fine piece of work sets this apart **from a lot of supernatural and paranormal books I have read.** If I was a betting man and with an outstanding Hollywood agent, **I could see this on the silver screen** with an outstanding soundtrack that will draw you into this fabulous read.'

RICHARDVALANGA
BLIND VISION

To see the evil dead is a curse...
It begins with the Roman exploratore Stasius Tenebris and the Calicem Tenebris (the Dark Chalice) - a vessel of evil that is brought back to life years later by Ethan Chance, a young man who was cruelly blinded by falling into an ancient Roman well when he was nine.

Was it an accident or did the spirits in the well choose Ethan for a reason? ...the Calicem Tenebris restores his sight but at a price.

This is the story of the chalice and the village called Darwell and the dark fate awaiting its inhabitants at the Festival of Healing.

Can Ethan, his friends and a knight from the Crusades save the day or is Darwell doomed to forever serve those who worship Mars, the Roman God of War.

'Blindingly good book'
This is the second book by Richard Valanga I have read and it's even better than his first, Complex Heaven. **If, like me, you enjoy fantasy novels that you can't put down then this author is for you.**

'Brilliant!'
'Although "Blind Vision" is primarily aimed at young adult readers I still thoroughly enjoyed this book, I was drawn into it from the very first page with **great characters and a truly intriguing dark supernatural story line**. Set in 2 time frames- present day and fantasy Roman/Crusaders the story comes together brilliantly in a very detailed and fascinating way.'

'Richard Valanga is a great writer who has a fantastic imagination and I would happily recommend "Blind Vision" to readers of any age - you won't be disappointed!'

'The end is very exciting. You can feel the tension in the air. You can't put the book down. You just want to read faster and faster to find out what's going to happen. It is absolutely amazing. **One of the best books I have ever read.**' – A Young Adult reader.

RICHARD VALANGA

THE SUNDERLAND VAMPIRE

Late at night, a man awakes in a Sunderland cemetery and is confused and alone. The man cannot remember what has happened and has no recollection of the events that have led him to such a cold and desolate place. Why was he there and more importantly... who was he?

It is not just his loss of memory that is worrying him though, it is the strange new urges that are calling to him from the surrounding darkness, unnatural thoughts that seem somehow familiar... and disturbing.

The Sunderland Vampire is a psychological paranormal mystery thriller and a ghostly gothic romance that ultimately leads back to the coastal town of Whitby.

"It oozes Anne Rice..."

"This is brilliant, wonderfully vivid, very detailed and sumptuous and a pleasure to read."

"Thrilling and intriguing, I love this book!"

"Great writing... great work!"